VIRAGO
MODERN CLASSICS
597

Angela Thirkell

Angela Thirkell (1890–1961) was the eldest daughter of John William Mackail, a Scottish classical scholar and civil servant, and Margaret Burne-Jones. Her relatives included the pre-Raphaelite artist Edward Burne-Jones, Rudyard Kipling and Stanley Baldwin, and her godfather was J. M. Barrie. She was educated in London and Paris, and began publishing articles and stories in the 1920s. In 1931 she brought out her first book, a memoir entitled *Three Houses*, and in 1933 her comic novel *High Rising* – set in the fictional county of Barsetshire, borrowed from Trollope – met with great success. She went on to write nearly thirty Barsetshire novels, as well as several further works of fiction and non-fiction. She was twice married, and had four children.

By Angela Thirkell

Barsetshire novels

Non-fiction

Collected Stories

AUGUST FOLLY

Angela Thirkell

virago

VIRAGO

First published in Great Britain in 1936 by Hamish Hamilton Ltd
This paperback edition published in 2014 by Virago Press
Reprinted 2014

A CIP catalogue record for this book
is available from the British Library.

ISBN 978-1-84408-968-0

Typeset in Goudy by M Rules
Printed and bound in Great Britain by
Clays Ltd, St Ives plc

Papers used by Virago are from well-managed forests
and other responsible sources.

MIX
Paper from
responsible sources
FSC   FSC® C104740
www.fsc.org

Virago Press
An imprint of
Little, Brown Book Group
100 Victoria Embankment
London EC4Y 0DY

An Hachette UK Company
www.hachette.co.uk

www.virago.co.uk

I

Railway Affairs

The little village of Worsted, some sixty miles west of London, is still, owing to the very defective railway system which hardly attempts to serve it, to a great extent unspoilt. To reach it you must change at Winter Overcotes where two railway lines cross. Alighting from the London train on the high level, you go down a dank flight of steps to the low level. Heavy luggage and merchandise are transferred from the high to the low level by being hurled or rolled down the steps. From time to time a package breaks loose, goes too far, and trundles over the edge of the platform on to the line, but there is usually a porter about to climb down and collect it. When your train comes backwards into the station, often assisted for the last few yards by a large grey horse and its friends and hangers-on, you may take your seat in a carriage which has never known the hand of change since it left the railway shops in 1887. If it is market day at Winter Overcotes your carriage will gradually fill with elderly women, carrying bags and baskets, who prefer the train to the more expensive motor-bus, children with season tickets coming back from school, and one or two old men who still wear a fringe of whisker. As your train pulls out on the single line which joins Winter Overcotes to Shearings, a small junction fifteen miles away, you are back in the late Victorian era. Up and down the single line, at rare and inconvenient intervals, run a few little trains, which can only pass one another when, at the stations, a second line emerges, only to flow back into the parent line a little further on. Engines and carriages are a striking relic of our earlier railways, and under their skimpy coats of paint may be read the names of long defunct systems.

The line meanders, in the way that makes an old railway so much more romantic than a new motor highway, among meadows, between hills, over level crossings. At Winter Underclose, Lambton and Fleece, the train stops to allow the passengers to extricate themselves and their baskets from its narrow doors. It then crosses the little river Woolram and enters a wide valley, the further end of which is apparently blocked by a hill. Just under the hill is Worsted, where you get out. The valley is not really impassable, for a few hundred yards beyond the station the train enters the famous Worsted tunnel, whose brutal and unsolved murders have been the pride of the district since 1892.

The line is staffed and controlled by three local dynasties: Margetts, Pattens and Polletts. If a Margett is station-master, you may be sure that there is a Patten in the goods yard, or on the platform. If a Patten is engine-driver, his fireman can hardly avoid being a Pollett. If there is a Pollett in the signal-box, there will be a Margett to open the gates of the level crossing and warn the signalman that the train is coming. All three families are deeply intermarried.

Mr Patten is the station-master at Worsted. His head porter is Bert Margett, son of Mr Margett the builder, and his nephew, Ed Pollett, whose father keeps the village shop, is in the lamp-room, and gives such extra help as zeal, unsupported by intellect, can afford. He also has a genius for handling cars.

The inconvenience of the hours of running is made up for by the kindness of the staff. They will hold up a train for any reasonable length of time if old Bill Patten, cousin of the station-master and father of the second gardener at the Manor House, is seen tottering towards the station half a mile away; or young Alf Margett, Bert's younger brother, from the shop, has forgotten one of the parcels he should have brought on his handlebars, and has to go back to fetch it. Since no trains can proceed until their various drivers have exchanged uncouth tokens of metal, like pot-hooks and hangers, or gigantic nose and ear-rings to be bartered with savage tribes for diamonds and gold, there is no danger.

Most of the land hereabouts is owned by Mr Palmer, whose property, bounded on the north by the Woolram, runs south nearly as far as Skeynes, the next station down the line. East and West are Penfold and Skeynes Agnes, where there is a fine Saxon church. Mr Palmer is a J.P., an excellent landlord, and owner of a very fine herd of cows which supply Grade A milk, at prices fixed by the Milk Marketing Board. His wife, in virtue of her husband's position and her own masterful personality, has taken the position female Squire.

Of other gentry there are few in the immediate neighbourhood. Lady Bond at Staple Park does not count, because she and Mrs Palmer have not for some time been on speaking terms. There are also the Tebbens, who live at Lamb's Piece, near the wood above the railway. At the moment when our story opens, on a warm June morning last summer, Mrs Tebben was in her drawing-room, reviewing a book on economics. Happening to raise her eyes to the window, she saw Mrs Palmer opening the garden gate, so she went to warn her husband. Mr Tebben was a Civil Servant during the week, from ten or eleven to six, or such later hour as his country might require, and carried an umbrella wet or fine; but in the evenings, and from Saturday to Monday, he gave himself entirely to the past, taking for his province the heroic age of Norway and Iceland, with excursions into the English Epic. During the War his knowledge of the Scandinavian tongues had been of great use to the censor's department, from which he had emerged scatheless owing to his great presence of mind in deliberately forgetting to acknowledge the official communication offering him an inferior order of the Empire he had served. He was at this moment sitting in his very small, uncomfortable study, drafting a letter to a learned Society of which he was President, and did not wish to be disturbed.

'Warning, Gilbert! Warning!' cried Mrs Tebben, putting her head in at the study door. 'Louise Palmer!'

As her husband only stared at her with the expression of a mad and rather obstinate bull, startled from its dreams, she began to insert herself into the room. To open the door wider was impossible because of the furniture. The house at Worsted had been altogether Mrs Tebben's doing. Her husband would have preferred to live permanently in London, where his books would all have been under one roof, but Mrs Tebben, feeling that her children, who were both at school in the country and liked London more than anything in the world, ought to have pure air for their holidays, had plotted and saved towards the purchase of a perpendicular field on the side of a hill near the village of Worsted. From her own earnings, for after taking a first at Oxford she had coached for many years, not letting marriage interfere, and had produced several useful and uninteresting textbooks on economics, she had bought the land and caused to be built Lamb's Piece, a local name on which she had pounced with educated glee, but no provision had been made for a study. After two miserable years of trying to work in a corner of the drawing-room, distracted by his wife's village activities, by his son's rudeness during school holidays and, later, University Vacation, by the ebb and flow of domestic life, Mr Tebben had insisted on a separate work-room.

Mrs Tebben prided herself on being able to argue like a man, with logic and without rancour. This very mistaken point of view was based upon her early passion for a young don, Mr Fanshawe of Paul's, whose courtesy to his women pupils cleverly concealed his contempt and abhorrence, which passion had consumed her during her last year at college, or rather, during that portion of the year spent in residence. After taking her degree she had done some research, gone on a Norwegian cruise, met and married Mr

Tebben, and settled down to coaching and the rearing of a son and daughter. Mr Fanshawe had determinedly ripened into an Oxford character, refusing to use any other than a small, flat, tin bath, and arguing with his women pupils with logic and without rancour; while for his intellectual equals he used every weapon fair and unfair, and nourished feuds which overflowed into every learned journal in Europe.

Mrs Tebben had therefore replied to her husband's plea for a study:

'Your point of view is perfectly reasonable, Gilbert. You are the wage-earner, therefore it is only just that you should be comfortable. I will send for Margett, and we will see what we can do.'

'Isn't it more a job for an architect, Winifred?' said Mr Tebben. 'Margett is only a builder, and look at the mess he made of Mrs Palmer's barn.'

'That was quite different. Mrs Palmer wanted to use the barn for Greek plays, so she had to have a fixed basin put in for the actors to wash before they changed into their ordinary clothes. Sandals do let the dirt in so frightfully. It is true that the basin did leak, but as there will be no fixed basin in your study, Margett could do it quite well.'

Mrs Tebben, thus open-mindedly arguing, or rather, trampling kindly over her husband, had summoned Margett, the carpenter and builder. After a long conversation, only two plans were found possible. One was to put the study in the basement, which owing to the perpendicular nature of the land was really a ground floor, the other to take a piece off the dining-room. Mr Tebben would have preferred the lower storey, from which he could escape straight into the garden and away down the valley into the woods, if pressed by enemies, but Mrs Tebben, who liked to have her household under her eye, decided to take a piece off the dining-room. The result was two rooms, both too small for human habitation. In the one the family took their meals, seated at a narrow table, the backs of their chairs grating against the walls, in the other Mr Tebben had made a little hole for himself among his books, where he sat with an oil-stove in winter, and fried in the sun in summer. An ancestral bookcase, with which he refused to part, almost blocked the entrance. It was as high as the room, it stuck out so far that the door could never be more than half opened, its shelves were edged with faded, scalloped fringes of red leather, which, disintegrating, shed dust and leathery crumbs. Owing to the great depth of the shelves the books were double banked. Mr Tebben always knew where a given book should be found, but could not always summon the energy to dig it out from the back row. Mrs Tebben rarely knew where any book she wanted was placed, but was willing to remove all the front rows, lay them with ready cheerfulness on the floor, and when she had found what she wanted, put them back in their wrong places. Their son, Richard, now in his last year at Oxford, had a deep contempt for these and all his parents' other ways, though, unlike Mr Fanshawe of Paul's, he did not attempt to conceal his contempt under a mask of courtesy, a social virtue which he condemned as hypocritical snobbery.

'Louise!' cried Mrs Tebben again, getting herself through the door and shutting it behind her. 'Her van will be upon us, before the bridge goes down!'

'Her van?' asked Mr Tebben, justifiably puzzled. 'Oh, I thought you meant she was bringing the milk-lorry down the garden. Well, I can't see her. I'm busy. I'm writing to Fanshawe. The letter ought to have been sent a week ago. Can't you stop her?'

'You'll have to see her sooner or later,' said his wife, 'if it's about her Greek play. You know she wants you to do Theseus, and she said she would take no denial.'

'I certainly won't be Theseus,' said Mr Tebben. 'I won't wear sandals and catch cold and wash my feet in that leaky basin of Margett's. I have never acted in one of her plays yet, and I never will. Besides, what does the woman know about Greek plays? Let Richard do Theseus when he comes down, or Margett, or Mrs Palmer's nephew that she's always talking about. I will not make a fool of myself. You really must tell her I am busy, Winifred.'

'So be it,' said Mrs Tebben. But it was not, for Mrs Palmer, who had annoyingly come round by the garden, in at the drawing-room window, and so through the hall, now intruded herself. Those who did not admire Mrs Palmer both disliked and feared her hectoring methods, but she was entirely indifferent to moral temperatures. Her husband avoided her activities as much as possible, and was very fond of her, having that affectionate reverence for his wife which is one of the advantages, from the female point of view, of the childless marriage. It is so much more difficult for a husband to cherish and revere the mother of several healthy children who take possession of her time and devotion.

Mr Palmer's only and much younger sister, Rachel, had married Frank Dean, the head of a large engineering firm.

The Deans had lived abroad a good deal, on account of Mr Dean's work, and their large family had made the Manor House a kind of headquarters. Of late they had not been down so often, and were not well known to the Tebbens. The nephew that, according to Mr Tebben, Mrs Palmer was always talking about, was Laurence Dean, the eldest son. He had been for some years in his father's firm and was eventually to inherit most of Mr Palmer's property. His aunt Louise was devoted in her high-handed way to him and his brothers and sisters, and made as much fuss over them as if she were the hen that had hatched someone else's eggs.

'News! News!' cried Mrs Palmer, waving a letter at the Tebbens. 'I had to come round and tell you, Winifred, and as I met your Mrs Phipps at the shop, I knew there would be no one here to answer the bell, so I came creeping round by the drawing-room. I shall just tell you about it and run away, for the great man must not be disturbed.'

Mr Tebben, who detested being called a great man, got up, but was unable to offer his caller a seat, as he had the only chair in the little room, and Mrs Palmer could not have squeezed her stout, imposing person behind the table. Luckily Mrs Tebben, who in some ways had never developed spiritually since the days of cocoa-parties in a bed-sitting room at college, remembered refreshments, and said to Mrs Palmer:

'You must have a cup of tea. Mrs Phipps will be back in a moment, and the kettle is just on the boil. We always have tea in the morning. Come into the drawing-room and Gilbert will join us.'

Rather suspiciously Mrs Palmer allowed herself to be led

into the drawing-room, where sofas and chairs heaped with papers showed that Mrs Tebben had been working. It was a pleasant side of Mrs Tebben's character that although her own books were described, by those who read them, as important, she was entirely modest about what she had done, and never dreamt of demanding elbow-room or solitude for herself, although she accepted their necessity for her husband. There were more bookcases, photographs of places in Norway and Iceland that they had visited before children put such an expense out of the question, and in a corner a small upright piano, celebrated for having belonged to Mr Tebben's mother, but possessing no other merit. Mrs Tebben, clearing an armful of papers and a huge tabby cat off the sofa, invited her visitor to sit down.

'It is about the Deans,' said Mrs Palmer. 'I have had a letter from Rachel. She and Frank and five, or is it six, of their children, are coming to the Dower House for the summer.'

'Mr Palmer's sister and her husband?' said Mrs Tebben. 'Gunnar, put your claws in!'

'Yes. Fred is so delighted, and so am I, because they will be able to help with my play. You know we are doing *Hippolytus* this summer. That is partly what I came to see you about.'

'I must see about the tea,' said Mrs Tebben, getting up again. 'I'll send Gilbert to you, if you'll excuse me for a moment. Gilbert! Gilbert!' she shouted as she passed the study door, 'Mrs Palmer is alone in the drawing-room. Entertain her. I must see about some tea,' and so disappeared into the kitchen.

Mr Tebben unwillingly rose, went into the drawing-room, saved Mrs Palmer from Gunnar, who was preparing to sharpen his claws on her skirt, sat down beside her, and said nothing.

'We are doing *Hippolytus* this summer, you know,' said Mrs Palmer, for the second time. 'We know that you are only free at weekends, but we are very anxious to get you. Theseus cries out for you in the part.'

'Greek isn't my subject,' said Mr Tebben. 'The Scandinavian languages are more in my line. Now, if you were doing something in the nature of a saga – but no, it wouldn't do. No, I positively couldn't act, even in a saga. Besides, I don't think the village would understand Norse.'

'But we aren't acting sagas,' said Mrs Palmer, 'it's Euripides.'

'Greek is much the same,' said Mr Tebben. 'They wouldn't understand Greek. No, I really don't think they would.'

'It isn't Greek, it's English – a translation.'

'I don't think they'd understand a translation either,' said Mr Tebben determinedly.

'My nephew, Laurence Dean, that you have so often heard me talk about,' said Mrs Palmer, trying a fresh point of attack, 'will be here for the summer. His parents, my sister-in-law and her husband, will be at the Dower House with some of their children, I mean Laurence to do Hippolytus. Now, if you did Theseus, we should at least feel that we had a nucleus.'

Mrs Tebben now came in, with a three-legged cake-stand, followed by Mrs Phipps, carrying a wavering brass tray of tea-things. When the tray had been balanced on an eight-legged folding stand, Mr Tebben got up.

'"Two legs sat on three legs, milking four legs",' he said meditatively. 'Dear Mother Goose. Well, I must get back to my work. That letter to Fanshawe should have been written a week ago. Goodbye, Mrs Palmer. Villagers understand nothing, so it really will not matter what you do.'

With which helpful remark he picked up the tabby cat, and going quickly back to his study resumed his letter to Mr Fanshawe, whose society held outrageous views about the Elder Edda.

'What a splendid Theseus he would make,' said Mrs Palmer, as her host went out.

'Milk?' said Mrs Tebben. 'I'm afraid you will never get Gilbert to do Theseus. In fact, I know he won't. Gunnar! Gunnar! Do you want some milk? Oh, Gilbert must have taken Gunnar into the study. You know he doesn't like the Greeks. Gilbert, I mean. He says they were uncomfortable.'

'Well, it can't be helped,' said Mrs Palmer, taking a note-book out of her bag and crossing out an entry. 'We shall have to find someone else. It isn't a big cast. Theseus, Hippolytus, a huntsman, and a henchman are all the men. Margett will be the huntsman, and Patten, my second gardener, the henchman. I dare say Pollett, at the shop, will do Theseus if Mr Tebben really can't be persuaded. And then, about Hippolytus ...'

'Richard comes down today and might be able to help. He will be here all the summer, I hope. He has been doing Greats, so he would know the play. Not in English, of course, but then he knows the original, and could get the *spirit*,' said Mrs Tebben, going into the trance of adoration which any thought of Richard always induced.

'Perhaps he would train the chorus for me, then,' said Mrs Palmer, with great presence of mind. 'That is where real skill is required. I had thought of Laurence for Hippolytus. He has had a good deal of experience. He is in his father's engineering firm, and they have an excellent amateur dramatic society.'

She did not add that, in her opinion, anyone whose ears stuck out as much as Richard's was naturally disqualified for a part which did not demand a wig.

Mother, and aunt by marriage, each eager in the defence of her absent young, were silent for a moment, massing their forces for the next move. Mrs Palmer, who had quicker wits than her friend, got in first.

'I wish there were a part for you, Winifred,' she said regretfully. 'Your Lady Montagu was such a success the year we did *Romeo and Juliet*. I could hardly ask you to do the nurse in *Hippolytus*.'

There was no inflection of interrogation in her voice, but Mrs Tebben chose to take it that there was.

'Of course I'll do the nurse,' she said obligingly. 'It's a longer part than Lady Montagu, but I learnt those two lines very easily, and it will simply be a question of application. I shall give myself regular hours for study, as I used to do in the old days. And what about you?'

Mrs Palmer had been thinking very quickly.

'I shall lead the chorus,' she said, feeling that by so doing she could foil any attempt on Richard's part to train the villagers in his own way. 'And my niece Helen, Laurence's sister, will do Artemis,' she continued hurriedly, 'she drives a racing car. That fat daughter of Mrs Phipps's, Doris, I mean, will have to do Aphrodite, because Mrs Phipps is helping with the dresses. That only leaves Phaedra. Neither of Dr Thomas's girls from the Rectory can act without giggling, and I don't want to ask Lady Bond, because we are at war about a fence. My sister-in-law, Laurence's mother, would take the part, I am sure, and she looks wonderfully young for forty-eight, but she cannot ever remember her words. What shall we do?'

'Margaret will be coming home next week,' said Mrs Tebben, suddenly remembering the daughter whom, in her worship for Richard, she often forgot. 'She has been at Grenoble with a family. Not Greeks, but highly cultured people. I think she said something about having met Laurence there in one of her letters.'

Because her mother could only think of Richard, Margaret, who was two years younger, was often forgotten like that. Her father also let her existence slip from his mind at times, not because he adored Richard, whom indeed he vaguely found rather trying, but because his mind was usually on letters to Fanshawe and similar subjects. So she had been sent to Germany and then to France when she left school, and there might have remained for ever if her father, suddenly remembering her existence, had not demanded her return. Mrs Tebben, arguing that as her husband was paying for the child's education he had a perfect right to see her, had agreed, and now came her reward, for Margaret would be a useful pawn to play against Mrs Palmer. As that lady had no alternative left, she was obliged to accept enthusiastically, only wishing that Margaret were rather more hideous than she remembered her, as so very pretty a person might attract Laurence, whom she destined for a good marriage.

'Then that's all settled,' said Mrs Palmer. 'Tell Richard to come over and see me as soon as he gets back – he might dine with us tonight, after the Choral. And tell Margaret too, of course, as soon as she comes home. We can't begin rehearsing too soon. And do you mind if I have Mrs Phipps on Wednesday afternoons? She can do a lot of machining for me, and I know you are nearly always in town in the middle of the week. Say goodbye to the great man for me. I shall just slip out again as I came in.'

Mrs Tebben watched her visitor go with mixed feelings. To have Richard refused for Hippolytus and Mrs Phipps commandeered for Wednesdays was intolerable. On the other hand, she as Nurse and Richard as chorus master would have the play a good deal in their own hands, and certainly Richard would not have wanted to play Hippolytus to his sister, of whom he thought as poorly as he did of his parents. If Mrs Palmer thought she could manage the chorus against Richard's wishes, let her try. And Gilbert was safely out of it, which reminded her that he had not had any tea, so she poured out a cup and took it into the study.

'I'm afraid it's rather cold and stewed,' she said, putting it down on the table.

Mr Tebben was used to it in that state, for it was one of his wife's economies to keep tea for hours, under a tea-cosy, or in the fender, rather than send for fresh supplies, so he pushed it kindly away and continued his work till lunch-time. Meals were no particular pleasure to him in his own home. What she ate was a matter of indifference to Mrs Tebben, who prided herself on being a good housewife, so she had forced her family into a small service flat in London, and had Mrs Phipps to cook in the country. Mrs Phipps, a born cook only in the sense that she had brought up a large family chiefly on tinned foods, had a natural gift for making meat appear grey and serving all vegetables in that water which to throw away (so scientists tell us) is to lose the most nutritious part of their natural salts. Today the meat, being cold boiled mutton, would have been grey in any case. The salad was from the garden. Mrs Phipps had indeed held it under the tap, but not long enough, nor had she shaken away the water (not, in this case, recommended as nutri-tious by scientists), so that the lettuces lay in a gritty pool.

'Well, Gilbert, I have rescued you from Louise,' said Mrs Tebben. 'I am sorry there are no potatoes, but Mrs Phipps didn't put them on in time, and knowing that you wanted to come with me and meet Richard at the station, I didn't like to wait for them to be finished. We could have them in if you like and just eat the outside part that is cooked, and have the rest properly boiled and use them up with the salad tonight.'

'No, thank you,' said Mr Tebben.

'Some cold caper sauce? There was just this little bit left, and it seemed a pity not to use it. If you don't want it, I will have it, so that it won't be wasted.'

'Are there any pickles?' asked Mr Tebben, though with-out hope.

'Alas, no, my dear. A breakdown in domestic arrangements. But the salad which is so good for you, is all our own.'

'When I eat green stuff,' said Mr Tebben, chewing away at a well-grown lettuce, 'I understand why cows have four stomachs. I am relieved to hear about Theseus. Nothing would have induced me to act, but I had no wish to argue with Mrs Palmer. Greek plays! I have always felt that the Greeks were easily amused. A stone seat under a burning sun, with the bitter wind that so often accompanies it, four or five people in preposterous boots and masks, plays with whose plots everyone had been familiar from childhood, and there they would sit for days and weeks. Now, the Vikings—'

'Excuse me, dear,' said Mrs Tebben, 'but which will you have? Here I have tinned apricots. The dish on the left, I will not disguise from you, is the remains of yesterday's rice pudding. I told Mrs Phipps to warm it up, but I fear she has forgotten. At least it is neither hot nor cold. Will you have both? And please go on with what you were saying.'

'I'll wait for cheese,' said Mr Tebben. 'The Vikings had more sense, so had the Icelanders. The very idea of an open-air theatre was abhorrent to them, if indeed they ever thought of it. Their national literature, stories of gods and heroes, was familiar to them, and they would have laughed, yes, laughed, at the idea of dramatising what was already in the highest degree dramatic. We find no traces of open-air theatres in Norway or Iceland. Practical people, they realised that an open-air parliament, for so, very roughly, one may describe the Thing, or All-Thing, was enough strain on anyone, without resorting to open-air entertainments. If they wanted to be entertained they sat at home, by a fire, and had their skald to recite to them.'

'More like the wireless,' said Mrs Tebben, sympathetically. 'Cheese, dear? We are just finishing up this hard bit before Richard comes, if you don't mind.'

'Wireless!' said Mr Tebben, taking the cheese resignedly. 'That is a thing the Icelanders would never have tolerated, not for a moment. Being a highly cultivated people, their chief pleasure in the long northern evenings was talk and song among themselves, while the women worked. A kind of talk of which, with the pleasant difference that no women are present, our University Common Rooms are in some sense the only survival.'

'I do so agree with you about open-air performances, dear. I can't think why the coffee is so nasty again. Will you have some? Luckily Louise has the barn centrally heated now. Do you remember what time Richard's train arrives?'

'Two-ten. We have plenty of time to walk down the lane.'

'But I am taking the donkey-cart for Richard's luggage, Gilbert; so will you get Modestine for me while I just look round Richard's room. The reading lamp by his bed is broken, and we seem to have run out of bulbs, so if you don't mind I'll put yours there till I can get a new one. I lent mine to the Choral Society and forgot to get it back.'

Mr Tebben hated Modestine, who was an elderly man, but literature must be served, more than anyone he knew. Mrs Tebben, always conscious that she must economise, for they were not well off and there were the children to be provided for, had decided that a car would be an extravagance and a donkey and cart would do very well to take them on little excursions and do their station work. There is no need to explain how wrong she was. Richard had firmly been ashamed of cart, donkey, and mother from the first moment that the plan was discussed, and refused to ride in, or be seen walking by, the little governess-cart which Modestine sometimes pushed backwards, sometimes caused to remain stationary across the village street, and occasionally ran away with down the main road. Nor would he catch nor harness Modestine, neither lead him to the forge to be shod. Margaret, kind creature, was always ready to do her best, but she had been away for a year. Therefore Mr Tebben had been forced – for Mr Phipps the gardener and odd-job man, who was also the sexton, was far too busy letting the vegetables run to seed – to be catcher, harnesser, and leader (when driving was of no avail), or rather puller of the hateful animal, chasing it in wet grass, pitting his strength unsuccessfully against a brute's. Though Mr Tebben had been a mountain climber in his younger days, his strength was as nothing against Modestine's, nor could he find any satisfactory method of retaliation when Modestine trod on his feet with hard little hoofs. If a god had granted Mr Tebben one wish, and one only, it would have been that Modestine should for a day have human feet, and he hoofs, that justice might be done. Mrs Tebben was not a good walker, so whenever they dined out in the immediate neighbourhood, she was conveyed by Modestine, a hurricane lamp tied to the front of the governess-cart, her husband driving or leading, as Modestine dictated, Richard, if he were of the party, a hundred yards in front or behind.

Mr Tebben caught Modestine, who was in a tolerant mood, gave him the rest of the cheese, and put him into the cart. Mrs Tebben, wearing a shapeless old raincoat, for the day though warm had been showery, and a battered garden hat, got into the cart. Her husband, under pretence of sparing Modestine, walked at her side along the green lane that led down the hill to the railway. As Modestine had a feeling about level crossings, Mrs Tebben drew up by the line. The train was already signalled, and Bert Margett the porter, elder brother of young Alf, was in the act of shutting the gates.

'Want to come through, mum?' said Bert.

'No thanks, Bert,' said Mrs Tebben. 'I couldn't get the donkey across. He doesn't like the lines.'

'I'll take him over, mum,' said Bert, going to Modestine's head.

Modestine, recognising him as one of the class who were his proper masters, nimbled elegantly across without a murmur.

'Goes nicely with old Bert, don't you, Neddy?' said Bert affectionately.

'Here, Bert, get them gates shut; she's coming,' shouted the station-master, Mr Patten, the uncle of Mrs Palmer's second gardener.

'Okey-doke,' shouted back Bert Margett. 'I'll come and take him across again, mum, when she's gone,' he added to Mrs Tebben, and resumed his task of shutting the gates.

No sooner had he done so than tank engine 17062, driven by Sid Pollett, a cousin of Mr Patten's who lived further up the line, came noisily round the curve, having waited to do so till Mr Pollett had received certain information from his fireman, a Margett, who had got out of the cab to reconnoitre, that Bert had shut the gates. For greater facility of communication with his cousin, the engine-driver drew up in front of the station-master's office, so that the end coach with the luggage van remained forlorn beyond the platform, marooning passengers and luggage.

A young man put his head out of the end coach.

'Hi! aren't we going up to the platform?' he shouted to Bert.

'Don't look like it, Mr Richard,' shouted Bert.

'Hell!' said Richard, climbing down onto the line. 'I've got no end of stuff in the van.'

'All right, Mr Richard,' said Bert, 'I'll see to it. Your father and mother and Neddy's outside.'

'Oh hell,' said Richard, 'they would bring that foul donkey. Look here, Bert, you'll find three suitcases and a packing-case of books that weighs about a ton in the van, and I've got a gramophone and a box of records and a lot of coats and things and my cricket bat in the carriage. And there's a pair of boots somewhere about, and for the Lord's sake be careful with those records. Hullo, Father, I wish you'd get a car. You can get a perfectly decent one for about twenty-five quid.'

'I don't think your mother would like it,' said Mr Tebben, sadly wondering why the inner affection he felt for his son should always be changed to embarrassed dislike at the very moment of meeting. 'She's outside in the donkey-cart. How are you?'

'Oh, all right,' said Richard, adding in a stage undertone,

'Oh, my God!' which was meant to show that he resented his mother's appearance in the donkey-cart and his father's unnecessary inquiry after his health and possibly his examination results, which would not be out for some weeks and were not his father's business, and he wished them to know it without the trouble of having to tell them.

In deep depression Mr Tebben led the way silently through the booking office to the little station yard.

'My dear boy,' cried Mrs Tebben, throwing her arms wide.

Richard recognised with disgust that she was wearing the raincoat which reminded him forcibly of the appearance of the wives of Heads of colleges at garden parties, and that her untidy bobbed hair was escaping in every direction from beneath a hat suitable for Guy Fawkes. That her face was irradiated with affection escaped his notice.

'Oh, all right,' said Richard. 'I'm afraid you'll have to get out, Mother. I've an awful lot of stuff.'

As he spoke, Bert and his truck came clanking out of the station, followed by Ed Pollett, the occasional or sub-porter, carrying the gramophone and records.

'But even if I get out, my dear boy,' said Mrs Tebben, preparing for a logical argument, 'Modestine could not take all that luggage. We must make two journeys.'

'Oh, don't fuss like that, Mother. The donkey can easily take my stuff. Do him good, the lazy brute.'

'But, my dear boy, Modestine cannot possibly drag all those boxes up the lane. You seem to have a great many records. Willingly would I walk if that would help, but as things are I see nothing for it but that I should drive some of your luggage up to the house while you and your father walk, which I know Daddy would love. You can then bring Modestine down again and fetch the rest of your things, and coming back you could just go round by the village and ask Mrs Margett if the Choral have done with my reading lamp.'

For twopence, or to be more exact, for the price of a ticket back to London, Richard would have dashed over the level crossing, jumped into the up train, whose driver was at the moment exchanging tokens with Mr Patten's cousin in the cab of the down train, and gone back to town. But having only two shillings he had to content himself with replying, 'Oh, anything anybody likes. All I can say is, it's always exactly the same, the minute I get back. Fuss, fuss, fuss,' and then feeling ashamed of himself.

'Don't you worry, mum,' said Bert. 'Ed'll run Mr Richard's stuff up in Mr Patten's car as soon as he's off duty, won't you, Ed?'

Ed nodded. Richard strode off up the hill alone, angry and mortified because the irritation which his parents always produced in him had for the thousandth time got the upper hand. He had promised himself again and again this term that next time he would make allowances, treat them with tolerant kindness, and now, before he had even shaken hands with his father, or let himself be kissed by his mother, everything had gone wrong. It was quite impossible to apologise to one's parents. They might be solemn about it and anyway it was not one's own fault. If Mother would go about in a donkey-cart, looking like that, when even the station-master had a car, and Father would look at one as if he wanted one to be sympathetic, hang it, it was enough to put any fellow on edge, especially when he knew that he had slacked all this year and probably hadn't done well in Greats. The next thing would be that they would begin to ask him what the exams were like, and Mother would want to go through some of the papers with him. As if anyone with any sense didn't know that a chap who had just come through the Schools would be gibbering with nerves till the results were out, and never want to hear of the beastly things again, and that having to stay with one's parents made it worse than ever. If only one's people would somehow have some more money, so that one could go abroad with other chaps instead of having to be cooped up with people who didn't understand one and had probably never been young themselves at all.

He turned into the wood and there abandoned himself to the deep despair of a young man who knows he didn't work enough in his last year, is even ruder and more intolerant to his parents than they deserve, and has let himself down before Bert and Ed.

Meanwhile Bert had put Richard's small luggage into the cart, led Modestine across the line and renewed his promise that Ed should run Mr Richard's things up as soon as he could get off duty. Modestine took his own way up the lane, for neither his passenger nor his passenger's husband had any heart to notice whether he plodded on or stopped to browse. Mrs Tebben, much too hot in the raincoat, sat staring in front of her, while Mr Tebben walked silently at her side. This time it was to have been different. Richard had had a hard year, they agreed, with Greats at the end of it, and each had secretly determined to do everything that might please him; placate was the word that each shrank from forming. And now, as always happened, the vacation was beginning with what was almost a scene, what would have been a scene if either of them had dared to answer back. Bitterly discouraged, yet unwilling to confess so early to defeat, they reached home in silence to find the house empty, Richard they knew not where, the last rankling thought in their mind being that the whole station had witnessed their disgrace.

But Bert and Ed, who were quite used to the Tebbens, gave no thought to these fine shades.

'Plenty of stuff young Richard has,' said Bert. 'You need as many hands as a opticus to carry all them cases and all.'

'That's right,' said Ed.

'I come off duty six-thirty,' continued Bert. 'It's the Choral tonight, up at the Manor House. I'll get my tea first and a bit of a wash and then you get the car and I'll come up with you, see?'

'That's right,' said Ed.

'Okey-doke,' said Bert.

2

Beginning of Romance

Driven in at last by the pangs of hunger, for it was nearly tea-time, Richard slipped into the house and upstairs. The attic, formerly his playroom as a little boy, now his bed-sitting room, was his only retreat, but even so not a safe one. His father, he must do him that justice, hardly ever came upstairs, and knocked and apologised if he did. But he never knew when his mother might come quietly and annoyingly in, kiss the top of his head, ask whose that interesting hand-writing was, rearrange one or two things that he had specially put where he wanted them and, just as she was going, ask him to run up to the shop, or get his bicycle and go over with a note to the Manor House. Richard felt so miserable that he was at the moment almost willing to recognise the possibility of some very small fault on his own side. Pausing opposite the looking-glass he gazed at himself, as if the mirror might tell him what was wrong. He only saw a rather bony young man, with fair hair and pale blue eyes, dressed with the studied carelessness of the undergraduate. The bat-like ears to which Mrs Palmer had taken secret exception, he rarely noticed, nor did his friends. Unless a young man's ears absolutely bend forward, it is strange how the eye, concerned with the more central features of the human head, skates over and discounts such peculiarities.

Of his long bony hands he was secretly proud, but annoyed by his even longer and bonier feet, which could hardly ever be crammed into ready-made shoes. He saw that he needed a shave, but decided to leave it till tomorrow. In the awful atmosphere of home, it didn't matter what one looked like.

His thoughts went back to the previous evening, and a party at the house of a friend who lived in London and had parents that could be relied upon to go out and leave the house clear, besides providing plenty of drinks. There had been no girls, thank heaven, and plenty of really serious discussion of intellectual questions. He smiled as he recalled to himself the one or two severe snubs that he had given to a young man from the London School of Economics, who thought he understood rationalising. The young man had not at first been convinced, and had quoted in argument a friend of his who was a Russian girl called Daria, but Richard had shown him exactly where he got off at. As for quoting what a girl said, Richard's gorge rose at the thought, for never yet had he seen a girl that was worth mentioning, and heaven knew there were enough at Oxford, the whole place simply crawling with them. Girls were the limit, and that was all one could say. After the party Richard and the young man had, with some condescension on Richard's side, sworn eternal friendship, which the young man, by that time far too full of beer, had accepted with tears. Richard knew neither his name nor his address, and no more was to come of it. But the party, or rather its after-effects, were possibly responsible for some of the depression which he felt today.

'A bit of a hangover, you know,' he said boastingly to himself in the glass, and then collapsed, as he reflected how little he would impress his parents with this, how they might quite probably not understand what he meant, and would certainly take it in the wrong spirit. Parents!

Just then the tea-bell rang.

'I'll just not say a single word unless it's a nice one,' said Richard to himself as he went downstairs. 'If they say something annoying, I'll simply hold my tongue.'

In pursuance of this virtuous resolve Richard, who usually spoke his mind freely and at length on every topic, sat in glum silence, broken by an occasional awkward Please or Thank you, which so wrought upon his parents that they would almost have preferred his natural discourteous loquacity. After tea his father, with great courage, asked him to come into the study and see the letter he had been drafting to Fanshawe. Richard, who was really interested in his father's work and knew something about it, was just beginning to become human when Mr Tebben was incautious enough to broach the subject of Richard's future plans which at once made him go out for a long walk and not be back till dinner-time, or supper, as Mrs Tebben chose to call it.

At this ill-dressed meal, consisting of sardines which he

loathed, tomatoes which he despised and a blancmange with the rest of the stewed apricots round it which he refused, his mother told him that Ed had brought up his luggage half an hour ago.

'He was on his way to the Choral at Mrs Palmer's,' said Mrs Tebben. 'By the way, Richard, Mrs Palmer is getting up *Hippolytus* and wants you to help. I'm sorry you don't like blancmange, dear. Do have some, it's a pity to waste it.'

'There aren't many parts for me,' said Richard, ignoring the question of the blancmange.

'That's exactly what I said to Mrs Palmer, but I told her you might be able to lead the chorus. Her nephew, Laurence Dean, the one she is always talking about, is to do Hippolytus.'

'He can have it,' said Richard. 'I don't see myself pretending to be dead on the floor of the Palmers' barn or being made love to by Mrs Phipps's fat daughter.'

'Is she to be Phaedra?' asked Mr Tebben. 'Well, possibly Phaedra was stout. Euripides does not tell us.'

'No, no, dear; Margaret is to be Phaedra.'

'My good mother, I must protest,' said Richard. 'It will be absolutely rotten for me if Margaret does Phaedra. One had one's conception of the part. Anything further from Phaedra one cannot conceive.'

'Phaedra may also have been good-looking,' said Mr Tebben.

'Oh, I didn't mean that. Margaret's all right, Father, but she hasn't the experience. I know a girl at Somerville who would do exactly. Mind you, I don't like her, but one must admit that she's the type: dark, handsome, wavy hair, fire, and she knows Life. She's been away for several weekends. She told me all about them.'

'I am not sure, or perhaps I would rather not be sure, what you imply,' said Mr Tebben.

Taking this, rightly, as a reproof for free-speaking, Richard mumbled something about being treated as if one were in the nursery, which his parents pretended not to hear. His mother, plunging into the breach, suggested that he might go over and see Mrs Palmer after supper.

'I can't go to old mother Palmer, that's flat,' said Richard. 'I promised to play darts at the Woolpack this evening.'

'But, Richard, my dear boy,' said his mother, 'I *told* Mrs Palmer you would go over; and what is more,' she added, laying down her pudding spoon dramatically, 'she asked you over for dinner and I absolutely forgot to tell you. There is still time, because they don't dine till late on Choral nights. Don't eat that cheese, dear, and you'll be able to manage her dinner. Perhaps Daddy would like it. No, Gilbert? Well then, Richard, give it to me and I'll finish it up with this little bit of bread.'

'I do wish to goodness, Mother, you wouldn't interfere. Just because Mrs P. has pots of money, she thinks she can order us all about. I'm going to the Woolpack.'

'But you can easily look in at Mrs Palmer's before or after your game and explain.'

'Mother, I can't.'

'Well then, dear,' said Mrs Tebben, remembering to look at things clearly, 'I must write a note to explain that you can't – I will take the blame entirely on myself – and then you can go over on your bicycle and leave the note at the

Manor House before you go to your game. I will write a little note now. Put my coffee down, please, Mrs Phipps. I have just to write a note for Mr Richard to take to Mrs Palmer's and then I'll drink it.'

'Why on earth can't we have a telephone?' asked Richard. 'My good mother, it won't hurt Mrs P. if I don't turn up tonight. I do loathe all this social snobbery.'

'I think, Richard, you might just look in,' said Mr Tebben, and whether Richard felt a command that he was a little afraid to disobey, or thought that his father was appealing to him as man to man, he grudgingly consented.

'Take a coat then, dear,' said his mother. 'It may be chilly coming back.'

Richard fled coatless into the warm summer night, disregarding his mother's cries to him to take the bicycle, and made his way by the field path to the Manor House. When he arrived, the Choral Society had just finished their rehearsal. Mrs Palmer was seeing them off in the hall and immediately pounced on Richard.

'Glad to see you,' she said. 'We are just going to dine. I always dine at a quarter to nine on Choral nights. Wait a minute, I must speak to Doris Phipps. Doris, tell your mother Wednesdays will be all right, and don't forget to learn your Aphrodite lines. You had better dine with us, Richard. Yes, I can see you aren't dressed and it's a pity you haven't shaved, but you'll get a good dinner here.'

'But I have had dinner at home, Mrs Palmer,' said Richard.

'Never mind. You can easily manage another one at your age,' said Mrs Palmer, insultingly. 'Sparrow, lay a place for Mr Richard.'

'Yes, madam,' said the butler. 'Would you care to wash, sir?'

Richard would have liked to say No, defiantly, but he valued the good opinion of Sparrow, the village's fastest bowler, and did not wish Sparrow to think him unclean.

'Anyone staying here, Sparrow?' he asked, as the butler led him away.

'Only Mr and Mrs Dean, Mr Richard; Mr Palmer's married sister and her husband, as you might say. I understand they are coming to the Dower House for the summer, themselves and family. Young Mr Dean, Mr Laurence that is to say, is an excellent all-round cricketer, I understand, and will be quite an acquisition to us. When you have washed, Mr Richard, and brushed your hair, dinner will be served.'

Much to his annoyance Richard brushed his hair, a concession he had never meant to make, and returned to the hall, where Mr and Mrs Palmer were waiting for their guests. Mr Palmer, a pleasant, white-haired man in a velvet coat, greeted Richard kindly.

'I expect you are ready for a good holiday,' he said. 'I know what that last year at the University is. You must get plenty of cricket and forget all about Oxford for the present. Louise, where are Rachel and Frank?'

'Not down yet,' said Mrs Palmer. 'They can't bear the Choral, for which I can't blame them, for the noise it makes is quite revolting. Sparrow!'

'Yes, madam,' said Sparrow, who had been hovering near the dining-room door.

'Tell Mr and Mrs Dean again that dinner is waiting. Tell them personally.'

Sparrow went lightly upstairs, and almost immediately returned, leading captive Mr and Mrs Frank Dean.

'This is Richard Tebben,' said Mr Palmer, 'and dinner has been ready for ten minutes. Come along.'

Without giving them time to shake hands, or even look at one another, he herded the party into the dining-room. Mr Palmer liked to dine by daylight in summer, and though dusk was filling the room, the only light was on the service table at the far end, so Richard could not see the Deans very well.

'Rachel,' said Mrs Palmer, leaning across Richard to Mrs Dean, 'this young man knows all about Greek plays. He is going to help me with the chorus. Richard, make Mrs Dean promise to act. And I must have a good talk with you after dinner, and show you exactly what I want you to do.'

'I'm awfully sorry, Mrs Palmer,' said Richard, 'but I've promised to play darts at the Woolpack. Some of the cricket team usually turn up, and I wanted to see them about our summer matches!'

'Darts!' said Mr Palmer. 'Why can't people drink beer in peace without throwing darts, I can't think. And the curate is always liable to look in and promote good fellowship. There's far too much good fellowship about here. I don't mean your plays, Louise,' he added hastily to his wife, 'but all these other affairs. One can't get an evening in peace. Now, Richard, you leave the Woolpack alone tonight, and stay here, and Louise will put you on the right track about her Greek plays. You'll learn a lot from her, a lot.'

'Of course, the whole English idea of the Greek chorus is fundamentally wrong,' said Richard, fortified by some excellent sherry. 'You should read what Professor Fosbrick says about it.'

'Fosbrick? Never heard of him,' said Mr Palmer conclusively.

'Fosbrick. Oh, *that* man,' said Mrs Palmer. 'I knew his first wife *very* well.'

Having disposed in this ominous way of Professor Fosbrick, she turned to Mr Dean on her left and plunged into technicalities about draining the field below the Dower House. As Mr Palmer enjoyed few things more than discussing and carrying out improvements on his estate, and his brother-in-law was a civil engineer, he added his voice to the discussion, and Richard found himself left to entertain Mrs Dean, who had not as yet spoken a word.

'Do you like Greek plays, Mrs Dean?' he asked.

'No,' said Mrs Dean, very kindly.

'It's a pity,' said Richard. 'You lose a lot.'

'But I like losing it. When you don't like a thing, it is money in your pocket to know it. I always know exactly what I don't like.'

'When you've seen *Hippolytus*, you'll feel quite differently.'

'No, I don't think so. It will be very dull and I shall hate it,' said Mrs Dean, her gentle voice composed, her calm unruffled.

Sparrow was now lighting candles on the table, and Richard was able to see his neighbour for the first time. If she had a grown-up son, she must be at least as old as his mother, Richard guessed, but no one would think it. With a backwash of irritation he compared his mother's untidy, shorn hair, her shabby trailing clothes, her maddening enthusiasms, with the still composure of this Mrs Dean, who wore her shining dark hair in a knot, was dressed in something shimmeringly white, and hated Greek plays. That Mrs Dean had always had enough money did not occur to him. There was something about her stillness that gave her a disquieting charm, which even Richard, very self-absorbed, and not at all sensitive except about himself, could not help feeling.

'I expect you will hate it, too,' she went on. 'My sister-in-law will bully you horribly. I am really very sorry for you, Mr Tebben. What else will you do this summer?'

These words might have been overheard by Mrs Palmer, who would have taken them as a joke, and doubtless Mrs Dean counted on this. But to Richard, sore after the day's misunderstandings, bullied as he had indeed already been by his hostess, the words came with the balm of sympathy and understanding. To be called Mr Tebben was also a delicate solace to his vanity, showing that this Mrs Dean regarded him as an equal, if not as a fellow conspirator against Mrs Palmer. But where a more modest young man would have held his tongue, Richard felt obliged to boast, and tell Mrs Dean rather noisily and very boringly about the village cricket club, from which recital she might have gathered, if she had been listening, that without his help the club might as well disband.

'I hear that your son plays a bit, Mrs Dean,' said Richard. 'I dare say I could find room for him if he likes to join us.'

'Which one do you mean?' asked Mrs Dean.

'Oh, I didn't know you had two.'

'I haven't. I have five. Laurence played for his school and

University, but now he is in Frank's business he doesn't have much time. I'm sure he'd love to join your club when he comes down here for his holiday. Gerald played for the Army, but he is in India with his regiment. The twins are both at sea now, but they played for their school and get a game whenever they can. Of course Robin isn't old enough. Are you a Blue?'

This question hit Richard, who had been at the tail of his college second eleven, rather hard. His good opinion of himself would not allow him to suspect any malice in it, but he was uneasy.

'I couldn't give the time,' he said, with doubtful accuracy. 'I was swotting for Greats all this year.'

'I quite understand. And I do think cricket excessively dull. Gerald and the twins used to talk of nothing else. Laurence is broader-minded. He plays tennis a good deal now, and so does Helen.'

'Is she your daughter?'

'My eldest daughter. She is quite uneducated, like me. She does a good deal of motor racing. Betty and Susan rather despise her, because they want to go to college. Betty has got a scholarship and Susan means to get one, but I think it is a good thing not to be too clever.'

'Are Betty and Susan your other daughters?' asked Richard, confused by a long vista of Deans, all brilliant at games and work, stretching away before him.

'Yes, they are the middle ones. Robin comes after them. He has just gone to his public school. Jessica is still in the nursery. She was a kind of afterthought,' said Mrs Dean, reflectively, with an expression of serene pleasure.

'Then you have eight children?' said Richard, awestruck.

'No, nine. But rarely all at home at once, I am sorry to say.'

The drain discussion, which had loudly raged through the rest of dinner, was now brought to a close by Mrs Palmer saying that they would have coffee and dessert on the terrace, a plan which gave universal dissatisfaction.

'Flies and moths on the terrace – and bats,' said Mr Palmer in an angry aside.

'Dear Louise,' said Mrs Dean, 'I don't think Frank ought to with his hay fever.'

'Didn't know you had hay fever, Frank,' said Mr Palmer. 'You ought to go to my man. He gives you injections. We'll have coffee indoors, Sparrow.'

'How long have you had it?' asked Mrs Palmer.

'Oh, off and on for some time,' said Mr Dean, looking at his wife.

It was a lover's evening of moonlight and nightingales and heavy perfume from the night-scented flowers, and though Richard's heart was entirely unoccupied, he felt nostalgic pangs which inevitably centred round Mrs Dean. He had seen a still beautiful woman, his first sight of her had been by candlelight, and that was the image that would remain with him. He would willingly have talked to her about himself all evening, but there was no chance of this, for as soon as they moved to the drawing-room she fell into a murmured conversation with her brother. As she talked she showed distinct and becoming signs of animation, and Richard wondered how Mr Palmer could have so inspiring an effect upon his sister. If he had been able to hear what they were saying, he would have wondered even more, for the subjects which brought light to Mrs Dean's dark eyes and a faint colour to her face were those of riding and tennis for Laurence, Helen, Betty and Susan, cricket for Robin, and the best milk for Jessica, subjects dear to Mr Palmer's own heart. He was a great deal older than his sister, and had married a woman of nearly his own age, so that he and his wife hardly seemed to be of the same generation as Rachel. The Palmers, childless, adored their nephews and nieces, while Rachel valued and admired her sister-in-law's generous affection. Had she been childless herself, she would never, she thought, have been able to love another woman's children without envy. But then, as she sometimes said, she could hardly remember a time when she had not got children, so she was no judge.

Mrs Palmer and Mr Dean, between whom there was no special affection but a good deal of mutual respect, were putting their practical, intelligent heads together over a slight alteration to the barn. Richard, feeling that the Woolpack would be lamenting his absence, yet unable to leave a house where he could look at Mrs Dean, remained miserably outcast from both groups, conscious of not being grown-up, not being good at tennis, and not able to ride. Of cricket he deliberately did not think. After what Mrs Dean had let fall about her elder sons' form, he felt that even the schoolboy Robin would be well above his class. As for milk, he hated it. Pulling his chair a little nearer to his hostess, he heard her say to Mr Dean:

'The acoustic is the trouble. You can hear very well in front and in the middle, but there is a kind of dumb spot at the back of the barn, and people do so shuffle and giggle when they can't hear that it upsets everyone.'

'Of course,' said Richard, 'what you ought to have is large earthenware jars in alcoves along the side walls. That is what von Bastow discovered at Terebinthos. You ought to read his book – it's translated. He gives marvellous accounts of the way jars improve the acoustics. Ten thousand people could hear distinctly every word that was said on the stage.'

As no one took any notice of him, he got up and walked away onto the terrace.

'From my own experience as a practical man, I should say that if the audience can't hear, it usually means that the actors aren't speaking plainly,' said Mr Dean. 'You'll have to rehearse your chorus better, Louise. Get Betty onto them. She produced her school play extraordinarily well last year. By the way, didn't you say young Tebben was to help with the chorus? You ought to speak to him about it. I thought he was here.'

Richard was pacing unhappily up and down the terrace. The country outside, drenched in moonlight, only increased his misery. In the distance the church clock sounded. Closing time. The Woolpack would now be ejecting its beer drinkers and dart players. He had been false to his promise and what had he gained? A very good dinner it was true, but otherwise he might as well never have been born. Mrs Palmer and Mr Dean treated him as a child and did not even take the trouble to consider his suggestion about earthenware jars. Mrs Dean had probably despised him for being so uncouth. If only he were indeed a child, perhaps she would like him better. She would at least take pains to find the best milk for him and a pony to ride, but as it was he might almost as well (though not quite) be at home. In great bitterness he stood still outside the window near which Mrs Dean and Mr Palmer were talking.

'It is disappointing about the pony,' said she, 'but perhaps something will turn up. Jessica is really too heavy for Nurse to wheel in the perambulator now, but if I could find a gentle pony, she could be led about.'

'I'll inquire,' said Mr Palmer, 'but since Margett's grey pony died, they have been very scarce about here. There are one or two over at Skeynes, but they are rather lively. Children ride them at pony meetings. Pony Clubs! No pony clubs when I was young. You got on and you fell off, and there you were. Is that light in your eyes? I'll put it out.'

'Mrs Dean,' said Richard, emboldened by the sudden darkness in the room.

Rachel looked up and saw, romantically surrounded by wistaria and honeysuckle, its large ears clearly outlined against the moonlight, the silhouette of Richard's head.

'Oh, Mr Tebben,' she said, 'I thought you had gone.'

'Mrs Dean,' said Richard, wounded but determined, 'I think I heard you say that you wanted a quiet pony. I mean, I wasn't listening, but I just couldn't help hearing the words. We have a donkey. He's about twenty years old and awfully quiet. If you liked I could bring him over and give your little girl some rides.'

'That's very nice of you,' said Mrs Dean, with that gentle animation he had previously admired.

'I haven't very much to do,' said Richard, 'and if you would say when it suited you, I could come over any time, and we've got a saddle. It's a bit mouldy, but I could rub it up a bit.'

'Thank you very much. That is very kind.'

'Well, good night,' said Richard, terrified of spoiling this idyll by another word.

'Good night, my boy,' said Mr Palmer. 'We must all get up early for these choruses of Louise's, eh?'

'Good night, Richard,' said Mrs Dean.

Richard, forgetting his hostess, reeled down the drive repeating his own name aloud. Never had Richard sounded so noble, so mellifluous a name. She had called him Richard. And her name was Rachel and both began with an R, at which thought Richard felt weak. That foul Modestine should be immediately shod and clipped within an inch of his life, his saddle cleaned and mended, and Richard himself would ride him until he was completely broken for any little girl's use.

As he passed the Woolpack, a few village men and lads were loitering at the door, among them Bert and Ed.

'Oh, hullo, Bert,' said Richard. 'I'm awfully sorry I couldn't get down in time for the game. I had to see Mrs Palmer about the play. I suppose you're in the chorus.'

'Looks like it,' said Bert, without enthusiasm. 'It's this way, Mr Richard. I go with Dawris Phipps, and Dawris seems to fancy a bit of dramatic, so there we are as they say. Not my idear of a chorus, Mrs Palmer's isn't.'

'What's Doris doing?' asked Richard.

'Well, I couldn't rightly say,' said Bert, 'but it's a solo turn.'

Here a slight scuffle which had been going on in the

background resolved itself into Ed, pushed forward by some of his friends with encouraging advice to speak up and tell Mr Richard.

'Hullo, Ed, what is it?' said Richard.

'I'm learning my lines,' said Ed.

'That's right, Ed's learning his lines. A line a day as the saying is,' said Bert, with what sounded like some hazy echo of a classical axiom.

'Splendid, Ed,' said Richard. 'You'll soon know them all at that rate.'

'No he won't, Mr Richard. You did ought to have remembered that,' said Bert reproachfully. 'Ed can't remember only the one line at a time. One gone another come, as they say. But he's as pleased as Punch down in the lamp-room, between trains, learning up his lines. Aren't you, Ed?'

A vague chorus from the men and lads at the Woolpack door indicated corroboration of Bert's statement and a certain pride in Ed's want of mental grip. After a few more words about the cricket club, Richard said good night and pursued his way homewards.

'Young Richard would make a good turn with that old Neddy of theirs,' said Bert to his audience. 'I'd laugh like anything to see them both wagging their ears.'

Unaware of this unfavourable criticism, Richard ran along the road and through the wood for the mere pleasure of running. His intention was to leap upstairs, leap into bed, as far as was compatible with having a bath, cleaning his teeth and other mundane considerations, and there to meditate till slumber claimed him on the perfections of Mrs Dean. But as he approached Lamb's Piece he saw to his great

42

annoyance a light in the sitting-room. It was impossible to get up those creaking stairs without being heard, so he walked in at the french window, defiantly determined to face the worst. His mother was sitting on the sofa, surrounded by papers, a writing pad on her knee. In front of her was a table with a tea-pot on it, covered by a red woollen tea-cosy.

'Did you have a good game, dear boy?' she asked, 'I have kept some tea for you. Did you explain to Mrs Palmer?'

'Oh, it's all right, Mother. No, I don't want any tea, thanks.'

'It seems a pity to waste it,' said Mrs Tebben, pouring out a tepid, black liquid. 'Was it nice at the Woolpack?'

'I didn't go. My good Mother, do you call this tea? It's stingo.'

'It is just the same that your father and I had. Besides Mrs Phipps let the kitchen fire out, and the Primus wouldn't work. But I could get you some lemonade, or there is the remains of that bottle of beer we opened on Tuesday.'

'I do wish you wouldn't fuss, Mother. Oh, Mrs Palmer wanted me to tell you that rehearsals begin next week, and can you come up and take the chorus two evenings a week in the barn?'

'Of course. And what was it like at the Palmers'?'

Richard made an ungracious and non-committal reply, but his mother gradually extracted from her increasingly sulky son an account of his evening. She particularly wanted to know what Mrs Dean was like, while Richard, unwilling to discuss that attractive woman in the squalid atmosphere of his home, assumed an air of oafish ignorance, and finally pleaded headache, a foolish move, which led to his mother laying her hand on his forehead to feel if it was hot, a liberty that he deeply resented. Owing to Mrs Phipps's lapse over the kitchen fire the bath water was cold, a final blow to break a man's spirit. Even in sleep fate pursued him with malignity, and instead of dreaming about Mrs Dean as was his fixed intention, he dreamt that he was standing before a wicket with a tennis racquet, being bowled at by eleven young Deans, each over ten feet high.

At the Manor House Rachel Dean, seated before a mirror, was brushing the long dark hair that she had never thought of cutting. Her husband, coming in from the dressing-room, drew aside a curtain and looked out on the garden.

'Darling,' said Rachel, 'if you leave that curtain open with a light in the room, bats will come in, and you know what happens with bats. They get their claws in your hair, and then you have to cut off all your hair or break their legs off, because they are too panic-stricken to rescue themselves.'

'Coward,' said Frank Dean, drawing the curtain again. 'Rachel, why did you tell Louise that I had hay fever? You know I've never had it in my life.'

'It was a deliberate lie,' said Rachel, placidly brushing her hair all the time. 'A noble lie. A lie in a good cause, because I didn't want coffee on the terrace, and I knew you didn't, and I knew Henry didn't. Frank, I think this will be a very pleasant summer. There is riding and tennis for Laurence and the girls, and there is a cricket club for Robin, and a donkey for Jessica, and the new drains for you. Louise's Greek play will be a little wearing, but I shall tell her I have a heart.'

'I don't like that, even as a noble lie,' said her husband.

'Well, it isn't quite a lie. You know Dr Masters did say that I had a murmuring heart, but he spoilt it all by saying it was of no consequence. What a lovely phrase a murmuring heart is, Frank. I should like to write a book called *The Murmuring Heart*. Yes, I shall have a heart all this summer, whenever Louise comes near me. So now everything is settled.'

'What do you think of that young Tebben?' asked Mr Dean.

'Poor boy,' sighed Rachel.

'Why poor?'

'I call anyone poor who gets into Louise's clutches,' said Rachel. 'He will never get his own way about the chorus. We must tell Betty and Susan to back him up.'

'I sometimes wonder,' said her husband, 'if you will have any time to think about me. It's the first holiday I've had since we were married.'

'Well, darling, you know you mostly won't be here, because whenever you say you will at last have a real holiday, you fall into some new work. But think of you I will. I always have, you know,' said his wife with an engaging smile.

'You agreeable object,' said Mr Dean. 'Lies or no lies, you are the most agreeable thing I know. Stop brushing your hair and go to bed, or I'll let the bats in.'

3

Introduction to a Family

For the next few weeks, Richard's life was largely ruled by Modestine. From a shed in the garden he rescued the old saddle and bridle, which he cleaned and polished into respectability. He accompanied Modestine to the forge, waited while he was shod, led him home, and began to train him for riding. His legs were too long for the donkey to be able to throw him off, but it could and did refuse obstinately to walk at all, so much to Richard's mortification Ed, who had mysterious powers over the brute creation, obligingly came up from the station every evening to put the unwilling animal through its paces.

When in due time the examination lists came out, Richard was hardly surprised to find that he had a third, for he realised that his faint hope that a miracle might have occurred since he did his papers was hardly reasonable. Mrs Tebben, who attached the importance to a good degree that only a woman who has got a first herself can understand, behaved extremely well, but it was impossible for Richard not to see that she had been crying, and her attempts to make light of it irritated him, though he knew that they were really an act of heroism. With his father Richard knew that he must sooner or later have the matter out. After skulking in the woods all day, he watched the house till his mother had gone to a rehearsal of the chorus, and with a very uncomfortable feeling knocked at his father's study door.

'Come in,' cried Mr Tebben, with false detachment. 'Oh, Richard. Come to see me, eh?'

'Not exactly, sir,' said Richard, standing on one leg till he nearly overbalanced.

'Well, going up to rehearsal?'

'Not just this moment.'

'Your mother's gone, I think.'

'Oh, has she. Well, perhaps I'd better go too. Old Mother Palmer will be having it all her own way.'

'Oh, before you go, Richard . . .'

'Yes, Father?'

'Er . . . wait a moment,' said Mr Tebben, bending over a drawer in his writing-table and hunting among some papers, 'where can it have got to? An old friend of mine, T. L. Platt, but the name wouldn't mean anything to you,' he continued, his head well down and turned away from Richard, and scrabbling violently and aimlessly among some old press-cuttings, 'he was at Paul's with me, and his sister married a man who shot himself in the Isle of Wight in ninety-four, or was it ninety-five; a very sad affair, and she was left with three children, but they are all doing very well now and two of them are married . . . Where on earth can I have put it?'

Richard, not unused to these discursive genealogical ramblings from his father and his father's old Oxford friends, waited with a growing feeling of sickness, and nervously fingering a box of paper-clips upset them all onto the floor. To stoop down and pick them up was a considerable relief to his feelings, and enabled his father to sit up again and take up the very ravelled thread of what he was trying to say.

'This man Platt, there was another Platt at Oriel at the same time, but no relation of his, I believe,' continued Mr Tebben, finding it easier to talk to his son's legs, which were sticking out from under the table, 'was ploughed in Greats, I remember, in the year before I came down. A very brilliant fellow, but uncertain.'

As he appeared to have come to the end of his depressing narrative for the time being, Richard spilt some more paper-clips and picked them up again.

'He did extremely well afterwards, curiously enough,' continued Mr Tebben, in a strained, unnatural voice. 'He read for the bar and became Chief Justice in one of the Colonies, I forget which. He was poisoned by a native who had some grudge against him. He did recover, but he has been a hopeless invalid ever since.'

Richard, issuing from his place of safety under the table, realised that this extraordinary speech of his father's was perhaps the kindest and most generous thing that he had ever known in his life. It meant that he was no longer an outcast, that his father still trusted him, that there would be no reproaches, and that if he had any good feeling and gratitude in him he would from this moment work like a nigger, and given any kind of chance would end his life as a hopeless invalid from poison administered by a vindictive native.

'Oh, here are the paper-clips, Father,' he said. 'I picked them up.'

'Thanks, Richard,' said his father. 'Well, well: Thought the harder, Heart the bolder, Mood the more as our Might lessens.'

On hearing this not very cheering quotation from the *Battle of Maldon*, Richard knew that he was entirely forgiven. Turning his back on his father, he examined the bound volumes of the *Transactions of the Snorri Society* with an interest which would have deceived no one.

'All right, my dear boy,' he heard his father say, 'all right. Piatt and I once had a very delightful walking tour from Grasmere to Seascale, going by Watendlath and then into Borrowdale and so over Stye Head Pass. E. P. Skellogg was with us, a first-rate historian, but sadly broken now. He had a stroke when his invalid sister died and his mind has been affected ever since.'

'Thanks most awfully, Father,' said Richard in a muffled voice, and rushed out of the room, banging the door.

Mr Tebben, left alone, picked up the rest of the paper-clips and went on with his work, his heart lighter than it had been for a long time. And though Richard was far from being a changed character, and indeed spoke with great intolerance to his parents at supper about driving his mother over to Skeynes in the donkey-cart, both he and his father were nearer to being friends than they had been since Mr

Tebben used to tell a small Richard the story of Burnt Njal in instalments after he was tucked up in bed at night. Richard even went so far as to consult his father about doing some reading for the bar, and though nothing was decided, chiefly because neither of them knew anything about it, a feeling of manly co-operation was born which was going to be a comfort to them both.

As the day of the Deans' arrival drew near, Richard moved in a state of exaltation which his parents found trying and incomprehensible. While his mother was delighted that he should at last make friends with Modestine, and his father was pleased to see that he shut himself in his room and read for several hours a day, they could both have wished that he did not find it necessary to show so freely his difficult toleration of their existence. If Mrs Tebben had known that his hours with Modestine were a vigil dedicated to Rachel Dean, if Mr Tebben had known that part of Richard's solitary hours in his room were spent in the composition and subsequent destruction of what even their author had to admit to be very bad verses, they would have understood his conduct a little better. But as to explain anything to parents who obviously can understand practically nothing, is simply waste of time, these things were not made known to Mr and Mrs Tebben.

One morning Richard, buying tobacco from Mr Pollett at the village shop, saw Doris Phipps at the other counter, where a modest drapery establishment was kept, consisting chiefly of spotted handkerchiefs and cheap scent.

'Hullo, Doris,' he said, 'nearly ready with your part?'

Doris, with blushes and giggles, said she didn't seem to have no time nowadays, because she was cleaning up at the Dower House for Mrs Dean when she come, and had been ordered by Mrs Palmer to take up the duties of kitchenmaid as soon as the family was there.

'They come tomorrow, don't they?' asked Richard, with assumed carelessness.

'That's right, Mr Richard. Mr Dean and Mrs Dean they're coming down in the car with nurse and the little girl and the other young ladies and gentlemen by train and the second chauffeur is bringing Mr Laurence's that's the eldest young gentleman's two-seater down tomorrow morning, and Mrs Palmer is sending up six quarts of milk a day and there'll be two parlour-maids and two housemaids and two in the kitchen besides me and they say the chauffeur's ever so nice and the second car is to go in Mrs Palmer's garridge because there isn't room at the Dower House for two cars besides Mr Laurence's that's the eldest young gentleman's and Miss Helen's that's the eldest young lady's and all the groceries come down from London twice a week,' said Doris, all in one breath.

'I suppose you don't know what sort of time Mr and Mrs Dean are expected?'

'Mrs Palmer said to dinner, Mr Richard, and cook comes tomorrow morning and the other girls and they say cook's temper is a fair treat,' said Doris.

Richard walked home on air, wondering how soon one could decently pay a call, and whether he ought to write a note to tell Mrs Dean that the donkey was ready, or tell her himself. Stumbling over a pile of books in the passage, he fell forward into the dining-room where his mother had already begun lunch.

'Dear boy, you are late,' said his mother.

'I say, Mother,' said Richard, too excited to resent this interference, 'I suppose you'll call on Mrs Dean at once. I think we ought to.'

'Well, dear boy, I shall call, of course, but I don't expect she will want visitors at once. Do you remember that Margaret comes tomorrow? I have to go to town for a night, to go to a dinner and a meeting with Daddy, so I shan't be back till tomorrow. Will you meet Margaret with Modestine? Her boat is due at four o'clock, and she ought to be here by the six forty-seven. It will be the up platform, because she is coming straight from the boat, so mind you don't miss her. And don't fall over those books in the hall.'

'Oh, all right,' said Richard. 'It'll do Modestine good to bring the luggage up. By the way, I told Mrs Dean you'd let her little girl ride Modestine.'

'Of course, dear Richard. But I fear Phipps can't be spared from the garden just now. I might drive Modestine over when I call on Mrs Dean and then the little girl could sit on him while I pay my call, if there is someone there to hold her on.'

'That's not riding, Mother. I'll take Modestine over myself every morning. We ought to be nice to the Deans, because of the Palmers.'

'But what about your reading, dear boy?'

'Well, Mother, there isn't really much sense in reading till I know exactly what I'm going to do. I dare say I'll go on the films anyway, so it's not much good wasting time reading. I suppose it's all right about Modestine?'

'Yes, dear, if you think he's up to it. Only you must get him shod.'

'I did.'

'Where?'

'At the forge, of course.'

'My dear Richard, I do wish you had told me first. The blacksmith at Skeynes is much better. It can't be helped now, but I do wish you would sometimes think, and not be so precipitate. Oh, Richard, did you put your pyjamas in the laundry basket? The laundry is calling tomorrow morning instead of Monday, something to do with the Oddfellows wanting the van for their Outing, but they didn't send the clean things last week, so it is all awkward. Or could you make your pyjamas do for another week? That is, if they don't return the clean things tomorrow when they send. But I sent them a postcard, so they are almost certain to bring them.'

'Oh Mother, the pyjamas can wait.'

'Very well, dear boy,' said his mother with exasperating meekness, 'I'll get the pyjamas myself tomorrow morning, before I go to town and put them in the basket. So don't stay in bed too late, or they won't go. I'll put them down on the washing list now and that will remind me.'

On the following morning Richard, inspired by love, was up early and put the pyjamas in the laundry basket himself. Going to his room after breakfast, he found his mother, ready dressed for her journey, opening and shutting all his drawers.

'The pyjamas,' she cried. 'I can't find them anywhere. Phipps broke the shaft of Modestine's cart this morning, so I am having to have Mr Patten's car to go to the station. You were still asleep and I didn't like to wake you, or you could have gone over on your bicycle and got Mrs Palmer's carpenter to mend it, but it doesn't matter now. Where *are* your pyjamas?'

'In the basket. I say, Mother, I do wish you wouldn't worry so much about them.'

'Well, dear boy, if I didn't look after things in this house I don't know what would happen. I hear the car, I must fly. I have to take all those books up with me to the binders and I forgot to do them up, so they must go loose in the car. Don't forget to meet Margaret.'

She hurried down to the hall, where Richard helped her to put on the shameful raincoat in which she preferred to travel, gathered up some bags and parcels, and entered the car, expressing her fear that the pyjamas had made her late for the train.

'It's all right, mum,' said Bert, who had been detached from duty by Mr Patten to drive the car, and was piling the books into it, 'Mr Patten said he'd keep the up train till you come if I hurried a bit.'

The car went off and Richard was left in peace. As the parents were away he could do what he liked all morning and needn't stay in for Mrs Phipps's horrid lunch, whose composition he could, from his memory of last night's dinner, accurately guess. It was going to be a real sweltering day, a day for laziness and books, and noble, melancholy thoughts. He took his books into the garden, and read there steadily till lunch-time, when he walked over to the Woolpack and ate bread and cheese and drank beer. After lunch he worked again in the garden for some time. The sun was benignantly hot, the newly mown grass smelt sweet, bees were humming in a stupefying way, Gunnar was purring beside him, and Richard could hardly keep awake. He fetched a few cushions from the drawing-room and lay down on the grass for a short refreshing nap, from which he awoke some two hours later with a feeling that something had happened. As consciousness returned to him, he suddenly knew what it was. It was now half-past five. Margaret was due at six forty-seven, the shaft of Modestine's cart was broken, and in spite of his promise he had quite forgotten to see about having it mended. The Phippses had vanished. There was nothing for it but to tie up the shaft as best he could and take the cart to be mended next day.

After rummaging in the shed he found some rope, improvised a kind of splint with the handle of an old croquet mallet, and with a hazy remembrance of Boy Scouting lashed the splint into place as tightly as he could. His clumsy fingers made a long job of it, and he had tied it up three or four times before it held properly. Modestine was in one of his unpleasant, coquettish moods, and by the time Richard had caught the reprobate animal and harnessed it, he was very hot and dirty and the train was almost due. Without bothering to wash or put on a tie he leapt into the cart and urged Modestine down the green lane. From the top of the hill he could already see the smoke of his sister's train in the valley, though the smoke of the down train, which passed it at the station, was not yet visible. But in spite of all his entreaties Modestine would not mend his pace sufficiently to get to the level crossing before the down train rushed into the station, checked violently, and stood noisily puffing. Almost at the same moment a white sports car of extremely rakish appearance came into the station yard, driven by a girl of whom Richard could see nothing except that her dress was white and her dark head bare. He began to wish that he had washed.

'Miss Margaret can't get out yet, Mr Richard,' shouted Bert from the Booking Hall, as the little entrance to the station was impressively called. 'Mr Patten's going to move her up the platform in a minute. I'll send Ed along as soon as she's in.'

From the Booking Hall came a loud, confused sound of voices. Ed appeared for a moment, carrying a couple of suitcases, was pushed aside and almost trampled underfoot by two tall girls and a boy in a school cap, and disappeared again.

'We won! We won!' shouted the three in chorus, rushing up to the sports car.

'No, you didn't. I was in the station before your train stopped. Ask him,' said the girl in the sports car, nodding towards Richard.

The schoolboy left the group and came towards the donkey-cart.

'Excuse me, sir,' he said, with great courtesy, 'but did you notice my sister's car drive up?'

Richard said he had.

The boy, who had a round, serious face, suddenly smiled a mystic smile, though his eyes remained gravely fixed on Richard.

56

'Then you can stop those girls quarrelling,' he remarked, as man to man. 'Did Helen's car get in first, or the train?'

'Your train stopped just before the car pulled up,' said Richard.

'Good,' said the boy. 'Thanks very much. Robin Dean.'

'Oh,' said Richard, 'Richard Tebben's my name. Are you coming to the Dower House?'

'I say, is that the donkey?' exclaimed Robin. 'My mother said you had a donkey for Jessica. Nan, Nan,' he shouted, as an elderly nurse came out of the station, leading a little girl by the hand and followed by Bert laden with suitcases, 'here's the donkey. Isn't it a decent one?'

Nanny, with the proper reticence of a nurse when in the presence of the gentry, even if they are unwashed and tie-less, merely remarked in a non-committal way that she said it was and not to bother the gentleman.

'I've got my bike with me,' said Robin to Richard, taking no notice of Nanny. 'Have you a bike? Both the brakes came off my bike last hols and I ran into some sheep and got a sprained wrist. Will you come for a ride with me and the girls?'

'Are those your sisters, then?' asked Richard.

'Yes, sir. That's Helen in the car. I betted her we'd get here first. She doesn't bike, but Betty and Susan do. Laurence,' he yelled to a tall young man, who inexplicably came out of the station with Margaret Tebben, 'Mr Tebben says our train got in first.'

'Richard darling!' cried Margaret. Richard got out of the cart and kissed his sister, feeling a little confused.

'Poor Ed came for my suitcases,' said Margaret, 'but when

he saw so many people getting out of the down train it was too much for him and he dropped them, so Laurence picked them up.'

'You see I met your sister abroad this winter, so I knew her,' said Laurence Dean. 'That's a good sort of donkey. Robin, go and see if Mother has found her spectacles, because they'll be wanting to start the train sometime.'

Robin went off. Richard, more and more confused, said to Laurence, 'But I thought your people were coming by car.'

'So they were, but something happened to the big car, so they came by train and we telephoned to Aunt Palmer to send a car or two for the luggage. Those look like her cars and the farm lorry. I wish she'd sent a donkey. I find donkeys so refreshing.'

If Richard had begun to regret not having washed, he now regretted it more than ever. It was bad enough to have Laurence Dean and that young Robin and the nurse see him so dirty, not to speak of the girls, who were still arguing, but now Mrs Dean, *his* Mrs Dean, would see him as he was, and regard him with loathing.

'I say, Margaret, hurry up,' he said anxiously. 'I'll put your stuff in the cart and we'll get along.'

Margaret, always obedient, smiled to Laurence and was just going to get into the cart when Ed came round by the side exit, pushing a heavy truck of luggage. Modestine, bored, and anxious to get back to his field, took one look at Ed, decided to treat him as a complete stranger of terrifying aspect, and began to back violently. Before anyone could stop him he had crushed the cart against the automatic chocolate machine and smashed the patched-up shaft to pieces.

Robin Dean, who was notorious for his luck in always being on the spot when anything really interesting happened, now came out of the Booking Hall. His face lighted up as he saw the wreckage.

'Gosh!' he exclaimed, 'your donkey's broken his shaft, sir. Nanny, Mr Tebben's *donkey* has broken his shaft. Mother, look! Mr Tebben's donkey has broken the shaft.'

Rachel Dean, issuing from the station with her husband, had but one thought.

'How nice of you, Richard, to bring your donkey for Jessica,' she said. 'But I think she must go straight home now, as she goes to bed at half-past seven. Tomorrow she would love to ride. You must come to lunch. What, Laurence? Oh, is this Richard's sister? You are Margaret, aren't you? You must come to lunch too. Frank, this is Richard's sister that Laurence met in Grenoble last winter. What is it, Robin? Oh, Richard has broken the donkey-cart? Well, then he must come up with us in the car and his sister too. What, Robin? Yes, you can bicycle and so can Betty and Susan. Laurence, suppose you take Margaret up with Nanny and Jessica, and Helen can take Richard. Father and I will go in Aunt Louise's little car.'

She led Richard to the white sports car.

'Helen dear,' she said, 'this is Richard Tebben. Laurence knows his sister quite well. Take him up to the Dower House. He has broken his cart.'

Richard would have liked to explain that it was Modestine and not he who had broken the shaft, and that he and his sister were trying to go home, but Mrs Dean had moved away, so he had to go on to Helen, 'I'm so sorry, but

I'll have to see about our donkey. I can't leave it at the station.'

'That's all right, Mr Richard,' said Bert, appearing at his elbow. 'I'll take old Neddy up. Old Neddy knows me, he does, don't you, Ned? You tell my dad to send down for the cart and he'll fix it up.'

'Thanks awfully, Bert.'

'Oke by me,' said Bert, touching his cap to Helen.

Richard got into the car.

'Do you drive?' asked Helen, without looking at him.

Richard had to confess that he couldn't, to which Helen made no reply except to accelerate. It was a nightmare journey. The way to the Dower House was a narrow winding lane between high banks. Helen in her car and her young brother and two younger sisters on their bicycles passed and repassed each other till Richard was extremely alarmed. Whenever a stretch of a hundred yards could be seen, Helen increased her speed, followed by yells from the bicyclists. When the twists and turns made it necessary for her to go more slowly, the riders shot ahead with shrieks of derision. Robin taking a short cut over the tennis lawn, reached the hall door first and celebrated his triumph by riding round the rim of a small lily pond till his father, alighting from the second car, told him to stop.'

'But, Father—' Robin began.

'Stop was what I said. And don't ever ride on the tennis-court again,' his father remarked, without raising his voice. 'Come in, Richard.'

Still perfectly dazed, Richard followed Mr Dean into the hall. The nerve-racking journey with an apparently contemptuous and angry young woman, the dizzy bicycling of the younger Deans, Modestine's behaviour, Margaret's apparently intimate acquaintance with Laurence Dean, his fruitless efforts to explain to all the kind helpers that what he really wanted was to get home with Margaret and her luggage, made him feel entirely at a loss. He caught sight of his own reflection in a mirror and wondered what Mrs Dean thought of him. Probably it was because he looked so loathsome that she sent him in Helen's car; and probably it was that loathly appearance that had made Helen despise him so much. It was impossible to explain. If only he could find Margaret he would go home. But he didn't know where she was, and he didn't know where her luggage was, and now his host had deserted him and it was all too difficult.

'I say,' said a voice, 'Helen's simply furious. What's up?'

Looking round he saw one of the younger girls.

'Excuse me, but which are you?' he asked in desperation.

'I'm Susan. Betty and I are practically twins. Betty's eighteen and got a scholarship to Oxford. I'm sixteen and I'll get one next year. Betty's classical and I'm a bit of a dab at maths. Is Helen angry because you said the train got in first?'

'I don't know. But it did get in first. Her car came in a split second afterwards.'

'Of course it did. Laurence and Betty and Robin and I all get sixpence off her. She drives in real motor races, that's why she doesn't like being beaten by a train. Did she frighten you in the car?'

'I believe you,' said Richard with conviction.

'She did that on purpose,' said Betty. 'Partly for revenge

on the train, partly to try you out. She always does that to new friends. Are you at Oxford?'

'I've just come down.'

'What did you get?'

'A third.'

'Well, that's jolly good,' said Susan. 'I mean, a good third is jolly good, for a man. And I know a man who got a fourth, and he manages the biggest cinema in South London, so that shows. What are you going to do?'

'Read for the bar, I think. But I'll never pass.'

'Of course you will. I'll get my uncle to coach you when he comes. At least his aunt married an uncle of Daddy's, but we call him uncle, and he's frightfully clever. Mother left her spectacles in the train after all, but that nice station-master rang up to say the engine-driver would bring them back and he'd send them up tonight. Are you stopping to dinner?'

'I don't think so. If I could find my sister I'd go home. I had to catch our donkey and harness it and I'm not very respectable.'

'Oh, that doesn't matter. We never dress the first night in the country. Is Margaret your sister? Laurence met her abroad and said she was very decent. She's stopping to dinner, because I heard Mother ask her. You'd better stop too. Come and have a bath. You look as if you needed one.'

So shattered was Richard by the events of the day and the way in which the Dean family ordered one about, that he was quite prepared to find that communal baths were one of their customs, and to resist the same, but Susan, throwing herself ungracefully into a chair with her legs over the arm, pointed upwards, remarked, 'Third door along the corridor,' and began reading the *Tatler*.

A little piqued by the off-hand manner of this girl, who wasn't bad-looking if one liked them generously built with fair untidy hair, he went upstairs, and in a steaming bath, with an extravagant amount of bath-salts, he was able to muse freely upon Mrs Dean and her exquisite carelessness in losing her spectacles. That his own mother invariably mislaid her spectacles in trains and was despised by him for so doing, did not enter into his musings, which were presently interrupted by a loud bang at the door.

'It's me, Robin,' shouted a voice from the passage. 'Susan said you were in here. I'm awfully sorry, but I left the bicycle pump in the bathroom. Could I come in?'

Richard draped himself in a bath-towel of surpassing size, and opened the door;

'Thanks, awfully, sir,' said Robin. 'Could I have the bath when you've finished? If I don't get it now one of the girls will want it, and if I use the upstairs bathroom Nanny will make me wash.'

'Fire away,' said Richard. 'I'm done. But don't say sir.'

'Oh, all right,' said Robin, rapidly divesting himself of his clothes and turning the hot tap full on. 'I thought Mummy said you were a kind of tutor. I say, Helen's in one of her tempers, so look out. She seems to have her knife into you. I can ride backwards on a fixed-wheel bike, can you? Oh, Gosh, that's the gong. I say, hurry up.'

'You'd better hurry up yourself,' said Richard, hastily putting on his shabby shirt and trousers. 'I say, I wish you wouldn't make the bathroom so steamy. I can't see my hair in the glass. There isn't a hairbrush about, is there?'

'You'll find a comb in my coat pocket,' said Robin. 'A chap has to have a comb, or one's hair gets so ghastly.'

'A chap doesn't have to have nail scissors too, does he?' asked Richard, looking at the black fringe on Robin's hands and feet. But Robin, occupied in squirting himself with the bicycle pump, ignored the question, so Richard smoothed his hair with the pocket comb and found his way to the dining-room, where some of the family were already seated.

'It is only a kind of scratch meal tonight, so we aren't dressing,' said Mrs Dean, exquisite in long white velvet draperies, as she invited him to sit beside her. 'Helen and Robin are still missing.'

'Robin is in the bath,' said Richard. 'I'm afraid it's my fault, as I kept him out of it.'

'He's a little beast,' said Susan from across the table. 'He bagged the bicycle pump so that I couldn't pump up my tyres and then he bagged the bath. That boy is a pest.'

As she spoke the pest entered, his round face as composed as ever. Passing by Richard he remarked: 'I'll leave that place next to you for Helen,' and took the other vacant seat. Helen, coming in a moment later, was obliged to sit next to Richard, but kept a stony silence.

Richard, afraid to speak to Helen, diffident about talking to Mrs Dean, who in any case was talking to her husband, also remained silent, considering that in the hubbub made by the younger Deans he would not be noticed. Margaret, between Mr Dean and Betty, was thinking enviously what

64

fun it would be to belong to a large family who all appeared singularly free from inhibitions. She knew that it was hardly fair to compare her hard-working parents scraping from their small income to educate Richard and send her abroad, with the Deans, to whom money obviously meant nothing, but she wondered if having to pinch really need make people so trying as her own dear father and mother, by whom any kind of relaxation appeared to be regarded as a crime. When she had arrived at Worsted station, tired and a little on edge, keyed up to the homecoming always so self-conscious and, after the first flow of her mother's questions, so full of nervous silences which were only just better than nervous talk, her heart had been oppressed. Even Ed's report that Mr Richard was waiting in old Neddy for her had not really raised her spirits, though she loved and admired her elder brother heartily. It was always fuss from beginning to end at home, and though one loved one's parents and knew what sacrifices they made, one always felt that to leave the soap in the bath, or send both sheets to the wash instead of a clean sheet for the top and the top sheet to the bottom would bring both their respected heads with sorrow, repeatedly and plaintively expressed, to the grave. Not so much Father's head perhaps but Mother would discuss it all so endlessly, would make such efforts to blame herself for what she hadn't done and what was after all not very blameworthy, that Father would become embroiled, feel called by loyalty to support her, and everything would be uncomfortable.

To see so unexpectedly Laurence Dean, to be rescued by him from Ed's panic-stricken inefficiency, had made everything different. Laurence, spending a few weeks in Grenoble on the firm's business, had happened to stay with the same family where she was au pair, teaching two children English. He had immediately fallen violently in love with a pretty professional at the skating rink, and had made Margaret, greatly flattered, his confidante. As Mademoiselle Rose was in great demand at the rink where she worked, and Laurence was busy all day and often engaged to dine by business acquaintance at night, his passion had to be nourished on an occasional waltz or tango at the evening session, but it throve on such nourishment, and Margaret was allowed to hear every detail. It was, she felt, real love, so to cherish a being from afar, and Laurence assumed in her young mind a halo of romance. When he left Grenoble, having never succeeded in seeing his goddess outside her rink, Margaret promised to send him what news she could collect. Within a week of his departure Mademoiselle Rose married the chemist to whom she had been engaged for some years, and retired from public life. Margaret, her heart sore for Laurence, wrote to tell him the news. Laurence, who had already almost forgotten his brief infatuation, thanked her on a picture postcard, while she, feeling that Laurence could take no further interest in her since Mademoiselle Rose's marriage, was too shy to write again.

To see Laurence, whom she had pleasurably imagined as pining away for love, looking so well and contented was a shock, but a shock that could be supported. Fortified by the presence of Nanny and Jessica she had accomplished the drive to the Dower House without embarrassment, while Laurence talked cheerfully on various subjects, but never of his lost love. Margaret still thought hopefully that he might be pining in a very secret and heroic way that did not show, but so far she had never had a moment alone with him to approach the delicate subject. Possibly during dinner, protected by the noise of the young Deans, she would be able to slip a word into his ear.

She was interested in observing his family, different, as people always are, from her imagination of them. Laurence and Helen alone of the children had their mother's dark hair and blue eyes. Helen, not so tall as her mother, had the anxious expressive face of an animal that does not feel secure among humans. Why she looked so anxious Margaret did not know, nor why she was sulking like a thundercloud at her innocent neighbour Richard. Betty was dark, with brown eyes and thick eyebrows, handsome when she was not scowling. Susan and Robin were like their father, fair and largely made. While Susan and Robin had not yet passed the very trying age that thinks its valueless thoughts aloud, Betty, oppressed by her own importance in going to college in the autumn with a scholarship, and by a secret grief of her own, found speech unnecessary.

'How are the rehearsals going?' Mrs Dean asked Richard at length.

'Oh, the chorus is getting on. But we couldn't begin full rehearsals till you came. Will you be acting at all?'

'No. I have a rather troublesome heart and mustn't do too much,' murmured Rachel Dean in a most upsetting way, 'but the children are quite ready. They don't really want to act at all, of course, but they don't like to disappoint their aunt. If only it needn't be a Greek play it

67

would be more bearable. Even Shakespeare wouldn't be quite so bad.'

'Oh, I don't know,' said Richard. 'If it was Shakespeare you'd have to give nearly everyone a part, and you can't imagine how awful it would be. With *Hippolytus* you can stick all the village into the chorus, and if half of them don't know the words it doesn't matter, one can put the ones that know them best in front. Mr Dean, do you think Mrs Palmer is right when she wants to make the chorus sort of intone? Rather like church, you know. I want them just to speak it, ordinarily. We rather fell out about it at the last rehearsal.'

'If Aunt Louise wants them to intone, they will intone,' said Helen. 'You can't stop her.'

The light accent that she placed on the word 'you' was very offensive to Richard.

'Your sister will be a lovely Phaedra,' said Mrs Dean, who had apparently not heard her daughter's remark.

Richard looked at Margaret, whose gentle young face and diffident manner appeared to a brother's eye eminently unsuitable for the part.

'Oh, utterly accurst
Be she of women, whoso dared the first
To cast her honour out on a strange man,'

said Betty, now breaking silence for the first time.

Everyone eagerly waited for more, but Betty, with a reserved expression, continued her dinner.

'Well,' said Laurence, who was the first to recover himself, 'it's no good saying be careful before the servants, because they'll know it all themselves by heart before long. Aunt Louise is bound to rope them in. And as Mother was saying, Shakespeare would be far worse. Do you know it all by heart, Betty?'

'Of course,' said Betty. She did not add that in her opinion she *was* Phaedra, and that to see anyone else, Margaret or any other, in the part, was going to ravage her heart and violate her deepest feelings.

'If Aunt Louise wants her chorus to intone, I could play my mouth organ,' said Robin. 'Mouth organs are jolly like intoning.'

'So they are,' said Richard, scenting an ally.

'It seems a pity to encourage Robin to be rude about Aunt Louise,' said Helen.

Mrs Dean, possibly to cover Helen's deliberate rudeness to a guest, said that they would ask Mr Fanshawe when he came.

'Is that Mr Fanshawe of Paul's?' asked Richard. 'I think he used to tutor my mother.'

'Of course it is,' said Susan. 'I told you before he's a kind of pretence uncle. He is coming here for a long visit, hurrah. He doesn't look old enough to tutor anyone's mother, though.'

'At Oxford a tutor need not necessarily be much older than a pupil,' said Betty.

'What a joke it would be if schoolmasters weren't much older than the boys were,' said Robin. 'Gosh, what a time we'd give them. There's a new junior master this term who was in the sixth a few years ago and we all make noises all the time when he takes us for history. There's a boy called Morland in my form, and he can imitate a cinema organ with his mouth, and Mr Jackson said, "Shut up, Morland," and Morland shut his desk with a bang, and Mr Jackson said, "Don't make that noise, Morland," and Morland said, "I thought you told me to shut it, sir," and Mr Jackson had to pretend he hadn't heard.'

'What little beasts you all are,' said Susan. 'What did you do with the bicycle pump, Robin?'

'I was trying to pump some water onto a sparrow and it fell out of the bathroom window into a gutter, but I'll go onto the roof after dinner and get it. You can come too if you like,' Robin added to Richard.

Just then the parlour-maid handed a note to Mrs Dean.

'Mrs Palmer's chauffeur brought this, madam, and he's to wait for an answer,' she said.

'Oh dear,' said Mrs Dean, after looking at it. 'Frank, they want us to have a rehearsal tomorrow evening. Charles Fanshawe will be here, and I did hope we could have his first evening in peace. I wish Louise weren't so energetic.'

'Tell Aunt Louise to boil her head,' said Robin. 'Can I go and get the bike pump now, Mumps?'

'Hang on, Robin, I'm coming too,' shrieked Susan, pushing back her chair and following Robin from the room. Betty also rose, saying something about work.

'What do you think, Richard? Couldn't Mrs Palmer put it off?' asked Mrs Dean, turning flatteringly to her guest.

'Well, it's getting rather near the time,' he said diffidently. 'You see the performance is at the end of the month and we haven't had a single full rehearsal yet, only the chorus and a bit of Theseus, only he can't always turn up punctually because of the shop.'

'The shop?' said Mr Dean inquiringly.

'Yes, sir. Theseus is Mr Pollett who keeps the village shop, and in Summer Time he is open till all hours. We really ought to be having the chief actors. You see we can't get the village people more than twice a week, and that means only six or seven rehearsals before the day.'

'If the children promised Louise to help, they must stick to it,' said Mr Dean. 'Laurence and Helen, isn't it?'

'Yes, Father,' said Laurence, 'and bitterly do they rue the day, as doubtless does Margaret, who is to be Phaedra. Mother, tell Aunt Louise we'll all come tomorrow and you bring Uncle Charles. He'll be able to back Richard up about the choruses. I know my part beautifully, though I must say it's a pretty spineless one. But anything to oblige an aunt. What about you, Helen?'

'Oh, I'll know it in time. I don't know why I ever said I'd do it.'

'Because Charles said you weren't a bit like Artemis,' said Laurence with the frankness of a brother, 'and you always squabble with him.'

Helen glared at Laurence but said nothing. Mrs Dean looked anxiously at her daughter, and sent a verbal message to the effect that they would all be at the Manor House at eight o'clock the following evening. A move was then made to the garden where, under a large mulberry tree, rugs and chairs were placed.

'In a few weeks,' said Mrs Dean, placing herself gracefully on a long chair, 'it won't be safe to sit here, but till the mulberries are ripe we might as well enjoy it. Richard, I'm afraid it's been a very dull, quiet evening compared with what you are used to. If only all the children were here. Then there is a little life. We do miss the others so much.'

Richard, feeling that even one more Dean would have driven him permanently insane, and wondering what kind of home life at Lamb's Piece Mrs Dean could possibly have invented for herself in comparison with which Richard would find other houses dull, said something about enjoying himself very much. Mr Dean lighted his pipe. Laurence, who had brought a small stringed instrument from the house, established himself in a crotch of a low branch and played sad little chords, while Richard, Helen and Margaret sat on cushions. The rich yellow stone of the Dower House was still glowing, and the sun still sparkled from the attic windows and gilded the lichen-grown slates of the roof.

Helen, casting dark looks of adoration and fury at her brother Laurence, was struggling with her own worse feelings without much light to guide her. Laurence, her senior by a year, was almost half of her life. When he was at school she lived for his holidays. When he went to the University and then into his father's firm and, being a companionable creature, found many new friends, she discovered that she was capable of a jealousy which was her constant and bitter mortification and shame. She took to motoring as a kind of discipline, trying to lose herself in a fierce concentration on speed, an incessant care for the machines to which she trusted her life. Laurence, by no means a complex nature, took her devotion for granted, was proud of her motoring achievements, and went his own way. What Helen wanted was to feel that he needed her, that she could sometimes advise, or sympathise, but with the greatest kindness she was given to understand that Laurence was entirely capable of looking after his own affairs. Sometimes he used her as a listener if there was no one else more exciting, and each time that this happened she hoped that at last the moment for eternal confidence had come. When he told her, to have an audience for his own mockery of himself, about the Grenoble affair, Helen was far less jealous of the unknown Frenchwoman than of the English girl who had been the recipient of Laurence's confidences. The Frenchwoman was married and forgotten, but here was his Margaret Tebben, who had been admitted to Laurence's secrets, living within a few miles. There would be almost daily meetings while the play was in rehearsal and Laurence, pleased as he always was with a fresh audience, would share with Margaret all the little jokes about Aunt Louise and the villagers that should by rights have been Helen's. From the moment that she had seen Laurence come out of the station with Margaret, she had been consumed with a jealousy that took outward shape in rudeness to Margaret's brother, whom she rightly judged to be defenceless. She could not show her dislike of Margaret, for that might offend Laurence, so she used the perplexed Richard as a scapegoat, without gaining any particular comfort or benefit from so doing. That she had lost the race against the train afforded an excuse for her evil mood, and she did not trouble to contradict her younger sisters and Robin when they teased her about it.

Her father, who had been abroad for most of the last four or five years, on his work, did not know her well. Her mother

73

did not suspect the reason of her unhappiness and so could be of little help. And Helen, knowing that her mother ought not to be unnecessarily troubled, folded herself into her own dark thoughts, and incidentally made everyone else very uncomfortable by her moods.

As the light waned she looked from time to time in Margaret's direction, and had to admit, with angry generosity, that this new sharer of Laurence's thoughts, glimmering in golden pallor through the mulberry leaves, was not ill-matched with Laurence, now fast becoming invisible on his branch, letting loose melancholy chords to the dusk.

The peace of this outwardly contented group was suddenly broken by piercing shrieks from the house. Susan and Robin, having found the bicycle pump in the gutter, had the pleasant idea of exploring the roof. The thick wide slates gave an easy foothold for bare feet, the slope of the roof was not too steep, there were leads where one could halt, gables on which one could perch. All had gone well till Robin, crossing a flat patch of leaded roof, had caught a glimpse through the night-nursery window of Jessica in bed and wide awake. Having made this discovery, nothing was easier than to attract Jessica's attention by looking in through the window upside down. Jessica, pleased at seeing company, got out of bed and knelt at the window in admiration. Robin showed off by every possible acrobatic feat. Susan, seated on a gable, applauded his performance, Robin, above himself, ended by snatching from his small sister a shabby stuffed elephant, invariable companion of her slumbers, and pretending to throw it over the parapet. At this Jessica began to scream with over-excitement, the whole party under the mulberry came hurriedly forward to see what was happening, and Nanny descended upon the night-nursery. Before Robin knew what had happened Nanny, who had been supreme over him till he went to school, and still gave him all the affection she could spare from Jessica, had hauled him into the night-nursery by the leg, wrested the elephant from him, tucked Jessica tightly into her cot, and dismissed Robin with an injunction to go to bed at once. She would come into his room in ten minutes, she added, and look at his ears, neck, fingernails and toenails. Robin went off, routed, but on the whole pleased with a well-spent evening, while Nanny, drawing the curtains, left Jessica to the sleep that was rapidly overtaking her.

Mr Dean, looking upwards, saw his third daughter on the roof, and inquired what had happened.

'Nothing, Daddy,' shouted Susan. 'Nanny sent Robin to bed because he was making Jessica scream.'

'Come down at once then,' said her father.

Susan disappeared.

A thing happened to Richard which he thought only occurred in books. While the others were calling to Susan, Mrs Dean, taking his arm, said in a breathless voice, 'Inside. Quickly.' Startled but obedient, Richard moved towards the drawing-room window and found that he was almost supporting Mrs Dean. Her hands were clinging to his arm, and then loosened their hold. Richard, made quite desperate by the emergency, managed to let her down, clumsily, but with the greatest reverence, into an armchair, where, after one look at him with appealing, terrified eyes, she lay speechless.

Richard was appalled. This responsibility for his goddess was too much. Half of him wished to chafe her hands and fan her brow, for such, he gathered from literature, was the way to treat swooning ladies. The other and larger half heartily wished that some grown-up person were there to take the responsibility. On a sigh he heard the words 'Don't tell Frank', which though noble in the extreme did not help him in his perplexity.

Most luckily Nanny, coming down to lay a complaint against Robin, saw what had happened, took charge, and sent Richard away, with strict injunctions not to alarm Mr Dean.

'It's not the first time, nor it won't be the last, with Miss Susan and Master Robin scrimmaging about like that, giving us all turns,' said Nanny grimly. 'Oh, she'll be all right, sir. I'm much obliged to you, I'm sure, for getting her in, and now she'll do nicely. Now, if you'll ring the bell, I'll get her upstairs and no one the wiser.'

Richard rang the bell and went out into the garden. The rest of the party had returned to the mulberry tree, but Richard was too much disquieted to join them at once. Susan and Robin were as good as murderers, but what was he, if not an accessory after the fact? If nurse had not come in he would probably still be rooted to the spot in adoration and incompetence. He would at once take lessons in first aid and learn what to do when people fainted. He had a vague idea that one ought to get their heads lower than their heels, but that was a thing one couldn't possibly do to Mrs Dean. She was so far above humanity that no ordinary measures would be suitable. If he had been, say, the Count of Monte Cristo, he would have drawn from his pocket a small and exquisitely wrought phial, two drops from which would have brought the colour to her cheeks. Her dark eyes might then have rested with gratitude on her deliverer; she might have languidly extended her hand for him to kiss, a thought at which he was so overcome that he had to stop for a moment and recover himself. But realising that these thoughts were a betrayal of Mr Dean's hospitality, he pulled himself together and strolled with elaborate ease towards the mulberry tree. Margaret's voice called him.

'Richard, we must be going home. Laurence is going to drive us back with my luggage.'

'You don't mind going in the dickey, do you?' asked Laurence.

Richard on the whole preferred it, for there he could meditate upon a deity in white velvet, lovely, defenceless in her trance, relying on him for help. He suddenly remembered the delicate dark shadow on her eyelids and thought of violets, unaware that Shakespeare and others had done so before him. From his own dastardly incompetence and pusillanimity he averted his mind.

Meanwhile Margaret, in front with Laurence, had her first chance of speaking to him about his lost love.

'Oh, Laurence,' she said, 'I never heard any more about Rose, or I'd have told you.'

'Didn't you? I did. She sent all her old friends and pupils at the rink such a whacking *faire part* of her wedding that I had to send her a present.'

'What did you send?' asked Margaret, feeling that even a diamond heart set in pearls, or a volume of Keats, would be inadequate for the occasion.

'Mother found me a ghastly old silver vase that she was given on her silver wedding day. Lord, what hideous legs that girl had.'

Margaret was shocked, but not displeased. It was appalling that true love could die so soon, and so indelicately, but her own legs were unexceptionable, though Laurence need not necessarily know it.

Goodnights were brief. Laurence drove away. Margaret and Richard went to bed without much conversation. Both were tired, both self-conscious.

'I never knew you knew Laurence,' said Richard. 'He's not a bad sort.'

'I knew him at Grenoble,' said Margaret, 'last winter, but I thought he'd forgotten me. How lovely Mrs Dean is.'

'Yes, she's rather nice.'

Brother and sister each felt that the other was a sensible, understanding kind of fellow. Both also felt how very lucky it was that their dear parents had not been at home on that particular day.

4

Rehearsal with Interludes

On the following morning Modestine, reduced by incessant grooming and exercise to a state as near nervousness as he was capable of, was led by Richard to the Dower House. Richard had blacked Modestine's hoofs with the family shoe polish and given the saddle and bridle a final touch. He was not quite sure whether one took a donkey to the front door or the stable yard, but his doubts were relieved by meeting Nanny and Jessica in the drive.

'Good morning,' said Richard, checking with some difficulty Modestine's determined progress towards some shrubs that he fancied. 'Is Mrs Dean all right?'

'Oh, yes, sir,' said Nanny, 'there's no call to worry. Dr Masters says there is no cause for alarm. But Mrs Dean doesn't like Mr Dean and the young ladies and gentlemen to be troubled. I'm sure it's very good of you, sir, to bring Neddy up for Jessica. Say How do you do to Neddy, Jessica, and give him the nice sugar.'

Jessica extended a fat hand on the palm of which lay two pieces of sugar. Modestine sniffed at them so hard that they fell onto the ground, which made Jessica laugh uncontrollably.

'Silly Neddy,' she remarked, picking up the sugar and putting it into her mouth.

Nanny pounced on her, removed the sugar, and threw it into the bushes. Jessica's face crumpled.

'Oh, I say,' said Richard, alarmed, 'don't do that. You'll frighten the donkey. His name's Modestine.'

'How do you do, Neddy,' said Jessica. 'Nanny, Neddy wants his sugar.'

'Well, he'd have had it if you hadn't gone and put it in your mouth,' said Nanny, with the logic of the nursery. 'Now, sir, if you'll hold Neddy, I'll put Jessica on his back.'

'His name's Modestine,' said Richard, forcing the unamiable animal to stand still.

'There's a good Neddy,' said Nanny approvingly.

Richard, giving up the question of Modestine's name, to which both Nanny and Jessica appeared to be impervious, now led the donkey up and down the drive. In spite of his efforts Modestine covered himself with disgrace, sometimes ambling in a mincing way, sometimes stopping dead in affected terror at the sight of a small stone. Jessica, with Nanny grasping a good handful of the back of her frock, sat him firmly. Richard longed to get into closer touch with Nanny, who might somehow impress Mrs Dean with his kindness and efficiency, but he suspected that she looked upon him as merely a slightly older member of her nursery charges, and had an uneasy feeling that the back of his neck

80

was being scrutinised by her with the all-seeing and critical eye of a professional washer of the young. Nor was his self-distrust lessened when Nanny said:

'You'd much better let me take Neddy, sir, and you hold Jessica on.'

Accordingly Richard grasped Jessica's frock, Nanny took the bridle, and Modestine with hideous discrimination at once mended his pace and went so well that Nanny led him into the field, where she urged him to a kind of trot. Jessica was then adjudged to have so good a seat that she need not be held on, and Richard sat down in the grass. He would like to have gone up to the house and asked for Mrs Dean, but was too shy. After nearly half an hour of donkey exercise a bell was heard.

'That's your dinner, Jessica,' said Nanny. 'Come along now, there's a good girl.'

Jessica, who had shown no sign of emotion of any kind during the ride, shrieked loudly as she was lifted down.

'Stop that noise and say Goodbye Neddy, see you again tomorrow, and thank you to the kind gentleman,' said Nanny.

'Goodbye, Neddy, see you again tomorrow, and thank you, gentleman,' said Jessica, offering her hand.

Richard shook it, Jessica and Nanny walked away, and he was left with Modestine. He was saved from the embarrassment of not knowing what to do with him by the arrival of Susan and Robin, who came tearing across the field on bicycles as fast as the long grass would permit.

'I say, can I ride your donkey?' asked Robin.

'Certainly, if you can stick on.'

'Can *you* stick on?' asked Susan.

'Yes. But then I've rather long legs.'

'I bet I can stick on,' said Robin. 'What's his name?'

'Modestine.'

'Gosh, what a name,' said Susan. 'R.L.S. and all that, I suppose. Get up, Robin, and I'll whack him.'

The scales fell from Richard's eyes. Of all the affected, ridiculous names that an elderly he-donkey could be called, Modestine was the worst. How right were Bert and Ed, how right were Nanny and Jessica to call him Neddy. He would at once point out to his mother, and with no uncertain tongue, her folly in choosing such a name.

'I say, where's your sister?' said Susan.

'She's walking over for lunch.'

'Oh, that's all right. Laurence thought perhaps she'd forgotten, and he's gone to look for her in the two-seater. I say, if your donkey's called Modestine, I ought to have a pin to prick it. Oh bother, I've not got one. Here, lend me your tiepin.'

Richard, taken by surprise, allowed her to remove the handsome Woolworth safety-pin which kept the end of his tie down, and fascinated, watched her apply it to Modestine's hindquarters. Modestine leapt in the air, Robin, prepared for the worst, clung on, hitting Modestine violently with his heels. Clouds of dust flew out.

'I say, you haven't dusted that donkey,' said Susan. 'I'll give it a proper rub down for you after lunch. I love grooming animals. I went over and helped with Aunt Louise's farm horses this morning before breakfast. Hi, Robin, my turn now.'

Robin pulled up. Susan swung one of her long legs across Modestine's back. Robin applied the pin, and away galumphed Modestine at what was for him full tilt. Richard, feeling that Modestine was now beyond human aid, and that he was not needed, went towards the house. Mrs Dean, looking more glorified than ever in flowered chiffon and an impossible floppy garden hat, called him from a chair.

'Nanny says you gave Jessica a lovely ride. It was so good of you,' she said. 'Can you come again?'

'Every morning if you like. Or afternoons if that's better. Or really any time.'

'Oh, but that's such a trouble and I know you have a lot of reading to do. Shall I send one of the men over to fetch your donkey?'

'No, please don't, Mrs Dean. I'd love to come. I'm not very busy really. You see,' he went on, anxious that she should not be under any illusion about him, 'I did rottenly in Greats and I don't know what I'm going to do now, so it really doesn't much matter if I read or not. Please let me come.'

His flushed, earnest face and urgent ears pleaded so strongly for him that Mrs Dean relented and said that so long as his parents didn't mind, she would like him to come. He must often bring his sister, and often stay to lunch.

'I say,' stammered Richard, 'I hope you're quite well again, Mrs Dean. I mean I really was most awfully upset about you last night.'

'It was only hearing Jessica scream and seeing the children on the roof,' said Mrs Dean. 'It wasn't a bit important. But I didn't want my husband to be worried. You were most kind and helpful. You won't mention it, will you? And don't tell the children that seeing them on the roof fluttered me, or they will feel unhappy. That is lunch, I think.'

Lunch, personified by the parlour-maid, said it was ready, and they went in. Mr Dean was not there and Richard gathered that he had gone to town for the day. Lunch was dominated by Susan and Robin's description of their feats on the donkey, which Susan proposed to christen ceremoniously with ginger-beer as Neddy after lunch.

The parlour-maid came in with two pieces of paper which she laid before Mrs Dean.

'Two telegrams come on the phone, madam,' she said, 'one for you and one for Mr Tebben. The exchange couldn't get onto his house, but they thought him and the young lady would be up here, and I've wrote them down.'

'That's Mrs Phipps's niece, Palmyra, at the exchange,' said Margaret. 'She's very useful, because she always knows where everyone is.'

'What an unusual name,' said Laurence. 'Is it local?'

'No, she's christened after Mrs Palmer.'

'My telegram is from Charles,' said Mrs Dean. 'He arrives at Worsted at six forty-seven. That's the same train Father is coming by, so I suppose they will travel together.'

'They'll have their work cut out,' said Susan, 'as Uncle Charles always goes third and Daddy first.'

'I'm so sorry, Richard,' said Mrs Dean. 'This is your telegram. I hope it's all right.'

'It's from Mother,' said Richard, 'but I can't quite understand it. It says "Arrive 647 bringing paddock supper meet us Modestine".'

'Perhaps she means a kind of outdoor supper,' said Helen, who, much to Richard's relief, was in milder mood than the previous evening.

'It isn't paddock, sir, it's haddock. I thought I had wrote it clear,' said the parlour-maid with umbrage.

'Oh, I'm sorry. I read it wrong. I suppose Mother's got a haddock for supper. Oh I say, Margaret, I never asked if the cart was mended. Could I ring up Margett, Mrs Dean?'

'The young lady at the exchange asked me to tell you that the cart isn't mended, sir,' said the parlour-maid, 'because Mr Margett has gone on the Buffaloes' Outing.'

'Well, that's torn it,' said Richard. 'One can't get anything done at this time of year, with the outings. Could I ring up the station-master, Mrs Dean, and see if his car is free?'

'But my dear boy,' said Mrs Dean, 'our car will be going down in any case to fetch Charles Fanshawe and my husband. It can easily fetch Mr and Mrs Tebben.'

'I say,' said Robin, 'we'll have a gymkhana this afternoon with Neddy and the bikes, and then we'll all go down to the station.'

The plan gave universal satisfaction. Helen offered to go over to Skeynes, where the shop was better, and get some prizes. She invited Richard to come with her and as Mrs Dean was going to rest after lunch he accepted, not without trepidation. Much to his relief Helen drove at a moderate pace, and though she did not talk the atmosphere was far from unfriendly. At Skeynes they ransacked the general shop for prizes. There was not much choice, but Helen bought pencils, pocket-knives and bright handkerchiefs as if she were fitting out a missionary ship for savage islands, with what seemed to Richard, used to making his own small pocket-money or slender allowance stretch to its utmost limits, reckless extravagance. When she had added chocolate to her parcels she said:

'We'll go back by Skeynes Agnes. I haven't been there for ages and I want to see the church.'

Skeynes Agnes was on a spur of high land, looking south to the downs. The little Saxon church with its round tower and shingled spire was off the main road, hidden behind farm buildings and among large yew trees. Helen twisted her way down the cart track that led to it and stopped the car where two stone steps led over a wall into the churchyard. The church door was locked. Richard, knowing the ways of the neighbourhood, looked among the beams of the porch for the key, but it was nowhere to be found.

'Shall I go and see if I can find the verger or someone?' he asked, but Helen said it didn't matter, and anyway the verger had probably gone with the Buffaloes, so they strolled round the churchyard. The south side, where the land fell away, was terraced. Its wall was pleasantly low on the inside, with a drop of ten or twelve feet on the outside. On it Helen leant her elbows and looked away over the country, olive green in its heavy summer leafage, to where the comfortable humps of the downs shimmered in a warm grey haze.

'I was rather beastly yesterday,' she said, her face averted.

Richard was not prepared to contradict her statement, so he said it was rotten luck that the train beat her car.

'Oh, it wasn't that,' said Helen. 'I really can't tell you what it was, and you wouldn't understand if I did, and you'd probably be offended.'

'I hope it wasn't me.'

'Oh no; not at all. I was only feeling very down, and I was horrid to you because I thought you wouldn't hit back.'

'It was perfectly rotten for you to feel like that,' said Richard, 'but I do wish I'd known. I thought you hated me because I said the train got in first.'

'Oh, that didn't matter a bit. I can't explain. It's all too mixed. I'm not clever and educated like you and the others, and you and your sister probably despise me.'

Richard could not see Helen's expression, because she was still looking away from him as she spoke, but she was obviously unhappy, and for anyone who felt despised he had the utmost sympathy. If she thought that he and Margaret were clever and educated, he could at least give her immediate comfort.

'You were at Oxford and your sister is marvellous at French,' she went on resentfully. 'Laurence met her abroad and he says she's frightfully good at languages.'

'That's nothing. I did absolutely rottenly at Oxford. I must say it was mostly my own fault and if I'd worked I'd probably have done fairly decently, but there it is. And Margaret only talks French because she lived for a year in France. And German. I mean she lived in Germany, too. Neither of us can drive a car, and I'm absolutely nowhere at tennis. Mrs Palmer says you're a bit of an ace.'

At these words Helen began to cheer up. For the first time in their conversation she looked at Richard as she said, 'Would you like to learn to drive my car? It's very easy. I could teach you in a few lessons.'

'Rather. I'd much rather do that than be good at exams.

Mother was so awfully good at exams that she expected me to be brilliant too, and you can't think how depressing it is.'

'If you had Betty for a sister you wouldn't say that,' said Helen. 'I can simply feel her despising me because I'm seven years older than she is and couldn't do an exam to save my life. And since she got the scholarship she's worse than ever.'

'I must say Betty does make one feel a bit of a worm. After all, she's not the only one to get a scholarship. My mother got one, and she got all the special prizes and a first in economics and a research fellowship, and she writes books, and she earned enough money to buy Lamb's Piece, that's our house and garden. I don't mean to boast, but Betty needn't be so superior.'

'She won't be when she knows about your mother,' said Helen. 'I'll rub it in. It's a pity your mother wasn't classical, as Betty thinks nothing else matters, but it'll just show her. Come on now. We couldn't be friends, could we, do you think?'

'Rather.'

'That's nice of you,' said Helen, getting into the car. 'Now, when you want to start her ...'

Richard applied himself with enthusiasm to Helen's instructions. They got back to find the gymkhana, organised by Susan and Robin, about to begin. The proceedings were inaugurated by Robin opening a bottle of ginger-beer over Modestine, baptising him Neddy, and sharing the ginger-beer with Susan. Neddy was then groomed by his sponsors till no dust was left in him, and entered for every event. Richard and Helen were joined by Laurence and

Margaret, but it was soon discovered that the promoters of the gymkhana intended to win all the events themselves and took no interest in competitors, provided they had an audience, so the elders lazed very comfortably under an elm tree, while the late Modestine was worked as never in his life before. When Betty joined them with an armful of books, Helen let fall her information about Mrs Tebben, which caused Betty to attach herself with embarrassing devotion to Richard, as the shadow of the sun.

'I suppose your mother knew Miss Pitcher-Jukes?' said she, naming a lady celebrated in the annals of female education at Oxford.

'Mother beat her for the Octavia Crammer fellowship,' said Richard carelessly, and Betty cringed.

Before tea Nanny and Jessica came out, and a special race was arranged for Jessica in which she was to run, while Susan and Robin went backwards on all fours. When she had received a first prize of a penny for coming in last in the wrong direction and Susan and Robin had divided all the pencils and chocolate between them, tea was ready, and after tea there was a general cramming into Helen's sports car and Laurence's two-seater, and a scouring of the countryside, winding up at Worsted station, where the Deans' big car was already waiting, just before the down train came in.

A little earlier in the afternoon Mr Dean, having finished his business in town, had arrived at Waterloo station. At the barrier he met by appointment his connection Charles Fanshawe, formerly a tutor, now Dean of St Paul's College,

Oxford. Mr Fanshawe was a tall, lean man in the late forties, with thinning hair and a deeply lined, rather ugly face. He was an excellent Dean of college, taking a sardonic interest in the young gentlemen in residence and never forgetting a name, a face, or a history. If any undergraduate at Paul's got into trouble with the university authorities, or appeared before him for a breach of college discipline, Mr Fanshawe could be relied on to do his best for the offender, followed by such acid comment as would make the young man wish he had never been born, and sometimes turn over a new leaf. As everyone knows, Paul's is famous for the great row or disturbance which took place shortly before the Crimean War, in consequence of which row Charles Ravenshoe, a gentleman of good family in the West, was rusticated for a year. If Mr Fanshawe had been Dean at that period, it is probable that Charles Ravenshoe's career might have been different, for Mr Fanshawe, unlike the Dean of Ravenshoe's time, was not in the least afraid of personal violence, though he had rarely had to meet it. On the only occasion when anything like a serious disturbance had taken place at Paul's under his rule, namely in the year when Paul's made twelve bumps in Eights Week, Mr Fanshawe had put on his largest mountaineering boots, which carried about two pounds' weight of nails, studs and so forth, and had walked about the quad, saying no word but scrutinising with his usual sardonic expression, the faces of the ringleaders. Somehow the fun of the thing had evaporated. The young gentlemen had gone to bed and Mr Fanshawe, having surveyed the empty quad with satisfaction, had uttered his customary ejaculation of 'Ha!' and followed their example. This incident, added to the knowledge that he had once climbed round the whole of the outside of the college without ever setting foot to the ground, had established his reputation for good.

'Ha, Frank,' said Mr Fanshawe on perceiving Mr Dean.

'Well, Charles,' said Mr Dean.

Both gentlemen produced their tickets for the inspector at the gate.

'I know you will always travel third,' said Mr Dean, 'so I got a third-class ticket, though, mind you, it's an extravagance when I can get all my expenses paid first class by the firm.'

'I,' said Mr Fanshawe, 'knew you always travelled first, but I knew you would go third today because you thought I wouldn't go first, so I saved myself the trouble of getting a first-class ticket.'

'That's double-crossing,' said Mr Dean, getting into a third-class smoking carriage.

'It's the result of using one's brains. I want an evening paper. Hi!'

Mr Fanshawe called to a boy on the platform and got his paper just as the train started.

'A couple only just caught it,' he remarked as he sat down. 'Man looks like Tebben. A good Norse scholar in his way. I correspond with him occasionally over the Snorri Society.'

'There are some people called Tebben at Worsted,' said Mr Dean. 'Their son is acting in that Greek play my sister-in-law Louise Palmer is getting up.'

'There was a young Tebben at St Jude's who got a poor third lately,' said Mr Fanshawe. 'His tutor was talking to me about him. He said he had brains and was too conceited to use them. How are the family?'

Mr Dean gave brief biographies of his nine children since the dates when Mr Fanshawe had last seen them, after which Mr Fanshawe did a crossword and Mr Dean looked through some papers.

The London train was late, so there was very little time to make the change at Winter Overcotes. Mrs Tebben, as she settled herself in a non-smoker with her husband, said she had seen a man getting into the train who reminded her extraordinarily of Mr Fanshawe, whom she had never seen since she was at Oxford.

'It might quite easily be Fanshawe,' said Mr Tebben. 'He is some connection of the Deans', I think.'

'That would be too extraordinary, Gilbert,' said Mrs Tebben. 'To have lost sight of him all these years and then see him again today.'

Mr Tebben secretly felt that if one hadn't seen a person for a number of years, it was not more remarkable to meet them on one day than another, but kept it to himself. Mrs Tebben fell into a dream of Mr Fanshawe and her youth. At Winter Underclose she was receiving the avowal that he had cared for her deeply and silently ever since he coached her, and remained single for her sake. At Lambton Mr Tebben was dead and Mr Fanshawe was speaking words of comfort. At Fleece she was refusing him for the children's sake. As the train pulled up at Worsted Mr Tebben had come to life again and she was telling Mr Fanshawe that if he had spoken then he might have won her, but now the father of her children must ever take the first place in her life. Seizing her parcels she got out of the train, and followed by her husband crossed the bridge and came out through the Booking Hall into the station yard. She looked round for Richard and Modestine, but they were not to be seen. In their place she saw three cars and a group of young people who were making so much noise that they had not noticed the train come in. With a mother's eye she picked out her son. With a mother's tactlessness she went across and pulled at his arm.

'My dear boy, I suppose you got my wire. I saw such a particularly fine haddock when I was near the British Museum this morning that I felt I must get it. Here it is,' she said, thrusting a slightly oozing parcel into his hand. 'Where is Modestine? Is Margaret there? I hope the laundry did call and that they brought back the clean things.'

As she spoke two girls and a boy detached themselves from the group, rushed towards the Booking Hall, and flung themselves on the two men who were coming out, explaining at the tops of their voices to their father and their Uncle Charles that the car was there, that dinner was at once, that old Aunt Palmer had a rehearsal at eight and everyone must hurry.

Mrs Tebben turned, opened her mouth, gasped, and spoke.

'Mr Fanshawe! You don't remember me.'

Mr Fanshawe stopped, put on a pair of large spectacles, and looked at her.

'Miss Ross,' he announced. 'You took an excellent first in Economics. A very good set of papers. You were specially strong in comparative sociology. You married a Civil Servant called Tebben, an old Paul's man. We correspond

93

occasionally over the Snorri Society. I never forget a pupil. Are these your children?'

Mrs Tebben looked to where Richard, Margaret, Helen and Laurence were standing.

'Yes. I mean two of them,' said Mrs Tebben, who was struggling with old emotions and an insane desire to kiss Mr Fanshawe's hand and call him Maître.

'Any particular two?' asked Mr Fanshawe. 'They can't be Helen or Laurence, so they must be the two that aren't.' He took his spectacles off again.

'That is Richard,' said Mrs Tebben, overcome by her old tutor's powers of reasoning. 'He has just got a third in Greats,' she added, to Richard's great embarrassment and annoyance. 'And this is Margaret. Margaret dear, I haven't seen you yet to greet you. She is just back from Grenoble.'

'Ha,' said Mr Fanshawe.

A great welter of introductions now took place between the Tebben and Dean families, and before Mrs Tebben knew where she was, she found herself being rapidly driven towards her home in a sports car with two young women.

'I say,' said the younger of them, 'Richard says you know Miss Pitcher-Jukes. Do you really? I think she is the most marvellous person in the world. I'm going to Oxford next term and I'll be in her college. What's she really like?'

Mrs Tebben was torn between her natural contempt for her rude and conceited old fellow-student Effie Pitcher-Jukes, better known as Pidge, and a kindly feeling for this eager child by her side, but her better nature triumphed.

'I used to know her very well when I was at Oxford,' she

said. 'She is a little difficult, but brilliant. I must tell her about you when you go up.'

'Oh I say, *thank you*. But you are marvellous, too, aren't you? Richard told me all the things you've done. It made me feel such a worm.'

That Richard should have spoken well of her to any of his young friends so touched and surprised his mother that for a moment she could not speak. As Helen skilfully swung the car into the awkward gates of Lamb's Piece, Mrs Tebben said to Betty:

'That's all a long time ago, but if you would care to come and talk to me any time about Oxford . . .'

She paused, diffident before the young who were so apt to despise her, but Betty's halting and ecstatic acceptance left no doubt that she really wanted to come. Helen apologised for hurrying on, as dinner would already be late, and drove herself and Betty away. A minute later Richard and Mr Tebben were put down by the Deans' car, followed by Margaret in Laurence's two-seater, and the Tebben family were united.

'We ought to have supper as soon as we can, Mother,' said Richard. 'There's a full rehearsal at eight.'

'All in good time, Richard dear. The haddock won't take long, and there ought to be some of that Swiss roll that we had for tea the day before yesterday. I told Mrs Phipps to make a trifle with it. What an extraordinary thing it was to meet Mr Fanshawe again, Gilbert. I can't get over it. Margaret dear, I expect you have a lot of things to be washed. Unfortunately the laundry called yesterday, but I dare say if I sent a postcard they could call again, or if not

95

we must ask Mrs Phipps to take them home and let you have them back the day after tomorrow.'

Margaret said she had very little washing, and what she had could wait.

'Then that's all right,' said her mother, a little disappointed, but prepared to look on the bright side of things. 'Gilbert, I don't suppose you will want to come to the rehearsal, so I'll tell Mrs Phipps to make some cocoa before she goes and leave it in the thermos, so that you can have it whenever you like.'

'I think I shall come up to the barn,' said Mr Tebben, who disliked cocoa. 'I would like to have a word with Fanshawe.'

'But Mr Fanshawe isn't in the play, Gilbert.'

'They are all coming from the Dower House,' said Margaret. 'Mrs Palmer wanted some audience, so Daddy will be very useful. You saw the Greek play at Bradford, didn't you, Daddy?'

'Bradfield. Yes, I did.'

Mr Tebben hesitated, as if searching for a word.

'And how?' his son kindly prompted him.

'Well, Richard, the locution is unfamiliar to me, but it appears to express my meaning.'

'Mother, we must hurry up with supper,' said Richard.

'Yes, yes, dear boy. I'll tell Mrs Phipps to do the haddock that nice way that we all like it. First in boiling water, just to take the salt out, and then in milk with a dab of butter.'

Twenty minutes later supper was on the table. Richard, fuming with impatience, herded his family into the diningroom.

'I didn't think to tell you,' said Mrs Phipps, as she put a dry and uninviting fish on the table, 'that the milk turned.

If you don't want me I'll be going now, mum, because Dawris wants me to go up to the barn.'

Mrs Tebben's distress was such that she forgot to mention the cocoa.

'I suppose I ought to have seen about the milk,' said Margaret apologetically. 'We were up at the Dower House all day, and I forgot. And Mrs Phipps doesn't frightfully like being asked about anything.'

It doesn't matter in the least,' said Mrs Tebben. 'Richard, if you really don't want any trifle, will you put Modestine in the cart? I am so tired after my night in London that I feel the little drive up to the barn will do me good.'

Richard then had to break the news that he had been at the Dower House the day before and had completely forgotten about the cart, and that today Mr Margett was away with the Buffaloes and couldn't mend it. Mrs Tebben was saying that she would be quite happy to stay at home alone, and would get some cocoa for them all when they came back, and they were on no account to worry, when a loud hooting was heard from the road.

'That ought to be Laurence,' said Margaret. 'He said he might come and fetch some of us. Let him take you, Mother.'

'I shall accept the offer of a lift gratefully,' said Mrs Tebben. 'What a nice sister of his that is, Richard, the one that is going to Oxford.'

'Oh, Betty. I haven't much use for her myself. She's one of those regular University women. Thinks of nothing but scholarships. I say, do hurry up, Mother. We mustn't keep Mrs D— Mrs Palmer waiting.'

*

97

The horsemen and the footmen, as Mrs Tebben said lightly to Laurence, were pouring in amain for the first full rehearsal, though not a dress rehearsal. Mr Palmer's large barn, which was no longer used for the farm, was open along one side and one end, so that the summer performances could be held partly by daylight. At the further end the floor was boarded over to the height of three or four feet with steps on both sides. Behind the platform were two dressing-rooms. The sun, still far from its setting, shone directly into the barn, making dusty gold of its gloom and dazzling Mrs Tebben as she made her way towards Mrs Palmer, who was giving orders to the chorus.

'Oh, here you are, Winifred,' said Mrs Palmer. 'Just in time.'

'Laurence very kindly brought me,' said Mrs Tebben. 'Modestine's cart is broken, and I was just making up my mind to walk, or to stay at home, when he came with his car. Richard and Margaret will be here in a few moments. They are walking with Gilbert. Is Mrs Phipps here? I want to tell her to remember to bring me some eggs from Pollett when she comes tomorrow.'

'She's over there. Doris is trying to have stage fright and Mrs Phipps is helping her,' said Mrs Palmer grimly. 'Why don't you get your eggs from us, Winifred? They are much better than Pollett's, and if you told Mrs Phipps how many you wanted, she could tell my second gardener, Percy Patten, who boards with her, and he would bring them up when he knocks off work.'

'Or,' said Mrs Tebben, who could not bear to be outdone in arranging people's lives, 'if I let Bert Margett know when he passes the house on the way up from the station, he could tell Doris Phipps and she could easily run over from the Dower House and tell Percy.'

'Well, we'll arrange that. There's no need for Doris to be running after Percy. That girl's a fool. I must go and see about her. We'll start as soon as she is in her senses.'

Doris Phipps, pleased at being the hysterical centre of attention, was working herself up to a good fit of giggles, and saying she couldn't never say her lines before everyone.

'Don't be a little fool, Doris,' said Mrs Palmer.

'She's always been like that, mum,' said Mrs Phipps. 'A real good girl, Dawris is, and the least thing upsets her. It's the idear of Bert Margett makes her act so nervous. They've been keeping company now for three years, or it may be four, and Bert's such a one for his jokes that Dawris says she'll be off if she sees him in the chorus.'

'Bert!' said Mrs Palmer. 'Bert Margett!'

Bert was pushed forward by his friends.

'If Doris begins to laugh again when she's saying her lines, I'll give her part to Miss Thomas,' said Mrs Palmer. 'If Aphrodite is going to giggle, she might as well do it with brains, which Miss Thomas has got and Doris hasn't. Now, Bert, you go right at the back with Ed and help him with his lines, and don't let me hear any more of this.'

Doris, sobered by the thought of losing her part, promised amendment, and Mrs Phipps, saying I told you so, which was quite untrue, withdrew to the back of the hall.

'Now then, Doris,' said Mrs Palmer. 'You are on the stage when the curtain is drawn. Up you go.'

'I haven't had a chance of asking how you are,' said Mr

Fanshawe to Mrs Dean, while Doris obediently went through her lines.

'I'm well enough, thank you. A little worried about Helen and Betty. Specially Helen. She is unhappy and I don't know why. Also her unhappiness makes her rather cross. If you can find out at all – she is fond of you.'

'Rachel,' said Mr Dean. 'I don't think you've met Mr Tebben, Richard's father.'

'Richard has been so kind to Jessica, my youngest,' said Mrs Dean. 'He gave her a donkey ride this morning. I hope you and your wife will come and dine with us soon. You do know Mr Fanshawe, don't you?'

Mr Fanshawe, who like most of his sex would enthusiastically neglect any woman, however charming, to talk to any man, however dull, at once engaged Mr Tebben in conversation. It appeared that Mr Tebben had been at Paul's just before Mr Fanshawe. In fact they had actually overlapped by a year.

'Bowen was Master then,' said Mr Tebben. 'A very able man, but no disciplinarian. He resigned just after I went down. What happened to him?'

'He took a living somewhere in the West. His wife's health was poor and the doctors recommended a milder climate, but she died soon afterwards and he married his housekeeper. A very sad affair. Was Elton up in your time?'

'A. P. or F. P.?'

'You may well ask,' said Mr Fanshawe with a grim chuckle.

'Oh, you know that story, do you?' said Mr Tebben. 'No, F. P., I mean.'

'I hadn't seen F. P.,' said Mr Fanshawe, 'for many years, till I ran into him in Majorca last spring. He has married a woman there and is completely dominated by her and her family, mere peasants. He showed me his draft for a critical edition of Pindar, but it was obvious that he would never be able to finish it. Drinks, no doubt about it, and he seemed sadly broken.'

'A. P. of course has done very well,' said Mr Tebben. 'They say that his last Budget speech was one of the ablest things he has done. But I hear that his eldest son is in a very poor way.'

From the continuation of this entrancing conversation Mrs Dean was able to gather that of all the men of their time Mr Fanshawe and Mr Tebben were the only survivors with any claim to sanity, health, or moral standing. She could have listened for hours to the misfortunes of the graduates of Paul's, but for an interruption. Doris, Laurence and Mr Margett, as Aphrodite, Hippolytus and Huntsman, had repeated their lines with accuracy if without enthusiasm, supported by a chorus of huntsmen. The moment now came for the chorus of women to make their first statement.

'Now,' said Mrs Palmer, 'divide yourselves. Half to the right and half to the left.'

The chorus at once coalesced like globules of quicksilver.

'Divide, I said,' repeated Mrs Palmer. 'You, Florrie Patten, and Mrs Pollett, and you others, go over to the right. That's it. Now, Richard, you go down into the barn and tell me if you can hear us. I shall lead the first chorus from this side—'

'Strophe,' said Betty aloud to herself in a contemptuous way.

'And Miss Thomas the second chorus from the other side.'

'Antistrophe,' said Betty, revengefully.

'Now we shall begin,' continued Mrs Palmer. 'And don't forget what I told you. We are women of Troezen, full of anxious foreboding for the young queen's— Where are Miss Thomas and Miss Dolly?'

A babel of voices informed her that the Rector, Miss Thomas and Miss Dolly Thomas were at the moment entering the barn.

'I'm so sorry, Mrs Palmer,' said Miss Thomas from half-way down the barn. She was a weather-beaten young woman of about thirty with a pleasant expression. 'Father thought he didn't feel quite the thing, but Dolly and I said, "You'll like it, Father, once you're there," didn't we, Father?'

'What dear?' said Dr Thomas.

'PHYL SAID YOU'D LIKE TO COME, FATHER, DIDN'T SHE?' said Miss Dolly Thomas.

'What did she say?' asked Dr Thomas.

Both his daughters laughed heartily.

'Father thought we were going to the Albert Hall,' explained Miss Thomas proudly. 'He's such an old pet. We can't think how he got the Albert Hall into his head unless it was Hippolytus. So we brought him along to cheer him up. I'll put him near Mrs Dean. He's so fond of her. He remembers her quite well when she used to come here when the children were little. YOU LIKE MRS DEAN, DON'T YOU, FATHER?'

Dr Thomas's face lighted up at the sight of Mrs Dean, who rose to greet him. His daughters installed him comfortably by her side and strode up onto the platform, where they took their places among the chorus.

'Now,' said Mrs Palmer, 'you lead the second chorus, Phyl, and Dolly, you come on my side. Now, both choruses together. There riseth . . .'

'THERE RISETH A ROCK-BORN RIVER,' said the Misses Thomas, dominating the whole chorus.

'What, dear?' asked Dr Thomas from his seat.

'Well, I *am* sorry,' said Miss Thomas. 'When we've been shouting at Father we quite forget. Hold in a bit, Dolly. It's all right, Father.'

These last words were spoken at the top of her voice, but as capital letters mar the effect of these well-printed pages, we shall make no further use of them, having sufficiently indicated to the thoughtful reader the points at which they may be imagined.

'Now, we'll begin,' said Mrs Palmer. 'Doris, as you can't behave, you had better go. You said your lines quite nicely and you'd better get off and be in bed early. There's plenty to do at the Dower House.'

'Very well, mum,' said the abashed Doris.

'Now, we'll start properly,' said Mrs Palmer. 'Chorus! I don't think you quite got the idea of the chanting when you were rehearsing separately with Mr Richard.'

Richard, approaching the platform and looking up at Mrs Palmer, said with great courage,

'Mrs Palmer, we weren't going to try chanting. Do you remember at the last rehearsal we discussed it and we thought it wouldn't work?'

'Well, we altered that since. It was the last rehearsal but

one that you were at, Richard. You didn't turn up for the last one, so we had to make our own arrangements.'

Mrs Tebben, remembering well that the rehearsal in question had taken place on the dreadful day when Richard's results came out, stepped forward to defend her offspring.

'Well, Louise,' she said, 'I was at that rehearsal, and I must say the chanting didn't go very well. I believe Richard is really right about just speaking it. Doris and her friends giggled so much that I despair of getting them into shape by the day. Of course, it used to be marvellous at the Court Theatre in old days, but somehow we seem to have got past that, don't we? I mean, it's rather like Maeterlinck and Celtic Twilights and all that sort of thing. Of course it's impossible to know how the Greeks really talked, unless of course one could get them on the wireless.'

'Till then, Winifred, we have to take the word of the best authorities,' said Mrs Palmer, whose temper for the first time that evening showed slight signs of fraying. 'That woman with one leg who recites so well, you know who I mean, the dwarfish one with the very fine profile that recited all three parts of *Henry VI* in drapery, has made a special study of the Greek chorus, and says that the method of intoning reproduces as nearly as possible their exact method.'

'Surely, Louise,' said Mrs Tebben with some dignity, 'if we wanted to do exactly what the Greeks did, we'd have to talk Greek. I feel it is too big a subject for me. I wonder what Mr Fanshawe would have to say?'

As each lady felt perfectly certain that Mr Fanshawe

would be on her side, Richard was deputed to ask his advice.

'Excuse me interrupting, Mr Fanshawe,' said Richard, 'but there's a kind of row going on. Mrs Palmer wants the chorus to sort of chant, and Mother and I think they ought to just speak. Mrs Palmer says what do you think, if you don't mind.'

Mr Fanshawe, unwillingly dragged from his conversation with Mr Tebben, put his spectacles on and looked straight through Richard.

'I have frequently noticed, Tebben,' said he to his old friend, 'that split infinitives have become part of Modern English Usage. I deprecate their use myself, but I realise that they have probably come to stay. Perhaps, as Charles Ravenshoe's friend, Lord Saltire, used to say, we should take our time from the young men, but the old Adam is strong in me.'

'I don't myself so much mind a split infinitive,' said Mr Tebben, 'as the expression "sort of". Young people appear incapable of speech without that meaningless qualifying phrase.'

'What am I to say to Mrs Palmer?' asked Richard.

'Anything you like, Richard,' said Mr Fanshawe. 'How the Greeks spoke is a matter of conjecture and likely to remain so. Do you remember, Tebben, the very interesting controversy that F. P. had with the Master of St Barnabas on the missing line in that Pindaric Ode which Bowen afterwards proved to be spurious? I have often wondered if there wasn't more behind that than met the eye.'

'You mean F. P. standing for the Ormroyd Lectureship?' said Mr Tebben.

Richard, finding himself an outcast, moved away. Mrs

Dean beckoned to him and asked what had happened.

'It's a sort of row,' said Richard, 'about the way the chorus is to speak, and Mrs Palmer sent me to ask Mr Fanshawe, but he is so busy talking to Father that he won't listen.'

'Tell Louise I'll ask Dr Thomas,' said Mrs Dean.

Richard went back with the message.

'Mrs Dean will never make Father understand,' said Miss Dolly, who had overheard. 'I'll go down and tell him.'

But she was too late, for Dr Thomas, having perfectly understood that Mrs Dean wanted to know what Greek sounded like, had opened, full-mouthed, on the sixth book of the *Odyssey*, choosing that book in preference to any other because Mrs Dean, surrounded by her daughters, reminded him, he said, of Nausicaa and her maidens. It was recognised by everyone in the barn that Dr Thomas, his eyes shining, gently beating the cadence of the verses with his long, thin hand, and in excellent bodily health, would go on just as long as he wished, and that they were highly privileged to hear him. No one but Miss Thomas or Miss Dolly could explain his mistake to him. Mrs Palmer begged them in a whisper to do so, but they refused flatly.

'Dear old pet,' said Miss Thomas, 'he just loves reciting Greek poetry.'

'It's an education for everyone,' said Miss Dolly. 'You girls at the back there, stop talking and listen to the Rector.'

When Dr Thomas had said as much as he wanted to say, he stopped. Mrs Dean thanked him warmly. Betty, who had been listening spell-bound, said at the top of her voice that he ought to be rehearsing the play. Her words reached him in a slightly mutilated form, and much flattered he got up and approached the platform. Mrs Palmer came down to meet him.

'Have you come to give us your judgment about the chorus, Dr Thomas?' she asked.

'Certainly, certainly,' said the Rector. 'When that dear child of Mrs Dean's asked me to supervise the play for you, I was delighted. I have, as you may perhaps know, written a good deal about the Greek stage. Now, to begin with I will tell all these young people a little about the worship of Dionysos, without which they cannot really enter into the spirit of Euripides.'

Mrs Palmer's heart sank. More than an hour and a half had already passed with little or nothing to show for her pains. Richard and Mrs Tebben, it was true, had not so far quite carried their point, but no more had she. She cast appealing looks at Miss Thomas and Miss Dolly. Miss Thomas, with considerable cunning, managed to persuade her father that he was hardly up to producing a play, and suggested that he should give hints to the principal actors, one at a time.

'Here, Betty, come up here,' she called down the barn. 'You know Greek. Take Father back to his seat and ask him about the play. He'll be quite happy, dear old soul.'

Betty, overawed by the honour, respectfully led Dr Thomas back to his chair, and seating herself beside him listened with rapt attention to a preliminary examination of pre-Dionysic cults.

'Now, chorus,' said Mrs Palmer. 'Winifred, are you ready? The Nurse comes on next.'

The chorus, which had broken into groups and was happily gossiping, hastily rearranged itself and plodded with cheerful and ungrudging want of comprehension through its part. Owing to the respect still felt for the gentry in that part of the country, no one presumed to speak simultaneously with Mrs Palmer or Miss Thomas, but bundled along after them like sheep following a leader. Neither Mrs Palmer nor Richard felt equal to another discussion.

'Splendid,' said Mrs Palmer, when they had got through their opening speech. 'Splendid. Now, once more the last three lines, and then a pause. There must be a feeling of doom upon us before I speak the Leader's verses, "But see, the Queen's grey nurse at the door."'

The chorus repeated the last three lines and waited obediently for the feeling of doom. Mrs Palmer stretched out her arm towards Mrs Tebben, in tense silence.

'Well, Louise, finished?' said Mr Palmer, coming onto the platform from the back entrance and turning up the lights, 'that's good, that's good. I've been looking at that basin in the men's dressing-room and it's still leaking. Bert, tell your father I want him to send up first thing tomorrow. Buffaloes' Outing? Yes, but bless my soul, he won't be a Buffalo tomorrow. Well, Phyl, well, Dolly. How's the Rector? No need to inquire, eh? Now come along all of you and have something to eat and drink. You look as if you wanted it.'

Mrs Palmer, not unthankfully, came down from the platform. Dr Thomas protested against the breaking up of such an enjoyable evening, but when Miss Thomas and Miss Dolly told him that he would like to go home now, wouldn't he, he said perhaps he would. With Betty he shook hands warmly, begging her to call on him and continue their most interesting discussion. While the lower orders adjourned to tea and cake in the racquet-court, Deans and Tebbens drifted across to the Manor House, where they were hospitably greeted by Susan and Robin, who had spent a pleasurable evening with Mr Palmer's cowman and were now ready for a hearty supper.

'I say,' said Robin, 'I nearly came with my mouth organ. Who won? Richard or Aunt Louise?'

'Nobody,' said Laurence. 'And if you ask me, nobody will. What the chorus wants to do, it will do.'

'Were you good?'

'No. I consider Hippolytus a poor sort of chap who wouldn't take a dare, and no inspiration to a man like me. In fact, the whole story is repellent and improbable. Margaret, do you feel Phaedra in your bones?'

'Not very much. People don't really hang themselves when they are in love. Of course the Greeks had very little to do.'

'Do you know what people are like when they're hanged?' said Robin, politely handing sandwiches. 'Their eyes turn right round in their heads, *right* round, and come popping out, and their tongues stick right out all black and swollen, and they look stinking. I'd love to be a governor of a jail.'

'Robin, you are horrible,' said Margaret. 'I don't see, Laurence, how anyone could feel Phaedra-ish nowadays.'

'They couldn't if they didn't understand her,' said Betty, favouring Margaret with a baleful stare. 'She was a noble woman under a doom. She had to die, because death,' said Betty reverently, 'is better than life.'

Having stunned her hearers with this announcement, she stumbled wet-eyed from the room and went home, sobbing loudly. Once safe in her bedroom, she took out a small diary from a secret place under her best stockings and began to write the events of the day. But hardly had she made the entry, 'Discussed Dionysos-worship with the Rector. Margaret Tebben is ignorant and heartless,' when Nanny, who looked upon all bedrooms as night-nurseries and thus under her jurisdiction, came in, and attributing Betty's red eyes and sniffs to hay fever, hurried her into bed.

The Tebben family all had cause for pleasure. Mr Tebben had, with Mr Fanshawe, run through the biographies of nearly two-thirds of the men who were up in their time. Mrs Tebben had been able to support Richard and had seen Mrs Palmer, if not routed, at least rendered powerless. Richard had also enjoyed Mrs Palmer's discomfiture. Margaret had thought Laurence was very good as Hippolytus and was on the whole glad that she had not had to speak. If they could go all through the rehearsals without her having to say her part, it wouldn't be so bad. In this pleasant state of mind they all went home. Mrs Tebben, prowling in the larder to get food for her family, who, full of Mrs Palmer's claret cup and sandwiches, had begged her not to, found Gunnar, locked up there by mistake, angrily eating the rest of the haddock. Everyone blamed Gunnar.

'Bad cat,' said Mr Tebben. 'The Vikings, it is true, ate quantities of dried fish, smoked or salted, but less from desire than necessity. When fresh meat was procurable they greatly preferred it.'

Margaret rubbed Gunnar behind his ears. Richard carried

him up to his room and allowed him to curl up on his pillow. But no sooner was Richard asleep than Gunnar got out of the window and boasted hideously to his friends in the village that he had broken into the larder single-handed and eaten all the next day's dinner.

Mr Dean drove his wife back to the Dower House. Mr Fanshawe chose to walk, accompanied by Laurence and Helen. Susan and Robin, having no lamps, preferred to bicycle.

'You didn't have much of a time,' said Laurence to his sister. 'I can't think why Aunt Palmer wanted you. Artemis doesn't come till the very end, and at the present rate of going it seems to me doubtful whether we'll ever get there.'

'I wanted to see the others,' said Helen.

As they neared the Dower House Robin came rapidly riding towards them.

'Come and bathe with nothing on in the pond,' he shouted to his elder brother. 'Susan's gone to bed, but I'm much too hot.'

Helen and Mr Fanshawe continued their walk.

'Let's pace up and down the terrace like people in books,' said Helen, slipping her arm through Mr Fanshawe's.

'How is everything?' asked Mr Fanshawe.

'Rotten.'

'Inside or out?'

'In.'

'Then what about turning yourself inside out and getting expert advice?'

'May I, Charles? I'm simply loathing myself.'

'Well?'

'I'm having jealousy to that extent that I don't know what to do.'

'Well?'

'Oh Charles, it's Laurence. You know he is my very particular brother, and I don't think I'd mind anything in the world that made him really happy, like being in love with the right person, but I can't bear his not telling me things. And he met this Margaret Tebben in France last winter and made friends with her, and if he wanted to marry her I wouldn't mind so much, but I simply can't bear their being friends.'

'Well?' said Mr Fanshawe, taking the hand that lay on his arm and holding it.

'Good old Charles,' said Helen huskily. 'I don't know. I like her, and she is very pretty and well-educated. I can't compete at all. But I am just grinding myself to bits with being jealous.'

'You had better cry,' said Mr Fanshawe, very kindly.

'I am,' said Helen.

'Good. You'll feel better presently.'

They stood still while Helen pressed her face against Mr Fanshawe's coat sleeve and cried.

'I am better now,' she said gratefully. 'How did you know?'

'How did I know?' asked Mr Fanshawe with a slightly bitter note. 'My dear child, part of my job is to put a few elementary facts into the heads of young women. They all get overwrought. Most of them cry. After that they cheer up.'

'Do they fall in love with you, Charles?'

'I regret to say they do. It means nothing. No woman in her senses would fall in love with me, but to adore one's tutor, however old and ugly he may be, is part of a university career. It does them no harm, whereas to adore a female tutor usually involves an emotional strain which often has a serious effect upon their examination results. I can safely say that no young woman ever got a lower class than she should in her final schools on my account. Tell me about young Tebben.'

'Richard?' said Helen, rather surprised at the turn the conversation was taking. 'He is rather nice.'

'Ha,' said Mr Fanshawe.

'He did very badly in his exams,' said Helen, 'and he's rather down. Perhaps you could help him a bit.'

'I don't suppose I could. Would you like me to?'

'Oh Charles, you would be a dear. Good night. And thank you very much for good advice. Can I come and cry again when I loathe myself?'

She kissed Mr Fanshawe with affectionate perfunctoriness and went indoors. Mr Fanshawe continued to pace the terrace and to remind himself that he was just twice as old as Helen Dean. He would have a talk with Tebben's boy and see what could be done.

5

Cooks in the Kitchen

Rehearsals continued without any particular incidents. Mr
Tebben went up to his office every day, sometimes spending
a few nights in town, sometimes returning in the evening
to Lamb's Piece. He had rather wished to take his autumn
holiday late in September, but to oblige a newly married
colleague he had altered it to the last fortnight in August.
Mrs Tebben was delighted, because then, she said, he would
be able to see exactly how the play was going. Mr Tebben
took no interest at all in the play, but was comforted for his
change of date by the thought of Mr Fanshawe's company.
There were still a fair number of their contemporaries unac-
counted for, and Fanshawe might know something about an
ex-Bursar who had gone into business and just been sen-
tenced to three years' hard labour.

Mrs Tebben and Richard were on slightly easier terms.
Mrs Tebben was still ridiculously touched by what Betty had
told her. If Richard had troubled to tell Betty Dean how

well his mother had done at college, it must mean that he took a little, if only a very little, pride in her past achievements. Of his contempt for her present doings she humbly had no doubt, but that he should find anything in her worth boasting about to outsiders was a comforting thought, and made her determine to overlook the hours at which he came down to breakfast.

Richard, who really thought very little of his mother's scholastic record, and had only used it to snub Betty, secretly admired Mrs Tebben's defiance of Mrs Palmer on the subject of chanting more than he could say. Mrs Palmer was unable to give much time to the next three chorus rehearsals, because she was superintending Mrs Phipps who had just machined the dresses for the chorus all wrong, so Richard and his mother were able to have things their own way, and the chorus made a good deal of progress in getting their lines. Miss Dolly Thomas kindly deputised as Leader in Mrs Palmer's absence.

At the Dower House life was equally peaceful. Mr Dean and Laurence were also away all day, but had promised to take a week off for the play. Susan and Robin bicycled all over the country, fished and bathed in every forbidden piece of water, and made excellent progress in tennis under Helen's coaching. Mrs Dean, living very quietly through the long, hot days, tried to forget the murmuring voice that was her companion. If sometimes its undertones rose to her consciousness she thought she would talk to Charles Fanshawe and perhaps be reassured by sharing a trouble, but whenever she began to approach the subject pride and an instinctive wish to procrastinate prevented her. To speak of a shadowed fear might give it a shape and bring it suddenly to life; kept in silence and darkness it might murmur unseen, unheard, pray heaven unfelt. So Charles, in spite of an abnormal sensitiveness to fine shades, could find little wrong with her unless she were anxious about Helen and Betty; and Mr Dean, content with Dr Masters's report, accepted her explanation that the heat was responsible for her languors. What Nanny knew was her own business, and she showed her solicitude by snapping at Susan and Robin and watching Jessica at every step. Meanwhile Mrs Dean, anxious to give her brother pleasure, made a point of going to all the rehearsals and telling Mrs Palmer how good they were. As she possessed the gift, so useful and in the end often so fatal to the owner, of being able to pay an apparently absorbed attention to something which hardly penetrated her consciousness, Mrs Palmer was as pleased as Rachel Dean had meant her to be, and Mr Palmer liked to see his lovely sister getting on so well with his wife.

Perhaps the two people who most enjoyed the rehearsals were Betty and Dr Thomas. As the weather was so fine and warm, Miss Thomas and Miss Dolly told their father that he would enjoy coming down to the barn for rehearsals, wouldn't he? They further said that he would like Betty Dean to come to supper first and then go along with them, wouldn't he? Dr Thomas said he would, and finding in Betty an increasingly interested audience, he gave her the benefit of his immense erudition, under the impression that she was taking an active part in the play. When he talked about the classics his faculties were alert, and Betty had no difficulty in making him hear her, without having to shout. Nothing was more pleasant to Dr Thomas than to sit in the barn in the glowing evening sunshine, expounding Orphism, or rolling out Greek verse in his fine voice. To be the chosen companion of such a scholar as the Rector was all that Betty asked. She hung on his words, made notes of his comments, was ready to listen for hours on end to what were really valuable lectures on the Greek drama. Rather disingenuously she let him believe that she was taking the part of Phaedra and listened respectfully to his analysis of the unhappy queen's character and motives. To her family she merely appeared to be Betty, in a better temper, thank goodness, than she was at the beginning of the holidays. To herself she was not only Phaedra, but Dorothea in *Middlemarch*; a Dorothea who would be infinitely kinder to Dr Thomas than the real Dorothea to Dr Casaubon. Not that she meant to marry Dr Thomas, but the situation, she felt, was much the same. Miss Thomas and Miss Dolly she tolerated as having their uses, and they were grateful to her for keeping their father amused while they rehearsed.

'Gilbert,' said Mrs Tebben at breakfast one morning, 'when you take your holiday next week, we must ask the Deans and the Palmers to dinner.'

'We can't manage more than six,' said Mr Tebben.

'Eight, dear, eight, with a little management. The Palmers, the Deans, and ourselves.'

'That is only six.'

'Eight, dear, with Richard and Margaret.'

'I thought you would want to ask Fanshawe with the Deans,' said Mr Tebben.

'I could easily have an egg in the kitchen and come in afterwards, if that would help,' said Margaret. 'So could Richard, couldn't you?'

Richard, who only came in as his sister spoke, said couldn't he what, in a way that held out but little encouragement to hope that he would. The situation was explained. Richard found it difficult to think quickly enough. If Mrs Dean was coming to dinner he must be there. On the other hand he knew that his parents, more especially his mother, would probably disgrace him. He did not like to think of Mrs Dean, used to wide spaces and luxury, sitting in their tiny dining-room, eating their uninteresting and possibly revolting food. He knew he would be ashamed of his surroundings and ashamed of himself for being ashamed. Mrs Tebben taking his silence for the early morning sulks, and perhaps feeling as Richard did that too much family would spoil the evening, said she would ask Helen Dean and Mr Fanshawe. Richard and Margaret could have a nice little meal by themselves and come in afterwards.

If Richard had not felt immortal longings for Mrs Dean's society, he would certainly have left home at the suggestion that he should not come in till after dinner, as if he were still a prep school boy, and would further have shown his contempt for convention by being late for lunch. But as things were he said 'All right' ungraciously and sat down to his breakfast.

'Then I will send a note to Mrs Dean and you can take it up this morning, Richard,' said Mrs Tebben. 'Louise I shall be seeing in any case about the dresses. If she would have the veils cut on the cross as I suggested, she would save at least two yards of stuff on the chorus. It all helps. We have a dress rehearsal on Tuesday week.'

'Oh I say, they can't have a dress rehearsal then,' said Richard. 'It's the match against Skeynes.'

'But my dear boy, a cricket match in the afternoon needn't prevent your rehearsing after supper.'

'My good mother, we may not be finished till heaven knows when, and anyway there'll be some sort of a blowout afterwards, there always is. And you know they never go back till the 8.10.'

'Surely, dear boy, for once—'

'Besides, Mother, Laurence is playing and you can't do without him.'

'Well, we shall have to alter the rehearsal, that's all. And Richard, did you remember to turn back your bed? If you don't, Mrs Phipps just covers it up again.'

Margaret, who had slipped out and in almost unnoticed, said Richard's bed was turned back. When Richard had finished his breakfast and got his sister alone, he asked who had done it.

'I did,' said Margaret. 'And I just put a piece of blotting-paper over the work you were doing on your table. I mean, I thought if Mother did come up ...'

'I know,' said Richard, blushing as he thought of the poem to Rachel Dean that he had left on his table, unfinished, at one o'clock that morning. 'I suppose you didn't see what it was, did you?'

'I couldn't. I saw it was something like poetry, so I shut my eyes and covered it up.'

'I can't tell you about it now,' said Richard importantly. 'Some day, perhaps. It's rather big.'

'Thank you,' said Margaret.

Later in the morning they took Modestine, alias Neddy, up to the Dower House. The christening had been kept from Mr and Mrs Tebben, as there was a general feeling that they would not see eye to eye with the public about the change of name. Before going, Richard discovered that his mother had asked the Deans not to dress. A slight wrangle took place, Richard maintaining that Mrs Dean had never not dressed in her life and wouldn't understand it, Mrs Tebben practically accusing Richard of snobbery. Mr Tebben's suggestion that the subject should not be mentioned, and the decision left with the Deans, was scouted by his wife, who wanted to know how she could then tell what to wear herself.

'But you'd wear your dark blue lace dress anyway, wouldn't you, Mother?' said Margaret. 'You said Mr Fanshawe used to like blue. Then Daddy and Richard could wear black ties.'

'Very well,' said Mrs Tebben, not displeased, 'so be it,' and her thoughts went back to a day when Mr Fanshawe, meeting Miss Winifred Ross on the Paul's barge in Eights Week, had said, in default of anything else to say, how nice her blue dress looked. It was blue muslin with white spots, confined by a blue petersham belt with a silver buckle. Her hair was puffed out under a large blue straw hat trimmed with poppies and cornflowers and skewered into place with silver-headed hatpins. The blue eyes of the middle-aged Mrs Tebben, writer of textbooks on economics, looked back into the distance of time and saw that Winifred Ross always looked her best in blue.

'That was a brain-wave,' said Richard admiringly to his sister as they went along the field path, Margaret sitting sideways on Modestine, Richard walking beside her. 'It's bad enough Mrs Dean having to eat one of Mrs Phipps's unspeakable suppers, without being asked not to dress. Anyway, my dinner-jacket suit is about the only decent one I have. My blue suit is too shabby for words, and my brown one's as bad, and I can't dine in flannels, and I won't see my way to getting any new clothes just now. It's simply rotten being poor and a failure. Do you suppose I'll ever get a job or anything? Reading law's all very well, but I ought to be earning something. Dash it, even Mother was earning money at my age. I say, could you do anything about dinner do you think? You know what Mother is, boiled mutton and steamed pudding.'

Margaret, who also badly needed new frocks and saw little prospect of earning money herself, was extremely sorry for her brother, assured him that he would quickly get a job, and promised to do what she could about dinner.

'I cook fairly well,' she said. 'I did a lot at Grenoble. If only Mrs Phipps could break her leg. If she's there Mother will insist on her cooking and there'd be awful offence if I tried to interfere in the kitchen. As a matter of fact I know what dinner will probably be, and it's a black look-out. Mrs Phipps has a cock that she wants to get off on us. It will be a tough roast cock, grey potatoes, not enough beans from the garden, a trifle, and raspberries and cream.'

'Not enough raspberries either,' said Richard gloomily. 'Nor cream neither too. Well, let's hope.'

At the Dower House Nanny as usual took over Modestine, and Margaret went to play tennis with Helen, Susan and Robin.

'Betty's down at the Rectory,' said Susan to Richard. 'We thought at first she'd gone all pi, but it's only Greek plays. Coming to play tennis?'

'I've got to give this note to Mrs Dean first.'

'All right. Mother's in the morning-room.'

Richard found Mrs Dean writing letters. The outside blinds were down, the room bathed in warm, rose-scented twilight.

'I brought you a note from Mother, Mrs Dean,' he said, knocking against a chair. 'It's about dining with us. I do hope you'll be able to come.'

'So do I,' said Mrs Dean opening the letter. 'As far as I know we are all free. I must ask Frank and Charles – Frank is up in town today – and I'll send over an answer. It's very kind of your mother.'

'Couldn't I come and get the answer after dinner tonight? It would save you the trouble of sending it.'

'That's very sweet of you, Richard. Frank and Mr Fanshawe and I shall be dining at the Bonds', but I'm sure the children will love to see you.'

This was not what Richard meant. A long peaceful evening with his lovely hostess had been in his mind.

An evening in which, at last, he might be able to tell her a little of what she meant to him without having a dry tongue and a roaring in his ears. But so long as she was happy, even if dining with those stuffy old Bonds, all was well.

'I say, Mrs Dean,' he said nervously, 'I wanted to ask you something.'

'Yes?' said Rachel Dean, who wanted to get on with her letters.

'I say, when you come to us, you couldn't possibly wear that ripping white trailing dress, could you?'

'The Callot or the Schiaparelli?' asked Mrs Dean, interested.

'I don't know exactly. I mean that ripping hanging sort of one you had on the night we sat under the mulberry tree and you were frightened when Susan and Robin got on the roof and Jessica screamed.'

(The night I had to hold you from falling; the night I saw the dark petals of violets on your eyelids.)

'Oh, that tea-gown. It was very sweet of you to like it, Richard, but I must dress up a little more when I am having my first dinner with your parents.'

'We don't dress much,' said Richard in an off-hand way.

'Well, I'll see. I do wish I could keep you here, but I know you will be wanting to play tennis, and the children have been waiting for you.'

'They've got a four, Mrs Dean. Do let me stay here.'

'That would be selfish,' said Rachel Dean, smiling radiantly. 'Helen says your game is coming on splendidly, so I mustn't keep you. Come again soon.'

She put out her hand. Richard raised it to his lips, didn't know quite what to do with it, put it down again and crashed out of the room. Mrs Dean sighed with relief and continued her weekly letters to her soldier son in India and the twins at sea. Richard's attentions were so kind, so like the ass turned lap-dog, but he was a pleasant sort of boy and the children liked him. Altogether it was a pleasant summer if one could forget the murmur which must not be heard, which must always be kept from Frank, which one might be able to share with Charles, the silent, the utterly reliable.

In due course Mrs Tebben's invitation was accepted, and Mrs Tebben, as Margaret had foretold, was hypnotised into ordering Mrs Phipps's tough old cock and hoped vaguely that there would be plenty of raspberries. Richard became a prey to anxiety which Margaret did her best to dispel, promising that even if Mrs Phipps didn't break her leg, she would somehow see that the dinner was eatable.

The day before the great party dawned as fine and hot as the day for a village cricket match should be. The Worsted eleven was strengthened by Richard, Laurence, Robin, and Mrs Palmer's butler Sparrow. At eleven twenty-three the Skeynes eleven, stiffened by Lady Bond's son and an ex-county player, arrived at Worsted station, where they were met by the Buffaloes' band and escorted to the cricket ground, at a fairly flat field up near the church. Worsted went in first and were still in after lunch when visitors began to dribble onto the ground. Mrs Palmer, arriving with her husband, was preparing to take her usual seat in the front row of the four rows of rickety benches which were the grand stand, when to her indignation she saw Lady Bond calmly sitting there. It was useless to pretend that she had not seen her, so she had to say How do you do.

'Bond was so sorry he couldn't come over,' said Lady Bond. 'He had to be in town, something to do with the House of Lords. I hear you have quite a good side.'

'So Bond's up in London, eh?' said Mr Palmer, who refused to be aware of the hostility between his wife and Lady Bond. 'Poor fellow, poor fellow. Must wish he hadn't taken the peerage. Why did he vote against Clause Three of the Root Vegetables Bill? Bad policy, you know, bad policy. I see your boy is playing for Skeynes,' he continued, looking at the card. 'We'll see him make a century, I expect.'

As he spoke the Hon. C. W. Bond missed an easy catch and fell down.

'Bad luck, bad luck,' said Mr Palmer sympathetically. 'Ought to get glasses if he can't see. Come along, Louise, must go and talk to the Rector.'

Mrs Palmer, a good deal restored, waved goodbye to Lady Bond and followed her husband. As she passed a knot of villagers she singled out a boy.

'Here, Ernie Phipps,' she proclaimed, 'tell your mother I'll want her to stay on a bit tomorrow. There are one or two dresses that need altering. I'll tell Mrs Tebben.'

'Yes, mum,' said Ernie.

Dr Thomas was sitting under a tree with a rug round his knees. He was too hot, but his daughters had said he would like to have it. Betty as usual was at his feet, listening to a glowing description of the athletic training of young Spartans.

'Don't move, Rector,' said Mrs Palmer. 'How are we doing?'

Dr Thomas smiled and took off his hat.

'What is the score, Dr Thomas? Mrs Palmer wants to know,' said Betty.

The Rector appeared to hear her without any difficulty.

'Worsted are ninety-two,' he said. 'Last man has just gone in, your man Sparrow, Mrs Palmer. Laurence made twenty and little Robin made a very pretty thirty-one. Skeynes have some good batsmen and it ought to be an even thing.'

A few minutes later, amid shrill cheers from the girls and the small boys who made up the more demonstrative part of the audience, the hundred went up, and when Worsted's last wicket fell Sparrow had knocked the score up to a hundred and twenty-three. Dr Thomas, to Betty's disappointment, had left the subject of Greek physical training for reminiscences of W. G. Grace and Spofforth, but as Worsted came out to field, his eye fell on Laurence and Robin, and his admiration of their form and bearing made it easy for Betty to guide him back to the ancients.

When Mrs Tebben drove up in Modestine, a misleading figure of speech which she and her family were in the habit of using, Richard was thankful that he was fielding and would not be publicly disgraced by being recognised as her son. Then Mrs Dean was driven up to the field. She walked about for a little, looking very lovely and slightly out of place, waved kisses to Laurence and Robin, who enthusiastically returned them, and drove away again to a garden-party. Richard thought that she had included him in her greeting. Inspired by this thought he entirely forgot where he was, till he was suddenly roused by a shout and saw a ball hurtling towards him. Mechanically his arm shot out, by a miracle the ball stuck in his hand. The shout was repeated, this time a shout of triumph from Worsted.

'Look, Winifred,' said Mrs Palmer, poking her friend as she sat in Modestine's cart. 'Richard has caught young

Bond. Good boy, good boy. Out for a duck too,' and she hit herself with rapture. Mrs Tebben sat in a trance of pride.

> "'And even the ranks of Tuscany
> Could scarce forbear to cheer,'"

she said aloud to herself. Susan beat Margaret on the back and Helen congratulated her warmly. Margaret, tearful with pleasure, protested that it was nothing to what Laurence and Robin would do, but though they did well in bowling, Richard remained the spectacular hero of the afternoon. When Skeynes were all out for a hundred and ten a small boy asked him for his autograph, and life was full of dazzling possibilities. The two teams, by long usage, then had a gigantic high tea in the village hall, after which Worsted saw the Skeynes eleven off at the station. Richard and Laurence, flown with tea and ham, sent Robin home, and themselves did the daring deed of mounting on the footboard of the train and accompanying their rivals through the tunnel. As all eleven rivals were in one carriage and the tunnel was full of boomings and reverberations, conversation was difficult, but they managed to arrange with the Hon. C. W. Bond, who was full of generous admiration for their play, to fly to Vienna in the autumn and go down the Danube to the Black Sea, a plan which had its birth and death at that sooty and ecstatic moment. On the other side of the hill the engine-driver, Sid Pollett, obligingly slowed down, having received instructions to that effect from Mr Patten the station-master before leaving Worsted. Richard and Laurence jumped off, the engine whistled, the Skeynes eleven cheered, the Hon. C. W. Bond dropped his cigarette-case onto the line, where the wheels of the last coach went over it, crushing it to pieces, and the two adventurers went back up the hill towards Worsted.

The path to the village led through woods and fields and past Lamb's Piece. As they approached the garden Richard recommended caution, in case either of his parents happened to be about, which would spoil the evening. But the house looked quiet, and no one was visible except Margaret, who was leaning over the gate looking away down the valley. Laurence suggested that they should call to her, but Richard said it would be dangerous to let their whereabouts be known, so they continued their way to the Woolpack, where they drank beer and played darts with the rest of the eleven. The curate did look in with the view, deprecated by Mr Palmer, of promoting good fellowship, but finding it already promoted to an almost alarming extent, he went away. Richard and Laurence saw each other home several times, till it was late enough for the Tebbens to be in bed, so that Richard could get to his room unquestioned. Laurence went back to the Dower House with a disquieting vision of a girl, left alone, looking over a gate into the distance. He wished they had stopped to talk with her. Then, considering her mother, he was glad they hadn't. But the vision remained.

Early next morning Richard woke, feeling happier than he had felt since the end of term. Trying to account for the feeling, he suddenly remembered the catch that had dismissed young Bond. There was a holy feeling about that catch, which appeared to have been directly inspired by the thought of Mrs Dean. He shot out of bed and did a dance of joy. In the middle of a bound, expressive of triumph over opponents, he stopped. His bedroom window was over the back door, and from the yard outside came voices. He went to the window and looked cautiously out. His mother, who was up early as usual, had been gardening. She had a trowel in one hand and was talking to Mrs Phipps, who had evidently just arrived, for she still had her husband's cap on.

'Well, mum,' said Mrs Phipps, 'when you said there was company coming to dinner tonight I said to Phipps, 'Mrs Tebben can't have remembered it's a Wednesday, and Wednesdays I have to go to Mrs Palmer about the dressmaking.'

'But why didn't you remind me, Mrs Phipps?' said Mrs Tebben miserably.

'I said to Phipps, "If Mrs Tebben has company on a Wednesday it's to be supposed she had her reasons," and I never was one to hold with interfering.'

'But if you had only mentioned it ... Well, could you come back after you have done Mrs Palmer's sewing and help me? We could perhaps do the chicken this morning and have it cold.'

'I'm very sorry, mum,' said Mrs Phipps, 'but Mrs Palmer sent up word yesterday by my Ernie as she'll be wanting me to stay on. Being as Wednesday is usually a light day, with you and Mr Tebben being in town, I didn't like to disoblige her, specially seeing as Ernie is to go to her for the boots and knives when he leaves school at Christmas.'

'I simply do not know what I shall do,' said Mrs Tebben

with a despair and an elocution that would have done credit to any Phaedra in her worst moments.

'If only Dawris was free, I'm sure I'd let her oblige,' said Mrs Phipps, 'but seeing as how she's up at Mrs Dean's and run off her feet as it is, I don't see how she could. It's dreadful the way that cook's at her all the time, if she as much as goes to the stable-yard or runs into the garden for a moment, making her learn sauces and all. Dawris says she likes it, but I say two chauffeurs is two too many where there's girls about.'

Mrs Phipps disappeared into the scullery and Richard saw his mother walk disconsolately round to the front of the house. He hurriedly dressed and came down to find out what was happening. Heaven seemed to have heard his and Margaret's prayers and removed Mrs Phipps. It now remained to see what Margaret could do. He found his mother seated at the breakfast-table in deep gloom and his father reading his letters.

'Congratulations, Richard,' said his father. 'I hear you made the catch of the season. Anything wrong, Winifred? Margaret, did you hear the owls last night?'

Richard mumbled his thanks, Margaret said she had heard the owls, also a nightjar. Mrs Tebben sat silent. Presently she said she supposed they would have to put their party off. Richard kicked Margaret under the table. Mr Tebben raised his eyebrows.

'Louise is really unpardonable,' Mrs Tebben burst out. 'Not only does she take Mrs Phipps on Wednesday afternoons without really consulting me, but I thought at least Mrs Phipps could come and help me to get something cold, or to wash up, but Louise appears to be more important than I am. And I have to go to Winter Overcotes for the Women's Institute meeting, I can't get out of that. Richard, you'll have to take a note over to the Dower House and apologise and explain. As for Louise, considering that she has taken Mrs Phipps, I really don't see where we stand. It is too vexatious. It would serve her right if I let her come here and find nothing to eat.'

'I shouldn't put them off, Mother,' said Margaret. 'If you didn't mind my trying I think I could manage dinner nearly as well as Mrs Phipps. Will you go to Winter Overcotes and forget all about it, and leave me and Richard to see about dinner? We'll give Daddy some lunch and everything will be all right.'

After a great deal of argument, during which Mrs Tebben explained at length how she had thought perhaps they wouldn't mind having biscuit and cheese for lunch and the rest of that blancmange, she was persuaded to let the dinner-party stand, and went down to the station in a happier frame of mind. When she had seen her mother off, Margaret went to the kitchen to look at the fowl. Mrs Phipps, a little abashed, offered to pluck it, but Margaret told her to go on with the housework and then she could go. It was a sultry day with no breath of wind, so she took a chair into the kitchen yard and began plucking the fowl, conversing occasionally with Gunnar, who had hopes of giblets. Presently the well-known sound of Laurence's two-seater came roaring up the lane and into their little drive. Margaret called to him. Guided by her voice he came round to the yard and was very much surprised by what he saw. When Margaret told him that his Aunt Palmer had annexed Mrs Phipps and so left them cook-less, his indignation against her was as unbounded as was his admiration of Margaret for undertaking the job.

'Aunt Palmer is really the outer limit,' he said, 'scrobbling your cook and then coming to dinner.'

'I don't suppose she knew,' said Margaret. 'Probably she thinks dinners just happen. And I like cooking. I cooked a lot at Grenoble.'

'I'll tell you what,' said Laurence. 'Let me help. I'll tie a white tablecloth round my waist and give a hand.'

'I expect you'll be more trouble than you're worth,' said Margaret, 'and as for a tablecloth, Mother would go pale if she saw you wearing one as an apron, but if you really want to help, get me a lot of beans out of the garden.'

Laurence found a basket and went down the garden. When he got to the bean rows he found Mr Phipps sitting on a wheel-barrow eating bread and cheese.

'Morning, Phipps,' he said. 'A bit early for dinner, isn't it?'

'A man like me as works in graveyards has to get his bite when he can,' said Mr Phipps.

'Much doing in the graveyard line?' asked Laurence as he picked French beans.

'Worst season I've ever known, sir, and I've lived in these parts nearly seventy year and been sexton thirty-three,' said Mr Phipps. 'Not a soul nor a body for three months. Seems like there's a curse on that new bit of ground the bishop consecrated last summer. Can't get no one to make a beginning. Don't you pick them beans too young, sir, Mrs Tebben won't like it. Cremation's the trouble, sir. To my mind it's against nature, but these young people they like a bit of life and you can't stop 'em.'

'Not much life in cremation, I should have thought.'

'It's this way, sir. It means a nice outing to Woking in a motor-coach for the friends and relations. You can't blame them for liking their bit of fun. I was the same when I was a young fellow. I'd think nothing of walking to the county jail, a matter of fifteen mile each way, to stand outside the day a man was hung. But I'm not what I was.'

'Well, I hope you'll live to see the hoodoo taken off the new burying-ground,' said Laurence.

'Thank you kindly, sir,' said Mr Phipps, brightening up. 'Maybe I'll be the first myself. It wouldn't look bad on my stone, "He was the first".'

'"That ever burst",' said Laurence mechanically, which made the gardener burst into a cackle and say he'd tell his old woman that.

Laurence took the beans back to Margaret and gave her an account of Mr Phipps's ambition. Richard, disturbed in his reading by their laughter, came down and helped Laurence to string the beans. Margaret then put the cock into the steamer and began washing the potatoes.

'What sort of pudding does your mother like?' she asked Laurence. 'We didn't have pudding much in France, but I can do omelettes. Do you think she'd like a jam omelette?'

'She'd like a rum one better,' said Laurence.

'I'm afraid we haven't any rum.'

Laurence said he would go and get some, and before Margaret could protest he was in the car, racing towards the village. By the time Margaret had finished the potatoes, he was back with an armful of parcels.

'Let's do it in style,' he said. 'Here's the rum, and here's a bottle of sherry for us to drink now, and I found some caviare at home, so I brought a jar along, and salted almonds and some lemons and chocolates and a bottle of Benedictine and a huge tin of asparagus and some cigarettes.'

'But, Laurence, they're your mother's things. We can't feed her and the Palmers on her own food. Besides ... '

She was too shy to go on, but she felt a little hurt to her pride. Her people were not well off, but they were not beggars. Laurence seemed to think that he could shower groceries on them as if he were Bolton Abbey in the Olden Time. One present of wine, or one jar of caviare anyone could take, but this wholesale distribution of food made her find, against her will, a certain lack of perception, even of delicacy in Laurence. Then she blamed herself for ingratitude.

'Rubbish,' said Laurence, rummaging in the kitchen-table drawer for a corkscrew. 'Anyway, I bought the rum and the sherry myself. The Woolpack has quite a pretty taste in drink. The Benedictine and the asparagus and the cigarettes I pinched off Sparrow. He thinks I am having a picnic, but he didn't bat an eyelid at my ideas of a gypsy lunch. So you see it's only paying Aunt Palmer back for taking your cook. Sparrow would give me the moon since we won that match against Skeynes. So it's only Mother's almonds and caviare. Do you mind? Drink your sherry and say you don't.'

Margaret drank her sherry and said she didn't. As there was nothing else to be done till Mrs Phipps's cock had been steamed to tenderness, they went into the garden and sat under a tree. Richard went in to get some more cushions.

'Richard and I saw you last night,' said Laurence to Margaret. 'You were looking over the garden gate, all melancholy and pleasant. We would have stopped, but we thought your mother would pounce on us.'

'I know,' said Margaret, seeing a future in which so many people would go by on the other side of the way for fear of being pounced on.

'Don't look so sad,' said Laurence. 'We are all here now. Have some more sherry.'

Margaret had the sherry and looked gay, but she was not happy. It was all very well to play at being cook and have Laurence to bring in the beans and fetch caviare, but she knew that this was only an interlude. There were careers and futures to think of. Richard must find a job. She must find a job too if she could, though it wasn't very easy for a girl who had no particular education. She could speak French and German fairly well, and cook a bit. That wasn't going to get one anywhere. Probably it would just come to this: living at home, trying to be patient and good, helping Daddy perhaps by looking things up or doing some typing, helping Mummy in the house. And always seeing Laurence, or others like him, going by on the other side of the way. Tears welled up in her eyes.

'Margaret, *darling*,' said Laurence. 'What *is* the matter? Do you need comforting?'

She did indeed want to be comforted, but as his idea of comfort appeared to be an arm carelessly thrown round her, Margaret thanked him very much and said she thought it was the effect of sherry at twelve o'clock, which she wasn't used to. Richard came back with cushions.

'I say,' he said apologetically, 'I found Father in the drawing-room when I went to get the cushions, and he looked so depressed I said he'd better come out here. Nobody minds, do they?'

'Come along, sir, and have some sherry,' said Laurence, jumping up and kindly welcoming Mr Tebben to his own garden. 'Richard, my boy, look after your father while I get my little instrument.'

He sped across the lawn to his car, from which he produced his guitar and sat down under the tree again.

Mr Tebben had been indeed depressed. He loved his wife and family very deeply, but there were moments when he felt it was all too much for him. The fiasco of Mrs Phipps at breakfast was a bad beginning, and he found it difficult not to wish that Winifred were a better housekeeper. He had just had a notice that some dividends were not to be paid. Richard's future lay heavily on his mind, and much as he loved his boy and had believed in his promises of work, he could not see that he was doing much. This Greek play with endless rehearsals, the young people at the Dower House, cricket and tennis, were taking most of his time. He liked all the young Deans, but he was morbidly afraid that Richard would get discontented from being with people to whom money was a matter of course. He must ask Fanshawe's advice. Perhaps Fanshawe, who had so much experience in helping young men with the beginning of their careers, could tell him how much a really good crammer for the Civil Service cost, or how long it would take Richard to eat dinners and pass examinations to be a lawyer, or, if he didn't pass the Civil Service examination or the law examinations, whether he could ever expect to earn anything, or how one approached the mysterious world of business. Margaret's future seemed equally dim. He was enchanted by the pretty, sweet-tempered daughter who had come back to him, but what was he to do with her? There was hardly room for her and Winifred, who managed or mismanaged everything near her, and didn't like help or interference. He hadn't been able to afford to send Margaret to a University, nor did he think that she was the type of girl to benefit by it, but when he retired on a pension, when he died, what was going to become of her? When Richard found him he was wandering about the drawing-room, forgetting what book it was he had come to look for, and repeating to himself his favourite quotation, Thought the harder, Heart the bolder, Mood the more as our Might lessens, but what was all very well for the Old Companion at the Battle of Maldon, or for a grown-up man who had not found life easy, was not right for a young girl. At her age it would be outrageous to be armoured against fate by the final courage of complete disillusionment and unbelief.

When he got into the garden Laurence's foolish and amusing talk, with interludes of strumming on the guitar, the sherry, the warm day, the absence of his wife, all united to soothe and heal him. He let some of his cares slip from him and relaxed. Laurence insisted on providing the lunch. He ran up to the village again in the car and brought back several bottles of beer and two and a half pounds of sausages, which he toasted at the kitchen fire, letting their juice fall into a pan in which he had put pieces of bread. He then let the bread frizzle in the fat till it was crisp, piled the sausages onto it, and carried the dish into the garden. Margaret fetched glasses and knives and forks, Richard picked all the raspberries, and they had a sprawling, uncomfortable, delightful meal. Margaret had two sausages, Mr Tebben three, and Laurence and Richard the rest, except a small one, which was given to Gunnar. After lunch Mr Tebben smoked his pipe and gradually fell asleep.

'Poor Daddy,' said Margaret to Laurence, while Richard teased Gunnar, 'he hardly ever gets any fun. I wish to goodness I could get a job and help a bit.'

'I'd hate you to have a job,' said Laurence. 'Promise me you never will. Gosh, I never ate five sausages before.'

'I dare say I'll hate it myself, but I must. You see, there's Richard to be provided for. It costs a lot to educate a man, and if he's to be a lawyer he won't earn anything for ages. I dare say I could earn something before he does – nursery-governessing or something, like a heroine.'

'If anyone's to have a job it ought to be Richard,' said Laurence. 'Don't go taking one without telling me, will you?'

'Come and wash up,' said Margaret.

What with washing up, putting the cock through the mincing machine, and getting everything ready for the party, the afternoon passed quickly enough. Mr Tebben slept till tea-time, with Richard reading near him, and when he woke was agreeably surprised to find a tray on the ground with excellent, very hot, fresh tea and piles of buttered toast. Margaret's heart smote her at the sight of her father's pleasure in so small a thing as tea freshly made, and she felt that a great many people might pass by so long as she could make him happy with such small attentions. Just as Laurence was going, a thought struck her.

'My goodness,' she said, 'we ate all the raspberries for lunch. Laurence, I hate to bother you again, but if I give you the money will you very kindly see if Mr Pollett has some at his shop?'

'I'll tell you what,' said Laurence, 'I'll go home and change, and then I'll come back with raspberries and help you and Richard to serve the grown-ups' dinner and wash up, and then you and he and I will eat the remains in the kitchen. There's the sherry. There'll be enough left to give your guests a drink when they arrive. Don't waste it on Aunt Palmer, she never finishes hers.'

Again to be treated as a pauper, to be given the remains of the sherry bottle, in a way that made it the equivalent of coals and blankets. Margaret sighed, blamed herself again for false pride, and put the minced cock into a basin to be steamed up and served as a timbale.

Mrs Tebben got back from her meeting by the 6.47, tired but content, for she had routed Lady Bond on the question of sending a local representative to the annual meeting of the County Women's Institutes, and found a bargain in floor polish at Woolworth's. Margaret made some fresh tea for her mother, alleging as excuse for this extravagance that tea made at four o'clock would be rather strong if kept till seven, listened to her account of her day, assured her that all was well with the dinner, and sent her upstairs to have a bath and change into the blue lace frock, which she had already put out.

'I had to alter your dinner a tiny bit, Mother,' she said, 'so

I hope you won't mind. Laurence had a little caviare and some of that fat tinned asparagus, so we thought you wouldn't mind having them.'

Very luckily Mrs Tebben's mind was too full of her recent victory to object to having tinned asparagus in summer, or to conduct her usual searching inquisition into what had been going on while she was away.

'I can't think why Laurence had caviare,' was all her comment, 'but young people do have peculiar things. There was that friend of Richard's at Oxford who kept a mongoose. Never shall I forget Lady Bond's face when my resolution was carried by sixteen to three. Mrs Bird was chairman, and a very good one. It is very nice of you, Margaret, to take so much trouble. It will be coals of fire on Louise's head.'

Margaret, humbly delighted to have one word of recognition unaccompanied with criticism from her mother, hastened to explain that she had really enjoyed preparing the meal.

'You had better go upstairs now, Mummy,' she said. 'It's a quarter-past seven and you'll want a bath. Richard and I have had ours, so you'll have no one to interfere.'

When Mrs Tebben came down a little before eight, she found the drawing-room looking tidier than usual. On a table was a tray with eight glasses and a decanter, at which her husband was looking with interest.

'I was just wondering whether it would go round,' he said. 'I think if I poured it into the glasses, a little more than half full, I should know better. I hope you aren't too tired after your committee. I wish you wore that dress oftener, Winifred. Do you remember the blue dress you were wearing on that Norwegian cruise?'

Mrs Tebben did remember Winifred Ross's blue dress. It was the blue muslin with white spots, five years old, on its last legs, altered, washed out, but good enough for picnics on the fiords. Miss Ross did not think that Mr Tebben, that nice young Civil Servant, had noticed it.

'It just goes round,' said Mr Tebben. 'What shall we do with the decanter?'

'Give it to me, Daddy,' said Margaret, who came in with an apron over her flowery dress. 'Everything's ready, Mummy. When you've finished each course, ring the little bell and Richard will be there at the door to take the dirty things, if you don't mind handing them out. It's no good his trying to get round the table because there isn't room. I've put your place nearest the door, Daddy, because you don't get so fussed as Mummy,' she added in a whisper to her father. 'I love you in the blue dress, Mummy, and you're doing us all great credit. I must fly back to my saucepans.'

Mr Tebben then noticed that one glass was a good deal fuller than the rest.

'I must have filled that glass fuller than the others,' he said. 'I will just quickly drink some of it and then they will all look equal.'

6

One Way of Love

Rachel Dean was resting in her sitting-room before the Tebbens' dinner-party. All her young except Laurence, unaccountably absent since the morning, and Jessica, now having her bath, were playing tennis, and the house was quiet. She rang the bell and told her maid to ask Mr Fanshawe to come to her room.

'I do so want to have a talk with you, Charles,' she said, as Mr Fanshawe entered.

'Does that mean that I am to listen to you talking about your children?' inquired Mr Fanshawe, stretching out his long legs in an easy chair. 'I'd rather talk about you. I am a kind of Jesuit, you know. I see and hear more than you'd think and I can give very excellent, subtle advice. You, Rachel,' and he pointed a long finger at her, 'are hiding something from me. And not only from me, from Frank. I have been gradually noticing it for some time. He hasn't noticed it yet, but he will, very shortly. Then, not knowing what the matter is, he will probably shoot young Tebben.'

Rachel raised inquiring eyes.

'Richard? But he doesn't need shooting. Be less impressive, Charles, and speak out.'

'I suppose you are about the least vain and self-conscious woman for your age and looks in the British Empire,' said Mr Fanshawe, 'but there is a moment at which unselfconsciousness becomes sheer idiocy. Haven't years of experience – you are nearly as old as I am – taught you to recognise calf-love? Young Tebben is perfectly damp with it. Highly suitable for him, but what about you?'

'Of course he is a dear boy, but excessively wearing,' said Mrs Dean. 'One cannot get away from him. He clings like a leech. But he is really very nice.'

'You are far too amiable, Rachel. If Caligula came to stay you would think he was very nice so long as he let you talk about the children. What young Tebben needs is a good job of work, or an interest in someone of his own age. Someone like Helen,' he said, with a little effort.

'I think, Charles,' said Rachel, suddenly taking the offensive, 'that it is you who are keeping something from me. Do you really want Richard to take an interest in Helen?'

'It would seem reasonable.'

'Reasonable!' said Rachel with gentle scorn. 'Helen is two years older than Richard.'

'But she takes an interest in him.'

'We all like him. But, Charles, did you ever talk to Helen at all? She has been so very aloof these holidays and is quite unhelpable.'

'I did. Even my Jesuit mind hadn't guessed what her trouble was. She has very few affections and they are very deep. The deepest at present is Laurence. She has always adored him. She wouldn't mind seeing him in love, or married, so I gather, but she resents his friendships. She knows it is silly and she has been making really heroic efforts to cure herself these holidays, but there doesn't seem to be anyone to help her. Your Laurence is as nice as a child of yours should be, Rachel, but I sometimes think he has one skin more than some of us. It is lucky for him, and a little unlucky for people who care for him.'

'When you say "these holidays", do you mean Margaret Tebben?' asked Rachel.

'I think I do. And she is a nice girl, and at present worth two of her brother. He is one of the late developers, trying to himself and to others. Laurence likes Margaret, and Helen is trying to take it well. She told me so herself, and telling someone, even old Uncle Charles, was a help.'

'Laurence likes so many people that I always lose count,' said his mother. 'But he can look after himself. It is my Helen that worries me. If only she could care for someone outside the family. But she has never cared for young men at all, except of course you.'

Mr Fanshawe turned his head sharply.

'Yes, Charles, I know you are the same age that I am, but young men was what I said.'

'I might retort, young woman, and with far more reason.'

'Oh, I don't look my age, I know,' said Mrs Dean, with the candour of a woman whose looks have never failed her, 'but that isn't being young. You climb rocks and ski and skate and tramp over passes. I do nothing.'

'You are a beautiful, lazy creature, Rachel. Why don't you do something? Keep up your tennis? You used to be uncommon good. Helen gets her game from you.'

Rachel hesitated for a moment. This appeared to be the heaven-sent moment for telling Charles her secret trouble, but, as always happened when she tried to speak of it, speech would not come at all. Charles Fanshawe came to her help.

'Is there some good reason for you giving up tennis?' he asked.

'Yes,' said Rachel, bereft of her usual self-possession, her voice veiled with fear.

'It can't be varicose veins,' said Charles judicially, 'so it must be heart. Is it troublesome?'

'Not exactly,' Rachel admitted, already reassured by his matter-of-fact question, and quite ready to laugh at herself for posing as an interesting invalid.

'Well, now, we'll get to the bottom of this,' said Mr Fanshawe, just as if Rachel Dean were an undergraduate. 'A, reason for heart; b, what your doctor says; and c, whether there is really anything for you to be anxious about. I knew something was up, but I thought it was Helen and Betty. Why on earth you couldn't tell me before, I don't know. Now: a, reason.'

He hitched his chair closer to her sofa and put on his spectacles.

'Dear Charles, you make me laugh. You make me feel guilty.'

'So you are. Now, out with it all. Reason.'

'Well,' Rachel began, twisting a wisp of handkerchief in

her fingers, 'it was really the year when Frank was building that bridge in South America. He didn't want me to come, but it seemed rather lonely for him, and the children were all at school, so I went out for six months, and I had fever, and it was rather alarming with natives and shooting.'

'Just like a woman,' said Charles, putting his spectacles away again. 'You go where you aren't wanted out of a mistaken sense of devotion. You spoil your husband's happy, care-free time. You get ill, imagine things about natives, and have to come home. South America – yes, I remember the year. Jessica was born soon afterwards and doubtless that finished the job.'

'You can't blame Jessica,' said her mother, slightly offended.

'I don't. I never blame women,' said Charles, quite kindly, 'because they are so silly. One might as well blame hens. I do blame Frank for letting you come.'

'But he couldn't stop me.'

'Ha,' said Mr Fanshawe. 'Well, what does your doctor say? Are you in pain?'

'Oh no, not really pain, only now and then rather wretched. Rather choking and a kind of disposition to crumple up. What really worries me—'

'Well?'

'It's not talking about it, Charles. I don't tell Frank much, because he would be so worried and think it was his fault. I wanted often to tell you, but I didn't like to intrude.'

'All beautiful women are fools,' said Charles. 'Why the dickens you shouldn't tell me if that's going to be any help, I don't know. I shall talk to Nanny. I will bet that she knows more about it than anyone. Does anyone else know?'

'No. At least I had a kind of faint when Susan and Robin got on the roof and looked in at the night-nursery window and made Jessica scream, and Richard was there, but Nanny happened to come in luckily, so I don't suppose he thought of it again.'

'From my extensive knowledge of young men, the sight of beauty in distress is fuel to their touching and ill-placed devotion.'

'Don't tell Frank, will you?' Rachel pleaded.

'Not unless he asks me. And, dear Rachel, I think there is very little to tell. From what you say, I think you have been terrifying yourself quite unnecessarily. Hearts mean nothing now. Where they used to put you to bed if your heart so much as murmured, they tell you to be sensible now, and you live for ever. You shouldn't read so much fiction. There's nothing romantic about dying with a heart, only a very unpleasant spasm as a rule. You might look horrid. Now you have told me all about it you will find that it won't worry you so much, and you'll probably make old bones. Do what your doctor says. If he says diet, diet. If he says rest, rest. And if those young devils Susan and Robin frighten you again, I will skin them.'

'I am rather ashamed,' said Rachel, in a small voice.

'So you ought to be. Tell Frank you are worried and you will be quite happy all in a moment.'

'Well, Charles, you are a darling, and as usual a tower of strength. How lucky it is that your aunt married into Frank's family. I suppose we must dress now for the Tebbens' dinner-party. Bless you and thank you,' said Rachel, rising from her sofa and ringing the bell. 'I would like to hug you.'

'Do.'

'Well, my maid might take it amiss if she came in. I'll try to remember all your good advice.'

When Margaret got back to her saucepans she found Laurence in his evening clothes, tying a large white cloth round his waist.

'It's all right,' he said, seeing her look anxious, 'it's one of Aunt Palmer's Greek draperies. I pinched it from the barn on the way over. And I got the man at the Woolpack,' said Laurence, taking off his dinner-jacket, 'to lend me a barman's white coat, a relic of his happier days. And I got Sparrow to give me all Aunt Palmer's raspberries and a pint bottle of cream, so we ought to do. What's the first thing?'

'Your caviare. Can you make the hot toast to go with it while I keep an eye on the next course?'

'I am the Great Toast Wizard. Where's Richard?'

'Brushing his hair. It wouldn't come quite right.'

In the drawing-room Mr and Mrs Tebben were receiving their guests. The party from the Dower House came punctually. The Palmers were a few minutes late. Mr Palmer's attempts to explain the cause of their delay, namely that he and his cowman had been waiting vainly since six o'clock for a bull which was visiting them professionally, were strangled at birth by his wife.

'We want to hear no more, Fred,' said Mrs Palmer. 'Well, Winifred, you are looking very fine tonight. How are the

Vikings, Mr Tebben? Though I must say that Lucasta Bond is really indescribable, Lucasta indeed. I know from our cowman that the bull was at Staple Park yesterday, and Lucasta has deliberately and insultingly kept him. How are you, Rachel? Well, Mr Fanshawe, when is the next book coming out? I buy all your books. But Lucasta shall not get away with it. There must be a bye-law about not keeping your neighbour's bull, isn't there, Fred?'

'It's always a pity to stir up trouble in the country,' said Mr Palmer.

'It sounds more like Leviticus,' said Mr Tebben. 'Have some sherry, Mrs Palmer.'

'Good sherry you have, Tebben,' said Mr Palmer.

'The Woolpack isn't bad,' said Mr Tebben carelessly.

'I never knew they had a taste in sherry,' said Mr Palmer, feeling considerable respect for his host. Mrs Palmer having refused to drink her sherry, Mrs Tebben herded her party into the dining-room, where Margaret had put name cards on the table. Mrs Tebben would have dearly loved to upset all the seating arrangements, but was too much unnerved by a sound of scuffling from the kitchen, and had to take her destined place at the far side of the table, with her back to the window, while her husband, as previously decided, was near the door.

The scuffling was a slight fracas between Laurence and Richard. Richard, descending with his hair at last smoothed to his satisfaction, intending to carry in the dishes and feast his eyes upon Mrs Dean, found Laurence, attired as a cross between a waiter and a barman, in the act of taking the hot toast, under a napkin, into the dining-room.

'Oh I say, I thought I was going to do waiter and you help Margaret,' Richard exclaimed. 'Here, let's have the toast.'

'If it's the tips you're after, Aunt Palmer doesn't approve,' said Laurence. 'If you touch Uncle Palmer after the port – is there any port by the way? – he'll be good for half a crown at least. But mind, union rules, fifty-fifty on the takings. Or, look here, we'll toss for it. Brown side heads, slightly burnt side tails. You're tails.'

He took a piece of toast from the napkin and threw it into the air. It fell back onto the floor.

'Tails,' said Laurence, picking it up and putting it back on the plate. 'All right, you carry on. Give Aunt Palmer the burnt bit, it'll do her good.'

Armed with his plate Richard entered the dining-room. Mrs Dean, in floating green draperies, was sitting with her back to him, next to his father. He was sorry that he wouldn't see much of her face, but the curve of her neck from behind and the way her dark hair was knotted were calculated to afford considerable pleasure to an amateur of the Beautiful. Also, to see her face might be so distracting, especially if she smiled, that one might be struck motionless and forget to change the plates. He greeted the company, put the plate down on the table, had the satisfaction of seeing Mrs Palmer take the burnt bit that had been on the floor, and retired to the kitchen to reflect upon the smile that Mrs Dean had given him over her shoulder.

Laurence inquired if all was serene and they had remembered to put slices of lemon for the caviare. Reassured on this point he turned to his task of helping Margaret. The minced and steamed cock was turned out of its basin and covered with a very professional sauce, the beans, well tossed in butter, were dished up. Laurence was allowed to sprinkle chopped parsley on the young potatoes, and the next course was ready. The bell rang. Richard plunged at the dining-room door. Mr Tebben, in spite of instructions, had quite forgotten that he was to collect the plates and hand them to Richard. Mrs Tebben began to advocate a method by which all plates would be passed to her and by her put on the window-sill, whence they could be collected either at the end of dinner, or by Richard going out into the garden and fetching them out through the window. Richard, knowing that Margaret wanted to wash them for the raspberries, was vainly trying to communicate with his mother when Helen came to his aid and with kind firmness rescued the plates from her hostess and passed them across the table to Mr Tebben, who, recovering his wits, gave them to Richard. The timbale, the vegetables and the hot plates were placed before Mr Tebben and Richard again retired.

'Come and have your caviare,' said Laurence, who was sitting on the kitchen-table with the jar beside him. 'I never did believe in muzzling oxes that tread corn, and heaven knows we've trodden enough today. Margaret, you must be exhausted.'

'No, really not,' said Margaret, digging a knife into the caviare pot. She wished she were if Laurence thought she ought to be. It would be much more romantic to be pale and exhausted, but if one felt very well and had a face flushed with the heat of the kitchen range, it was out of the question.

'How goes the feast?' Laurence asked Richard. 'I bet your

father has forgotten to give them anything to drink. My people don't mind, but Uncle Palmer is a thirsty bird. Let's go and look.'

The two young men approached the dining-room door and looked in. Mr Tebben had served the timbale and everyone was provided with vegetables, but the glasses were dry. Richard went up to his father's chair.

'I say, Father,' he said in a low voice, 'you remember we put the white wine in the revolving bookcase just behind you. Shall I get it for you?'

Mr Tebben, looking guilty, twirled the bookcase and took out a bottle. Mrs Dean refused wine and asked if she could have lemonade, or orange juice. Margaret, who was behind Laurence, made a frantic face at him to show there wasn't any.

'Control yourself, Mrs Dean,' said her son. 'It damps everything if you don't drink. Let me give you a finger of this excellent white wine, and if you are bent on spoiling your evening I'll put some water in it.'

He did so, and was rewarded by a grateful look from Margaret.

'You boys make very good waiters,' said Mrs Palmer. 'Glad to see you being useful, Laurence. I didn't know Mrs Phipps cooked so well, Winifred. Congratulations.'

'I think, Louise, that if you reflect you will remember that Mrs Phipps is at the Manor House tonight,' said Mrs Tebben. 'She said you wanted her. Margaret is doing her best.'

'Good girl,' said Mr Palmer. 'An excellent dinner, excellent. Caviare couldn't be better. Same that I gave you at Christmas, Rachel.'

'Of course Margaret didn't cook the caviare,' said Mrs Tebben.

'No, no, of course not. Eat it raw, that's right. Or comes all ready cooked, what? I don't know what this stuff is we're eating, but it's excellent. Clever girl your Margaret. Why is Mrs Phipps at the Manor House, Louise? I've been telling that woman to get her teeth seen to for the last ten years. No sense those people, no sense.'

'I can tell you why she won't have false teeth,' said Mrs Palmer. 'It's all Lucasta Bond's doing. She told them at the Women's Institute that false teeth spell a ruined digestion.'

'Well, that's where her toes turn in,' said Laurence, who had established himself as a species of compère to the dinner-party, leaning against the dining-room door, with his fellow cooks hovering in the background. 'False teeth spell false teeth, as Lady Bond will know to her cost one day. There may be an anagram, but I doubt it.'

'Some day!' said Mrs Palmer indignantly. 'Lucasta had all her teeth out seven years ago.'

'Then she must speak of ruined digestions from personal experience,' said Mr Fanshawe. 'You are hard on her.'

'Heaven is my witness that I am not,' said Mrs Palmer dramatically. 'When I think of Lucasta – Laurence, did you hear what has happened? She is keeping the bull.'

'Is it a pub?' asked Laurence, interested.

'No, no, Laurence, the bull that we were expecting. Rushwater Rubicon, that bull of Leslie's,' said Mr Palmer.

'A story of a cock and a bull,' said Mr Fanshawe.

'Or the Rape of Europa, as one might say,' added Mrs Tebben, at which Laurence and Richard exploded into a

153

guffaw and fell away into the kitchen to have their laugh out. Mr Fanshawe and Mr Tebben indulged in the soundless hilarity peculiar to scholars. Mrs Tebben, pleased at her success, began to argue with Mrs Palmer across the table about the material required for the chorus's veils.

'What on earth are Richard and Laurence doing?' Mr Fanshawe asked Helen.

Helen looked round, and seeing her Aunt Louise deep in controversy with Mrs Tebben, she said:

'Aunt Palmer scrobbled Mrs Tebben's Mrs Phipps; it was rather unfair of her, I think. Laurence told me about it before dinner. He found Margaret doing the cooking this morning, and he thought she needed some help so he is in the kitchen, he and Richard. It must be rather fun. I'm not being jealous,' she added hastily, 'only feeling a bit out of it. They do sound as if they were having such fun in the kitchen.'

'So they do,' said Mr Fanshawe, as sounds of revelry came from the other side of the door. 'But have you reflected how dull it would be for me if you weren't here? You are a good girl, a very good girl. You will probably find that just as l'appétit vient en mangeant,' said Mr Fanshawe, who had a remarkably good French accent, 'so it decreases by not eating, i.e. don't be jealous the first time and you will probably be less jealous the second.'

'I dare say that's true, if illogical.'

'Logic has nothing to do with it. Logic I keep for people I despise. People I prize don't need it.'

Helen looked at him, but his face was as inscrutable as ever, and before she could continue what was promising to be an interesting conversation, she was addressed by her

Uncle Palmer, who wanted a new audience for his views on the Root Vegetables Bill, thus leaving Mrs Tebben at liberty to talk to her old tutor.

As she turned to address him the years fell away from Mrs Tebben, mother of two grown-up children; or if they did not, she felt that they did, which comes to much the same thing. Again she was Winifred Ross, that brilliant girl who wasn't exactly good-looking, but so nice. Again her guest was, as indeed he had never ceased being and was still at the present day, Mr Fanshawe of Paul's.

'I can't tell you,' said Mrs Tebben, whose hair was as usual in straggling disorder, and who had forgotten to put on any powder, 'with what tremendous interest I have followed your books. I have got them all, those I can understand and those I can't. I want to ask you a very great favour.'

'I will write my name in one of them with pleasure,' said Mr Fanshawe, who through long practice knew exactly what was coming. 'But let us talk of something interesting, your own works. I have not had time to read them all, but your little textbook on Intervaluations was, if I may say so, a really lucid exposition of the subject. I may say without shame, as it is not in my line, that I never began to understand the subject clearly till I had read your book.'

'Oh, Mr Fanshawe,' was all that Mrs Tebben could say, just as Winifred Ross might have done when her tutor had praised an essay.

'I hear that Richard is well thought of at Oxford,' he continued. 'I know he behaved badly over Greats, but his tutor tells me he has brains. What are his plans?'

Mrs Tebben, enchanted to find her old tutor interested in

her son, poured out to Mr Fanshawe all their hopes and fears for Richard, the necessity for him to earn, their own ignorance of the world and what strings to pull.

'In a way,' she continued in a lower tone, 'I wish the Deans weren't here just this summer. It is so distracting and Richard ought to be reading, but he is always at the Dower House. Helen is teaching him to drive a car, and has improved his tennis wonderfully, and they are always together, but it takes up so much of his time.'

'It won't do him any harm for a bit,' said Mr Fanshawe, conscious of a pang in his heart. 'And as for reading, it's a dog's job to read when you don't know what you are reading for. I'd like to have a talk with him.'

'Oh, how very kind of you. Gilbert! Gilbert! Will you ring the little bell? We have quite finished, I think.'

Mr Tebben rang, Richard appeared, collected the plates and brought in the asparagus.

'I knew you'd forget the sauce,' said Laurence, following him with a sauce-boat. 'This exquisite mousseline sauce, ladies and gentlemen, is the joint work of Miss Margaret Tebben and myself. I suggested it and she made it. On with the meal, let joy be unrefined.'

'What are you wearing, Laurence?' asked Mrs Palmer, suddenly fixing him with a glance.

'A barman's jacket, aunt.'

'Yes, I see that. I mean round your waist.'

'Well, as you have spotted it, my dear aunt, I may as well confess that it is a bit of drapery or whatnot from your chorus, because I hadn't an apron. I hope you don't mind, but I like to dress the part.'

156

Mrs Palmer, who always found it impossible to scold her eldest nephew, warned him not to dirty it. Mrs Tebben said now she could show her exactly how the veils ought to be cut.

'Your respected mamma,' said Laurence to Margaret, who was just finishing her omelette, 'is telling my Aunt Palmer exactly where she gets off at about the veils for the chorus.'

'Just warm the rum, will you,' said Margaret, pushing a saucepan towards him. 'Yes, Mother is a little like Mrs Norris sometimes.'

As Laurence didn't answer, she wondered if he had perhaps never heard of Miss Austen, blamed herself for the ungenerous thought, then, just to make herself plain, added nervously, 'Miss Austen, I mean.'

'Well, it does my heart good to hear you say Miss Austen like that,' said Laurence. 'Omelette ready? Right. Observe. I pour the rum over it. People who say Jane or talk about Janeites revolt me. The sort that can walk with kings and not lose that common touch. "Miss Austen to you" is what I feel inclined to say. Now, where are the matches? Hi! Richard, catch hold quickly.'

Richard's entrance with the flaming omelette was greeted with cries of admiration. It was variously compared to the funeral ship of a Viking (Mr Tebben), that jolly kind of dish they used to do so well at that little restaurant in Jermyn Street whose name he couldn't remember, but everyone would know it (Mr Palmer), a plum-pudding (Mrs Dean, whose simple point of view nearly made Richard swoon with adoration by its exquisite, childlike quality), Guy Fawkes (Mrs Tebben, who rather wondered what she meant when she had said it), a motor-car on fire at Brooklands (Helen), the Cities of the Plain (Mr Fanshawe), and a rum omelette (Mr Dean).

Laurence, who had made and drunk two rum cocktails while the omelette was in the making, felt obliged to explain to Richard and Margaret how very funny his father had been.

'Though, mind you,' he said, 'it wasn't a rum omelette. I mean not rum at all. A really good, ordinary omelette. And when I say ordinary, I mean extraordinary. What do we do now?'

'Start washing up,' said Margaret.

'No, I'll tell you what. Put all the washing-up things in the scullery and clear the kitchen-table, and then while the grown-ups guzzle raspberries we'll eat what's left. You wouldn't feel like making another superb omelette, would you?'

'If you haven't drunk all the rum,' said Margaret a little tartly.

Richard hurried on the raspberries, gave a last respectful look at Mrs Dean's back, and the three cooks sat down to a feast of remains, enlivened by more rum cocktails. Richard was longing for the moment when they could join the ladies. Unfortunately, from his point of view, his father happened to have some really good port, his one luxury, bought from his old college, and in this he knew that Mr Palmer would dearly love to indulge in a gentlemanly way.

'Oh my goodness, coffee!' exclaimed Margaret, as the sound of chairs being scraped back reached them. 'Look, Richard, I'll make it now at once, if you'll take it in, and then we might as well all go into the drawing-room and leave the washing up till later, or we'll never see the party at all. I'll go and tidy myself as soon as I've made it.'

Richard hastily washed his hands at the sink, took a look at his hair and picked up the tray with coffee and the Benedictine. He took it first to the dining-room, where his father offered him a glass of port as one man of the world to another, and Mr Palmer invited him to hear the real truth about Root Vegetables, but Richard excused himself, saying that he had to take coffee to the ladies, and went to the drawing-room. Here, to his chagrin he found Mrs Dean listening with such apparent intensity to what Mrs Tebben was saying to Mrs Palmer about the veils, that he had to talk to Helen. She, finding that, as Charles Fanshawe had said, trying to be good made one a little bit better, did her best to entertain Margaret's brother, but without much encouragement, for his eyes and attention were wandering all the time. When Margaret and Laurence came in, a shifting of seats took place, and Richard at last found himself by Mrs Dean who, looking like a wood-nymph (so Richard considered) in her green dress, with a wreath of green leaves in her hair, submitted with great fortitude to a very boring dissertation on cricket averages. Presently the men came in. Mr Tebben went to open the window. Gunnar, suddenly materialising, leapt through it and disappeared. Margaret crossed over to her father.

'I quite forgot to take the empty sherry glasses away,' she said. 'What luck that Gunnar didn't break one.'

'It is an extraordinary thing,' said her father, 'but we left a glass of sherry in here and it has gone. I mean the sherry, not the glass. Mrs Palmer didn't drink hers. Do you think it could be Gunnar?'

'It might be, Daddy. You remember the day he ate the rest of the pickles. He has such peculiar tastes for a cat, and he is so inquisitive. Was it a nice dinner, Daddy?'

'Perfectly delicious. We must have that omelette again. Could we, do you think?'

Father and daughter looked at Mrs Tebben who, Laurence's ex-apron in her hand, was laying down the law to Mrs Palmer.

'We might try,' said Margaret, thinking of the eggs and the rum that had gone to that confection. She might even swallow her pride and ask Laurence for the rest of the rum, if it would please Daddy. 'Perhaps one evening when we are alone? I'll just take these glasses away. Poor Gunnar, he must be repenting his crime.'

The evening would have passed pleasantly enough if Mrs Tebben had not found it necessary to amuse her guests. She produced slips of paper and pencils, and forced them to play games, which resolved themselves into a trial of wits between herself, Mr Fanshawe, Mr Dean and Laurence, the rest being nowhere. Mrs Dean excused herself very cleverly without giving a reason, and Margaret was only too glad to keep her company. Richard, unused to so many rum cocktails, was inclined to be noisy and boastful, and was only saved from making a nuisance of himself by Helen, who took him under her wing and bullied him into good behaviour. Mr Fanshawe, watching, wondered what she could see in young Tebben, and resolved all the more to help him if he could. When Mrs Dean at half-past ten said they must really go home, Mrs Tebben approached Mr Fanshawe.

'If I might ask what you so kindly promised,' she pleaded, enigmatically.

'Which book shall I write in?' asked Mr Fanshawe, pulling out a fountain-pen and putting on his spectacles, thus destroying his hostess's romantic treatment of the subject.

'They are all there,' said Mrs Tebben, proudly waving her hand towards a shelf. 'I have a peculiar fondness myself for your *Platonic Liberalism*.'

'You may well have a peculiar fondness, for it is a peculiar book. Worst I ever wrote,' said Mr Fanshawe, in a disheartening way. 'If I had time I'd rewrite it entirely. What shall I put in it?'

'That is for you to decide,' said Mrs Tebben, nearly adding Maître.

'I can't say "For Mrs Tebben from Charles Fanshawe", because I didn't give it to you. How will this do?'

In a laboured, cuneiform handwriting he inscribed on the fly-leaf, 'Charles Fanshawe wishes that he had given this book to his old pupil, Mrs Gilbert Tebben.'

'Oh, Mr Fanshawe,' said his old pupil, overwhelmed.

'There is an amendment,' said Mr Fanshawe, who was enjoying himself vastly. Running his pen through the word 'old' he substituted 'former'.

'It would, of course, look better if I had thought of it at first,' said Mr Fanshawe, removing his spectacles, 'but the English language is at fault.'

'Gilbert! Gilbert!' cried Mrs Tebben. 'Look what Mr

Fanshawe has written in his *Platonic Liberalism*. I really can't thank my old – or shall I say former – tutor enough.'

'You take my point so quickly,' said Mr Fanshawe, and then feeling that he had really given Mrs Tebben a long enough run for her money, he said good night and followed Mrs Dean and her party. Mrs Palmer, still unconvinced about the veils, took her husband away, and the Tebbens were left alone.

'A great success, I think,' said Mrs Tebben. 'They all enjoyed it thoroughly. How slow the Palmers are at games. We shan't have anything to finish up tomorrow except the raspberries. I had no idea there were so many left in the garden. Mrs Phipps might make us a summer pudding with the rest of them. You know, that nice pudding we all like, when you line a basin with bits of stale bread and soak it in fruit juice and fill it up with fruit and breadcrumbs. She does that quite nicely.'

Richard said darkly that he wished Gunnar liked raspberries. This was unfortunate, for it led to a command from his mother to search for Gunnar, who might otherwise have been happily forgotten. As Gunnar did not respond to cries of 'Milk' accompanied by the waving of a saucer, or 'Fish' (a deliberate lie on Richard's part), Mrs Tebben felt at liberty to worry about the washing up.

'You and Daddy go to bed, Mummy,' said Margaret. 'Richard and I will see to the glasses and things.'

'Well, don't tire yourself, dear,' said Mrs Tebben. 'Richard looks done up. Mrs Phipps must wash up tomorrow. She always resents a morning wash-up, but if she deserts me for Louise, she must take the consequences.'

When Margaret went into the kitchen with the coffee cups, she found Laurence, his coat off and his shirt sleeves rolled up, stoking the kitchen fire with a very professional air, and Richard filling kettles.

'Your hot-water furnace seems to have died on us while we were junketing,' said Laurence, 'so we are boiling kettles for the wash-up. Though why one speaks of boiling a kettle, I don't know. The French in their logical and unromantic way prefer to speak of boiling some water.'

'But I thought you had gone home,' said Margaret.

'He would have if he had any sense,' said Richard. 'I'm half asleep myself. It's been a long day.'

'All right, go to bed,' said Laurence, 'and I'll give Margaret a hand. Only make up that boiler thing first, because I can't get any sense out of it, and you'll want hot baths tomorrow.'

Sleepily Richard stoked up the furnace, said good night, and went staggering away to bed.

Margaret and Laurence wasted no time. Helped by an occasional drink Laurence carried kettles, dried dishes, scoured saucepans, and by half-past eleven the kitchen was clean and tidy. At twenty minutes to twelve Margaret had had her first proposal.

'Oh goodness, I'm tired,' she said. 'Thanks awfully, Laurence, for helping, and good night. Is your car there?'

'Yes. Would you like a drive?'

'No, thank you. I am simply falling asleep on my feet.'

'Oh, lord!' said Laurence, looking into the dining-room. 'If we haven't forgotten the dessert plates and the glasses. I'll get them out and it won't take a minute.'

He got a tray, collected the glass and china, swept all the crumbs onto the floor, and returned to the kitchen, where Margaret was sitting on a chair, drooping with fatigue.

'My poor child,' said Laurence. 'You are all in. Have a drink.'

Margaret shook her head and tried to smile.

'Then I'll feed you with apricocks and dewberries, as many as the guzzling blighters in the dining-room have left,' said Laurence, taking a raspberry between his finger and thumb. 'Open your mouth. That's it. Now another. You are just like a bird, Margaret, a small bird with a large beak, waiting to be fed. No, that's not polite. A large bird with a small beak. That doesn't sound much better. Anyway, a bird, and I adore you.'

Margaret had been taking the raspberries obediently and mechanically, sleepily enjoying being cared for, but now, to her horror, she saw through sleep-glazed eyes Laurence's face getting larger and nearer until it blotted out everything. She was enfolded and crushed. It was not altogether unpleasant, looked at abstractedly, but through her bewilderment and fatigue she remembered how lightly Laurence had treated her and her people that day, and her honest resentment revolted against his easy love-making.

'There, what was that like?' asked Laurence.

'Disgusting.'

'What?'

'Disgusting.'

'But why? I embrace you respectfully – note, I didn't even kiss you – and you call it disgusting. I thought people liked being respectfully embraced.'

'They may. I don't. You've been beastly all today and this puts the lid on it.'

'But I'm asking you to marry me, and you call it beastly.'

'You haven't asked me to marry you, and everything is beastly and horrible.'

'No, it isn't. It's divine. I ask you to marry me now, over the tongs or per special licence, just as you prefer, because really, Margaret, I do adore you extremely. My darling, I do.'

'How dare you,' said Margaret and got behind the kitchen-table. 'You simply despise me and all of us and you shower groceries on us as if we were the Workhouse Christmas Treat, and bring bottles of sherry because you want a drink, as if we couldn't afford a bottle of sherry of our own, and graciously let us keep the dregs for our guests, and just because you are well-off you think you can be lordly to me about taking a job, and how such an insensitive, selfish person as you came to be in such a nice family I don't know. Oh, go away, I wish to goodness I'd never seen you and I wish I'd never been born and I can't even cry.'

Her voice rose to a muffled wail on the last words, as she untied her apron and flung it on the floor with a gesture that appeared to mean, though with no particular reason, 'Now, tyrant, do your worst.'

'I see,' said Laurence. 'I've been tactless.'

'If you really cared for me you wouldn't need to think of tact. You'd just have it.'

'Social sins are more difficult to condone than sins of the heart,' said Laurence sententiously. 'I see I had better put on my coat and go home. I suppose this trifling esclandre is not

165

going to upset Aunt Palmer's *Hippolytus*? That would be perhaps too much self-advertisement.'

'If you mean that I want anyone to know how beastly you've been, that's where you're wrong,' said Margaret. 'I simply wouldn't trouble to let them know, or really ever think of the matter again at all. It's all those rum cocktails. Tomorrow you'll have forgotten all about it. And as for the play, if you'd taken the trouble to read it, instead of just learning your own words like a parrot, which is all you are, you'd know that Hippolytus and Phaedra are only once on the stage together and don't speak, and as far as the play goes the audience wouldn't have an idea of what was happening if it weren't for that horrible, idiotic, interfering chorus. I hate them. I hate everybody.'

Worn out by the strain of a furious quarrel which had to be exhaustingly conducted in hoarse whispers for fear of disturbing Mr and Mrs Tebben, overwrought after her long day, Margaret began to sniff.

'Oh, don't,' said Laurence. 'I don't mind your telling me off, but the gulps and the chokes I cannot bear. Darling Margaret, let me comfort you.'

Margaret walked in a dignified way to the kitchen door.

'Good night,' she said, with chilling disdain and impeded articulation, and shut the door carefully behind her.

Laurence, with an uncomfortable feeling of guilt, a sentiment to which he was almost a stranger, slowly turned down his shirt sleeves and put on his coat. Just as he was wrestling with the back door, the kitchen door opened again and Margaret looked in.

'I don't ever want to speak to you again, except in public,' she said, 'but don't make a noise as you go out. The back door is very stiff. Here, you'd better let me do it.'

Sweeping past her rejected suitor she pulled back the safety catch and opened the door. Laurence stepped over the threshold and stood in the backyard, looking down on her.

'I could squash you to death, you enchanting bird,' he said.

'Oh,' said Margaret, and shut the door. She heard his footsteps cross the yard, heard him start up his car and drive away. He was safely gone, but she could not move. Leaning against the dresser she went through again in her mind the horrible scene that had just taken place, altering and improving some of her own remarks as she did so. To be called a bird was perhaps the most melting, the most astounding thing that had ever happened in the world. No one else could ever have been called a bird before, or at least not in that voice. Enchanting bird. Oh, word of magic, of freedom, of bliss, of old life forgotten, new life begun. Oh moon, oh nightingales, oh love. Oh, arrows of desire.

The kitchen alarm, which had been set by Mrs Phipps to twelve o'clock to remind her to call Phipps to his dinner, did not know the difference between noon and midnight, and suddenly went off. Margaret, roused from her trance by the need for action, leapt on it and stifled it. Then she went up to her room and looked out of the window, till a bray from Modestine and the distant voice of Gunnar, unmelodious in the charmed night, roused her to go to bed.

A few minutes earlier Modestine, lounging about in the little shed down in the field that was his summer quarters, saw two points of fire approach.

'I suppose that's you as usual,' he said ungraciously to Gunnar. 'What's the news?'

'Nothing particular,' said Gunnar, settling himself on some old sacks. 'The usual dull evening. The people from the Dower House came to dinner. Now, there they do keep a good kitchen. Chicken nearly every day, so the cat there tells me, young Kitty Dean.'

'I dare say,' said Modestine. 'Some like chicken, some don't. I don't.'

'Know what I did tonight?' asked Gunnar.

Modestine only went on chewing some grass.

'Drank all their sherry,' said Gunnar, who needed no encouragement to talk about himself. 'They left it in the drawing-room while they ate chicken in the dining-room. Never offered me chicken, so I drank their sherry.'

'Was it good?' asked Modestine. 'I don't hold with sherry. Give me a nice pail of water, or a good green pond, and I'm perfectly satisfied.'

'Ignorant, that's what you are,' said Gunnar, 'and prejudiced. Vegetarians always are. I dare say you'd wear Jaeger underclothes if you had the chance. The sherry was poor, very poor. Mere cat-lap. Now, give me a saucer of milk and I know where I am.'

'Young Richard was calling "Fish" for you,' said Modestine.

'They don't catch me that way. You need to be up to their tricks, I can tell you, my good ass.'

'Don't call me your good ass.'

'Well, what shall I call you?' asked Gunnar, slowly stretching himself and walking round in an annoying way.

'Nice little donkey that takes little girls for rides every day? I'd like to see them try to make me take that Jessica for a ride.'

'I don't mind Jessica,' said Modestine, edging a little nearer to Gunnar. 'She gives me sugar. But if they put me in that donkey-cart again, I'll kick it to pieces, I will. I'll smash it to matchboard, and I'll throw old Mother Tebben over the hedge, and I'll kick old Tebben to death and join the army.'

'Oh, yeah?' said Gunnar, sitting down and staring rudely.

'Yeah,' said Modestine at the top of his voice and he trod on Gunnar's tail.

Gunnar with a shriek and a crackle of curses sped away into the night, while Modestine laughed quietly, and went on chewing.

7

The Day of Misfortunes

The following day was so dreadful that Susan, who participated in some of its more unnerving moments, christened it The Day of Misfortunes, and as such it was for ever after known in the Dean family. To begin with it was Sunday. During the night the fine weather had broken. The thermometer had gone down ten degrees and the world was shrouded in steady, hopeless rain. At the Manor House the Palmers' cook overslept herself. Breakfast, always an hour later on Sundays, was an hour and seven minutes late, which annoyed Mr Palmer inexpressibly. He was a stickler for punctuality, and as he always woke at the same hour, he detested having to wait for his breakfast once a week. At half-past nine he was at the breakfast-table. The lamps were lighted under the sluggard's friend, plates were warming, but no dishes of eggs or sausages were keeping hot. He rang the bell. Sparrow appeared.

'What's happened to breakfast?' he asked.

'I am sorry, sir,' said Sparrow, 'that Mrs Heeling overlooked the hour this morning. Having been wakeful with the toothache, as I understand, she in fact overslept herself. She is endeavouring her utmost to make up for lost time, sir. In fact, I think I hear her At It.'

He stepped without undue haste to the service hatch, behind which an unseen agent was scrabbling. Opening it he took out two silver dishes and placed them on the sideboard. While he put the coffee on the table, Mr Palmer lifted the lids.

'What does she want to skin the sausages for?' he asked angrily. 'They burst all over the place and look like nothing on earth.'

'I am sure I couldn't say, sir.'

'Louise,' said Mr Palmer to his wife as she came in, 'I wish you'd tell Mrs Heeling not to skin the sausages. I like a sausage that is a sausage. Sleep well?'

'No.'

'Nor did I. Worried about that bull. Worried. Good Lord, here's a letter from Bond in the paper about the Root Vegetables Bill. They'll print anything nowadays, anything. Sparrow! Has the bull come?'

'I couldn't say, sir, but I can inquire.'

Before Mr Palmer had finished annoying his wife by reading aloud Lord Bond's letter very indistinctly with his own running comments, Sparrow returned.

'I regret to say, sir, that the bull has not arrived, and they are of the opinion that he will not travel on Sunday owing to the amount of traffic on the road.'

'If Alured Bond would stop being in the House of Lords

and writing letters to the papers, and would have a telephone put in at Staple Park,' said Mrs Palmer, 'he wouldn't be such a fool as he is. But I suppose that is impossible. Sparrow, where are the cigarettes?'

Sparrow blenched slightly.

'I will get them from the boudoir, madam,' he said, making for the door.

'No, no,' said Mr Palmer, 'there was a new box of a hundred in here, only opened yesterday or the day before.'

'I think, sir,' said Sparrow deprecatingly, 'that Mr Laurence may have been At Them.'

'Been at them? He can't smoke a hundred cigarettes in a day. What do you mean?'

'It was not so much that he smoked them, sir, as that he took possession of them, as it were. Mr Laurence come here yesterday before lunch in a great hurry and said had I any cigarettes. Not wishing to offer him those I keep for my own use, which are Junior Whifflets, sir, and not what Mr Laurence would fancy, I thought you would not mind if he helped himself from your box.'

'Well, he seems to have helped himself to the box,' said Mrs Palmer. 'And he took some drapery out of the barn. Did he take anything else, Sparrow?'

'Now you come to mention it, madam, he did,' said Sparrow, with an air of great candour.

'Well, what?' said Mrs Palmer. 'Am I to hear that he took the Women's Institute collecting box?'

'Oh no, madam,' said Sparrow, shocked. 'It was only that bottle of Benedictine that we had up on Friday, and Mrs Heeling did say something about a tin of asparagus. I think, madam, that Mr Laurence was contemplating some sort of outdoor entertainment, a fresco meal as you might say.'

'Well, heaven help him if that's his idea of food for a picnic,' said Mrs Palmer. 'Fred, I grudge your nephew nothing, but if he is going to treat us as the Army and Navy Stores I must draw the line.'

'Quite right, Louise, quite right. Sparrow, if Mr Laurence wants to go for another picnic, send him to me.'

'Very good, sir,' said Sparrow and made his escape.

'Louise, what is a seven-letter word meaning "the most eternal"?' asked Mr Palmer, who had never managed to finish a crossword puzzle in his life, but much enjoyed the mental exercise. 'I've got E-blank-E-blank-E-blank-blank.'

'Say it again.'

'E-blank-E-blank-blank — no, *blank* only — E-blank-blank.'

'I can't possibly tell unless I see it. What is it, Sparrow?'

'Excuse me, madam, but Mrs Heeling thinks you would wish to know that there was no raspberries sent in this morning, and young Patten says Mr Laurence had them.'

'Well, it's exactly the sort of thing I wouldn't wish to know on a Sunday morning when nothing can be done about it. Fred, you must send word to Patten that Laurence is not to have the raspberries without asking.'

'No, no, he mustn't. Wonder why some fellow can't invent a raspberry without seeds. Get under your plate and hurt like blazes. You don't think it could be "Element", do you, Louise?'

'What could be?'

'A seven-letter word meaning "the most eternal". E-blank-E-blank-E-blank-blank.'

'Pardon me, sir, I think "Everest" might fulfil the required conditions,' said Sparrow.

'"Everest", eh? All right, I'll put it down, but it doesn't seem to make sense. Oh yes, so it does. Well, Sparrow, tell Patten Mr Laurence is not to have any raspberries. Is Thomas preaching today, Louise?'

'I don't know. Is the Rector preaching, Sparrow?'

'Such is his intentions, madam, but the Reverend Moxon is to be ready to perform in case of need. Miss Thomas has just phoned up, madam, to ask if you could call for her and the Rector.'

Mrs Palmer looked out of the window at the grey dripping world and ordered the car to come a little earlier, so that they might pick up Dr Thomas and his daughters. She was distinctly annoyed with her favourite nephew. The borrowing of the drapery she had condoned when Laurence was there, but in his absence his crimes looked graver. As her thoughts went back to the previous night, and Laurence's appearance as an habitué of the Tebbens' kitchen, a lurid light began to dawn on her. It was her asparagus, her Benedictine, her cigarettes that had fed the party, her raspberries on which they had feasted so profusely. And Fred had said that the caviare was the same that he had given to his sister at Christmas. Not for a moment did she suspect Mrs Tebben of being a party to what was a very questionable use of other people's property; she knew that Winifred was capable of eating roast peacock at her own table, when really interested in conversation, without noticing it or having the faintest idea where it came from. But towards the innocent Margaret her thoughts were not friendly. Margaret appeared to her to be using Laurence as a cat's-paw. The boy was probably going through one of his infatuations and Margaret was taking advantage of it. Had it not been for the *Hippolytus*, Mrs Palmer would have had no scruples in tackling her on the subject of letting Laurence, Fred's and her heir, make a fool of himself, but she could hardly afford to offend her Phaedra with the performance only a week off and the final dress rehearsal to come. If only she had not given in weakly to Winifred; if only she had let Phyl or Dolly Thomas take the part. If only she had not asked Laurence to take a week of his holidays just now on account of her play. She could only hope that when it was over and the young people less thrown together, that the affair would simmer down. Laurence's affairs, in her experience, usually did.

The car came to the door. Mr Palmer did not improve his wife's state of mind by keeping her waiting while he looked through the dictionary for all the words beginning G-R-A.

'It's an extraordinary thing, Louise,' he said, as they drove to the Rectory, 'but whenever Thomas preaches it rains. I don't know if you've noticed it. I wish I knew about that bull. John can't take his time off till we know for certain if he is coming or not, and it's all most inconvenient. Could the word be "Grazed", do you think? The clue is, "Would you be called this when you are in your last home?" "Grazed" doesn't seem to fit in somehow.'

By pretending not to hear, Mrs Palmer managed to keep her temper till they got to the Rectory, where Miss Dolly, in gum boots and a mackintosh, was standing at the gate.

'It's awfully good of you to fetch Father,' she said. 'Phyl has him all ready. When he saw the rain he thought he'd let Mr Moxon preach, but Phyl and I can't stand Moxon, so we promised Father you'd take him in the car. I hope you don't mind. I had to go down to the church and do the flowers this morning because Father was so interesting last night that we forgot about it. Wasn't it shocking? Your nice niece was here, and she and Father read Greek aloud to us. Here, he comes, the dear old soul.'

Dr Thomas came down the flagged walk on Miss Thomas's arm. As the day was chilly he had been wrapped in a large shepherd's plaid, and looked like a picture of a famous Edinburgh professor. With many courteous thanks and apologies he was helped into the car by his elder daughter and the chauffeur.

'Come along, Phyl, or we'll be late,' said Mrs Palmer. 'Are you coming, Dolly?'

'I'd disgrace you in these togs,' said Miss Dolly in a voice already affected by her father's proximity. 'I'll walk. Do me good,' and she strode off by the short cut across the field.

Dr Thomas was safely delivered at the vestry door, where Miss Thomas unwound him from his plaid. The Palmers went to the Manor House pew, a comfortable, old-fashioned square box, commanding an excellent view of the congregation.

About six o'clock that morning Susan and Robin had gone over to the Manor House farm, where they made the enchanting discovery that a bull might be expected during the day. If Mr Palmer could have heard the hearty partisanship with which they entered into John the cowman's denunciation of Lady Bond's infamous conduct, it would have done his heart good.

'I call her a stinking hog,' said Robin. 'Will he have a ring in his nose, John?'

'Yes, Mr Robin, but there won't be much need for the rope; he's a sweet-tempered chap so long as he isn't crossed.'

'I bet I could jump on his back and hold on to his horns,' said Robin.

'The last man as tried that got his back broken for his trouble,' said John. 'You and Miss Susan had better keep right away from him. When he's in the half-acre paddock, nice and safe behind the wire, that's the time to see him.'

'When is he coming, John?' asked Susan.

'Well, miss, I couldn't rightly say. Her ladyship did by rights have ought to have sent him over yesterday from Staple Park, but she didn't, and your uncle was fair put out. He said to me it wasn't likely her ladyship would let the bull come over today, because of the traffic, but there's something tells me we'll be seeing him march in some time this afternoon. They can bring him by the lanes all the way. And my old woman had a stranger in her tea last night, a great big one.'

'There's a boy at school called Morland,' said Robin, 'that can look a bull between the eyes and the bull is mesmerised.'

'I'd like to see him do it,' said Susan scornfully. 'I bet he's only boasting. Isn't it a pity we can't have a bullfight? I could ride Modestine and you could bicycle, and I'd have Jessica's red flannel dressing-gown and throw it over his head, and Modestine would get gored.'

'No, you don't, Miss Susan,' said John, alarmed. 'If either of you young ladies and gentlemen goes a step nearer than I say, I'll tell your aunt of you.'

The project was regretfully abandoned, but Susan and Robin went home in such good spirits that even being caught by Nanny, who had views about what she called 'them vicious cows', and being forced to have a bath before breakfast, did not damp them. Even church became a thing to be contemplated with equanimity as a way of passing the time till the bull came marching in.

Mr Fanshawe had had an early breakfast and gone for a walk, Mrs Dean did not come down, and Laurence had not appeared, when Susan and Robin joined their father, Helen and Betty in the dining-room.

Mr Dean inquired whether his family had any plans for the afternoon. Helen proposed to overhaul part of her car and give Richard a lesson. Betty was going to tea with Mrs Tebben. Mr Dean said that Mrs Palmer wanted some of them to go over to the Manor House for tea, so Jessica might ride if it wasn't too wet, and the rest of them could walk.

'We'll be having the car for your mother to go to church,' he said. 'Anyone who likes can drive. I'm going to walk.'

Susan and Robin preferred to bicycle, however wet, so Helen said she would go with her father. Betty was being an agnostic at the moment, so no one asked her, for fear she should feel called upon to bore them.

When the others had finished, Helen lingered behind in

case Laurence came down. When he did he looked so low that Helen saw something was wrong. She kissed him and provided porridge and cream. When he had eaten his porridge in silence he went over to the sideboard to inspect the food. From this strategic position, away from the light, his back to the room, he addressed his sister, asking her whether she knew what it felt like to be a fool. Helen said she did.

'Rotten, isn't it?'

'Why don't you tell Charles, whatever it is? He is awfully kind and helpful.'

'I don't know if I ought to. It isn't all my trouble.'

'Could you tell me?' asked Helen hopefully.

'I don't suppose you could understand.'

'I could listen.'

Laurence, having put a pining lover's portion of bacon, sausages, fried eggs, tomatoes and mushrooms on his plate, sat down at the table.

'Coffee, please,' he said.

Helen poured it out and brought his cup round to him. When she had set it down she stood behind him, gently ruffling his hair.

'I'm glad you don't have your hair slinky, like Richard's,' she said. 'He seemed to have his hair on his mind last night.'

'It's about all he does have,' said Laurence morosely.

'Was he a bore in the kitchen last night?'

'Fairly. Did you hear me come in last night?'

'Yes. You were late, so I supposed you had stopped on at the Tebbens'.'

'I was helping Margaret to wash up. Richard couldn't take his rum omelette like a man and had to go to bed.'

'Was it nice washing up?' asked Helen, her hands still busy among her brother's thick hair.

'Nice! If you call being turned down nice!'

Helen's hands were suddenly still.

'You might as well go on rumpling me, I like it,' said Laurence. 'I suppose I'd overdone the rum myself a bit. Anyway, I asked Margaret to marry me, or I meant to. All that happened was that revolted her. And now there's Aunt Louise's blasted *Hippolytus* to be got through. I don't suppose she'll ever look at me again.'

Helen was glad that Laurence couldn't see her face. She could not trust her voice, and her knees felt like water. That Laurence had actually proposed was something unexpected. That Margaret should have refused him, incredible. She hardly knew whether to be grateful to her for turning Laurence down, or very angry with her for giving him pain. It appeared to her that her duty, the one essential thing, was to help Laurence. If he wanted to marry Margaret, she must be forced to the altar. If he had taken his dismissal for good, he must be comforted. Her attitude to Margaret would depend on her brother. She sat down by him and could find nothing to say.

'Well, it's no good talking about it,' said Laurence, and for ten minutes told his sister about the evening; how hard Margaret had worked and how enchanting she looked; how she was tired and he had tried to cheer her up and was rebuffed. As he told his story, laying indignant emphasis on her scorn of his comfort, Helen began to falter. To Laurence's very quick friendships and casual love affairs she was used, and had spent a good deal of time making friends, for his sake, with young women with whom she had little in common, whose names she forgot as soon as they and Laurence had lightly parted company. But Margaret wasn't quite of Laurence's world. She belonged more to the world of their parents, when girls took things more seriously. Helen, as her mother said to Charles Fanshawe, had never cared for a young man except as a companion, and almost fiercely aloof herself, she began to feel sorry for a girl, after all only a very young girl, not much older than Betty, who had perhaps liked Laurence and then had it all spoilt for her by his selfish haste.

'If anyone proposed to me as off-hand as that, in my own kitchen and on a diet of rum,' she said, attempting to speak easily, 'I'd throw a spanner at him.'

'She did, metaphorically,' said Laurence. 'And the worst of it is that I care so much. Last night I felt I was rather the Bold Baron, and sauntered away with a word of badinage on my lips. But when I got home and put the car away I felt like hell. I nearly came up to tell you, but I didn't. Then I felt hellish all night, and this morning it's like the Morgue. When I woke up I wished I were dead, or that this ghastly play were over and I could go back to London. I say, Helen, you couldn't say anything to her, could you? I simply daren't.'

The last splinter of ice melted in Helen's heart as she said she would do what she could.

'I can't exactly go and ask her to marry you,' she said, 'but if I can say a word I'll say it. And I'll tell you what, I might be specially nice to Richard. He's a bit of a strain sometimes, but Margaret is awfully fond of him, and if she sees him having a good time with the car and enjoying himself, she might look more favourably on the family. And Betty is going to tea with Mrs Tebben and will simply adore talking about Oxford, and that will all make a good impression.'

'That's perfect of you. I don't believe that the family will be much help, but one might try. I really don't know what I'd have done unless I'd had someone to talk to,' said Laurence, giving his sister a hearty hug and hitting her on the back. They went into the hall, and met Mr Fanshawe, just coming in.

'I've been for a tramp,' he said, 'and I'm just going to get into respectable clothes and take your mother to church.'

He went upstairs. A bad night and a six-mile tramp had not in the least helped him to forget that Helen took an interest in young Tebben. On the landing he ran into Betty, who was carrying a pile of books. Several of them fell on the floor.

'Sorry,' said Mr Fanshawe, stooping. 'My fault, I wasn't looking where I was going. I'll pick them up. Are you coming to church? Marcus Aurelius, Emerson, Tolstoi? Is it a holiday task?'

'I find conventional religion of no use to me,' said Betty. 'Going to church is merely a drug and doesn't exercise the mind. I prefer something that makes me think.'

'Of course if Emerson does that, you are doubtless right,' said Mr Fanshawe, automatically dropping into the courteous manner he reserved for his pupils. He pursued his way to his room, reflecting with sorrow that it would be at least four years before Betty could stop being a prig.

*

Breakfast at Lamb's Piece was not without incident. Mrs Tebben was roused at eight o'clock by a banging at the back door. She hurried down in a dressing-gown to find Mrs Phipps waiting severely in the yard.

'I'm sure I didn't want to disturb you, mum,' said Mrs Phipps, 'but the safety catch was down on the back door. Of course if I'd known you wasn't wanting me so early I needn't have come. I'd have been glad enough of a lay in bed.'

'Did you have a nice time at the Manor House?' asked Mrs Tebben brightly.

'Mrs Palmer didn't want me for the whole evening after all, so I could have come if you'd only let me know. I said to Phipps, 'If Mrs Tebben knew I was free she'd be on the door-mat like a shot wanting me to come up to her place.' I knew you'd be missing me.'

'Well, we managed splendidly and Miss Margaret cooked a lovely supper. Your cock was so nice. And you'll find the kitchen all clean.'

The implacable Mrs Phipps did some sotto voce grumbling about people in her kitchen, and began to get breakfast.

'We seem to have a great deal of bread and crumbs on the floor,' said Mr Tebben, eating his too softly boiled egg.

This was unfortunately overheard by Mrs Phipps as she brought in the marmalade which she had forgotten and resented being reminded of. She explained that she was give to understand that the young ladies and gentlemen had tidied up last night, and when those that weren't brought up to it did it, it would better have been left alone. And what was she to do with the rum?

'The rum?' said Mrs Tebben. 'But we never had any.'

Mrs Phipps brought in a bottle, two-thirds empty, and banged it down on the revolving bookcase, saying she dessaid it had walked there of itself.

'But how on earth did rum get here?' asked Mrs Tebben again.

'Laurence brought it down to make an omelette,' said Margaret. 'I did tell you last night, Mummy, he had brought some things for the party.'

'What else did he bring?' asked Mr Tebben.

'Only some sherry, Daddy, and some cigarettes and the asparagus. Oh, and the liqueur and the almonds. That was all, except the raspberries and some cream. We ate all our raspberries at lunch.'

Mr Tebben looked curiously at his daughter. He, also, felt that Laurence was perhaps presuming too much, but as he never interfered with his children if he could possibly help it, he said nothing.

'Will you harness Modestine for me, dear boy?' said Mrs Tebben. 'I'll have to drive to church. Perhaps you will come with me, and Margaret and your father will walk.'

Rather to her surprise Richard, instead of his usual sulks, consented with a fairly good grace, only stipulating that he should have Modestine in the afternoon as Jessica would not be having her morning ride. When Mrs Tebben drove to church it was always necessary to start early, so that Modestine could be put up in Mr Pollett's shed, behind the shop. Wearing the shameful hat and mackintosh, with a waterproof carriage rug over her knees and holding a large umbrella, she made her progress up the hill, past the Woolpack and down the street to the church. Here she got out, while Richard, who had dutifully walked at his enemy's head, took him down to the shop and stabled him. As he returned, the Manor House and the Dower House motors were disgorging their occupants, Susan and Robin were parking their bicycles in the lych-gate, much to Mr Phipps's annoyance, and Margaret with her father came up on foot. Laurence was hanging about, waiting for a sign from Margaret who, with great skill, managed not to include him in her greeting to the family. Laurence, anxious to turn the knife in the wound, deserted the Dower House pew, which was just behind the Tebben family, for the Manor House pew. From this point of vantage he could embarrass Margaret and make himself miserable by looking at her all through the service. Mrs Palmer looked grimly at her nephew as he sat himself down between her and his uncle, but she could not scold him in church and he was quite unconscious that she was in any way annoyed.

Margaret was so conscious of Laurence's gaze, fixed on her in a way that she felt the whole congregation must notice, that she could hardly think of anything else. She was not at all sure whether she liked or hated him, but if she hated him she would like it to be clear that he could not sit in the Palmers' pew staring at her, Sunday after Sunday. He had such a very nice face and its present harassed appearance smote her to the heart. If he behaved again as impertinently as he did last night, she would have her wits about her and tell him exactly what she thought of him, though what she did think was far from clear to her. The only thing she was really certain of was that she wished they could have the scene over again. She would either be more cruel or more kind. It would indeed be pleasant to be more kind. She decided to speak to Laurence after church, coolly, but quite nicely, as a woman of the world might speak to a presuming boy.

Mr Moxon, whom the Misses Thomas so disliked, was a breezy young man with a great belief in words, especially his own. He was scoutmaster of the Worsted Boy Scouts and was devoted to Boys in the abstract. He had run a club for them in the East End before he came to Worsted and went to a Boys' Camp every summer. About individual boys he was not very intelligent, but Boys in the lump were meat and drink to him. He rattled optimistically through his part of the service and helped his aged Rector up the pulpit steps with an obtrusive deference that made Miss Dolly Thomas shake her fist at him in secret. Dr Thomas's age and learning, his benevolent disposition, had made him much loved by his flock, who listened with affectionate toleration to his learned sermons. While he disported himself like Leviathan among Greek and Hebrew references, Mr Palmer, who had long ago given up trying to hear the Rector, began to read the prayer book. Suddenly Laurence felt his uncle stiffen, as if he were a pointer who had noticed an uncommonly good piece of game. His uncle dug him in the leg. He turned. Mr Palmer was holding out a book and signing to him to pass it to Mrs Palmer. Laurence did so. Mrs Palmer looked at it, raised her eyes in question, and shook her head, once in despair of guessing what her husband meant, and again to tell him to keep quiet. To Laurence's alarm his uncle then formed with elaborate shapings of his mouth and a loud whisper the letters G-R-

A-V-E-N. Mrs Palmer, after considering the possibility of her husband having suddenly gone mad, then realised that "Graven", was the word that had nearly made them late for church. She frowned angrily at her husband and turned her head away. By the time the service had come to an end her annoyance with him had reached such a pitch that Laurence's misdeeds were entirely forgotten. If anything else were needed to put Laurence and his affairs well in the background, it was the conduct of Susan and Robin, who had good voices and good ears and took a second to the hymns in the manner of Mr Frank Churchill, slightly, but correctly, to the great surprise of their neighbours.

It was in the churchyard after the service that the first Great Misfortune took place, when Dr Thomas introduced his curate to Mrs Dean, who with mistaken amiability asked him to come back to lunch. Mr Moxon said that would be simply ripping, and he'd love to have a talk with the Young People. They always, he said, as he got into the car, where he and Mr Dean stood, uncomfortably bent at a right angle, both refusing to take the seat next to Mrs Dean, came to him in all their difficulties. Rachel called Laurence to come with them, but he said he would walk. Lingering near the gate he hoped for a word with Margaret, just to say that if she would let him come to tea, or go for a walk with her, there was a great deal he could explain. Margaret came out, her head very high, walked straight past him, and went home to do as much crying as could be done before lunch without rousing attention.

Lunch at the Dower House fell alive into the hands of Mr Moxon. Worsted, Mr Moxon said, was the most delightful place and Dr Thomas an absolute saint. The scouts were not yet perhaps all they might be, but they got together jolly well. It was marvellous, he said, how by merely allowing the spirit of fellowship to pour into you, all things became possible. Robin who, usually very sweet-tempered and tolerant, had taken a violent and well-grounded dislike to the curate at sight, muttered that fellowship wouldn't milk a cow. Mr Moxon pounced on him, cheerily forced him to repeat his words, and laughed heartily. That, he said, was exactly what fellowship would do. When his boys' club went to Kent for their holiday camp none of them could milk. By the end of the week, owing to the wonderful spirit of fellowship prevailing among them, three of them, splendid boys whose fathers were out of work, were accomplished milkers, and if the camp had gone on longer he had no doubt that the whole fifty would have acquired the art. Susan said she was sorry for the cows and had to be suppressed by a look from her father. Mr Moxon said he would take lemonade if it was all the same to Mr Dean. Not, he said, that he had any personal objection to alcohol, for he always thought that the sin lay rather in the abuse of strong drink than in its use. He himself, he said, took a glass of beer as readily as any man, but for the sake of the Boys, he never took anything stronger.

Mr Fanshawe said 'Ha' and helped himself to a very strong whisky and soda, a drink which he rarely touched.

Mr Moxon, his eyes streaming with tears owing to too much horseradish sauce, said how delightful it was to see the whole family at church and that was what he called practical fellowship.

'Not quite all really,' said Rachel, apologetically. 'You see my second boy is in India and the twins are at sea, though, of course, they have to attend prayers, but the times being different make us not all be at church at the same moment, and Jessica isn't really old enough to enjoy it and Betty doesn't go.'

'And why does not Miss Betty go?' asked Mr Moxon, who had washed the horseradish away with lemonade. 'We must open the gates of fellowship wider for her.'

'To anyone who thinks and reads,' said Betty, staring at Mr Moxon as if he were in a cage, 'religion is useless. Every intelligent person has grown out of religion now. One has to go of course, as a matter of convention from time to time, but it means nothing. And as for fellowship, I am an Individualist.'

'Betty is also a disciple of Marcus Aurelius,' said Mr Fanshawe gravely.

Mr Moxon said that as a 'Varsity man himself he must of course have a fellow feeling for that Fine Old Pagan, and he and Miss Betty must have a really rousing argument someday. Betty looked balefully at him and made no answer beyond an unpleasant curling of the lip, a trick which she had brought to perfection before her glass. Mr Fanshawe asked if Marcus Aurelius were a University man, and when Mr Moxon laughingly denied any special knowledge, Mr Fanshawe said it was the use of the word 'myself' that had confused him. Mr Moxon said that there were men at his dear old Alma Mater who held as broad views as any, but all were inspired by fellowship. Mr Fanshawe inquired what particular Alma Mater Mr Moxon affected, and on hearing that it was extra-collegiate said 'Ha' again, in a way that temporarily froze the guest.

Mr Dean, feeling that his duty as a host was, however unwillingly, to protect his guest, diverted the conversation to South American engineering works. Mr Moxon had been for two months in the Argentine. He had studied the whole question ('What question?' asked Laurence, unheard) and had come to the conclusion that fellowship would solve everything.

'But you can't have fellowship with natives,' said Susan. 'One has to shoot them if they are too troublesome. One tried to murder Daddy in his tent so he shot him. It went against the grain, but he had to.'

Mr Moxon, who had never before sat at a murderer's table, said he was grieved to hear it, but things were better now, implying, to the fury of the young Deans, that their father's departure had considerably raised the moral tone of the place. Mr Moxon said he would like Mr Dean to come down and talk to the scouts and bring the little chap (at which Robin scowled). Several of his lads, he said, were pretty good with the gloves and would give the young man a rousing bout. He hoped the lad (his ingenuity in finding names for Robin made that young gentleman sulk violently) would come to camp with them next summer. They went over to Staple Park and camped in Lady Bond's barn, where they had a jolly camp-fire and sing-songs every night, which he was sure our young friend would thoroughly enjoy. He must, he said, be getting along now, and had had a simply ripping time.

'It has been so nice to see you,' said Rachel, adding in desperation, 'but we are all going away, I am afraid, for ever so long, I don't quite know where. Would you like to be run down to the village?'

Mr Moxon laughingly replied that Shanks's mare was his favourite steed and the young people nowadays seemed to have forgotten what a real good tramp meant, and so departed.

'I never thought I would live to hear anyone really say Shanks's mare,' said Susan. 'I say, Betty, you blipped him jolly well.'

'I simply spoke as I felt,' said Betty.

'I do not know,' said Mr Fanshawe, 'why young men who selflessly devote their time and energy, and in many cases their means, to that very noble task of organising and helping boys less happily placed than themselves, should almost invariably be conceited bores.'

By the time Mrs Dean had had a rest and everyone had more or less got over Mr Moxon, the rain had stopped and Richard arrived with Modestine. Mr Dean and Laurence were working, Betty had gone to Lamb's Piece, so Mrs Dean and Mr Fanshawe decided to walk to the Manor House, while Nanny led Modestine with Jessica on her back.

'You'd better come too, Richard,' said Susan, as she and Robin got onto their bicycles, 'you might see the bull.'

'Uncle Fred said the bull wouldn't be here today,' said Helen, 'and I'm going to show Richard how to mend a bit of the car.'

'Well, John has a feeling that he will. He gets feelings about cows and bulls and they're usually right.'

'All right, Richard and I will come as far as the park, and then we'll go back.'

Richard attached himself to Mrs Dean, who seemed to him somehow even more exquisite in tweeds than she did in her summer dresses, while Helen and Mr Fanshawe sauntered behind, and Susan and Robin skirmished round Modestine on their bicycles.

'Let's go for a good tramp,' said Mr Fanshawe to Helen, 'instead of sitting at the Palmers'.'

'Yes, do let's. Oh, but I forgot, there's the car. I promised I'd show Richard how to take a bit of her down. What about after tea?'

Mr Fanshawe agreed, but he felt chilly and grown old.

Just before they reached the lane to the Manor House they heard shouting. Susan and Robin, violently excited, said it must be the bull.

'Do get off your bicycles then,' said Mrs Dean. 'Nanny, stop the donkey.'

Round the bend in the lane Rushwater Rubicon came, gently trotting, an immense animal with a body shaped like a petrol tin, a curly fringe, and wide nostrils through which he puffed fire, or so Susan afterwards said. Lady Bond's cowman and another of her men, who were bringing the bull over, were running behind him. Mr Palmer's cowman came hurriedly down the track that led to the half-acre paddock to try to head Rushwater Rubicon off, but was just too late.

'Get over the wire,' he shouted to the walking party, 'he won't hurt you there.'

There was a moment's panic. Susan and Robin were over the fence in a moment. Rushwater Rubicon, annoyed by their excited voices, gave a mild bellow. Charles Fanshawe and Helen, some way behind the others, came running up, but before they could reach the spot Modestine had stopped dead and Jessica shot off over his head. Nanny, for once losing her presence of mind entirely, began to scream. Rushwater Rubicon walked up to Jessica and blew at her. Richard, quite convinced that it would be his last moment, sprang to Modestine's head and turned him across the narrow lane, blocking it, while with his foot he rolled Jessica behind him. Nanny picked her charge up and ran back with her to Mrs Dean while Richard, not knowing what to do next, stood holding Modestine's head and staring at the bull. Rushwater Rubicon was perplexed. Cowmen he understood and visitors on Sunday, but Modestine he suspected of being something barely human and when that unemotional animal, wrenching round his head, looked at him with his lip drawn back over his upper teeth, the bull was thankful to find his cowman at hand to rescue him, and was led peacefully away into the half-acre paddock, glad to get away from a lane where one met such monstrosities. Richard then sat down in the ditch and wondered if he were going to die.

'Gosh, you were marvellous,' said Susan's awe-struck voice, sounding very far away. 'Put your head down between your legs if you feel queer. I say, you are absolutely marvellous. You saved Jessica's life. Put it right down,' and a strong hand pushed his head almost to the dust. Robin, large-eyed and rather frightened, stood staring.

'Here, Robin,' said Susan, hitting her young brother with her free arm, 'get your bike and go and tell Father, quick. Perhaps Jessica's hurt or something.'

Robin obediently shot off. Presently Richard got rather

shakily to his feet, and he and Susan went back to where Mrs Dean was standing with Helen at her side, and Mr Fanshawe holding Jessica unconscious in his arms. Nanny was crying loudly. Mr Palmer's cowman, who had been hanging about, joined them and explained how the accident had happened. A passing motor-bicycle had startled the bull, who had pulled the rope out of his attendant's hand and run quietly away. John's distress over what was entirely the fault of Lady Bond's cowman and assistant was so great that Mrs Dean managed to say something comforting to him, and he thankfully went after the bull. In another moment Mr Dean was there in the big car and had taken Jessica and most of the party away. Susan and Richard were left in the lane with Modestine and the bicycle.

'I think we'd better walk home,' said Susan. 'I feel all groggy. Oh, poor little Jessica. Do you think she'll die, Richard?'

Richard, knowing nothing at all about it, said he was sure it was all right and they walked back in silence, except for an occasional yelping sob from Susan. When they reached the Dower House they were afraid to go in. They took Modestine to the stable yard, where they found Robin, trying to comfort himself by giving the stable cat some milk. Susan couldn't stop crying, and Richard had to sit with her on the old horse-block while she sobbed herself into a kind of stupor and he rhythmically patted her shoulder. After what seemed like several hours Nanny came out with red eyes.

'Oh Mr Richard, I'd never have forgiven myself if anything had happened,' she said. 'The doctor has been and he says Jessica only has a mild concussion, poor little lamb, and she's in one of the spare rooms with a hospital nurse, and she'll be all right in a day or two. And to think of her laying there, and I don't know what we'd have done without you. You were a hero, sir. It does seem a shame for Jessica to have a nurse, and not her own Nanny nor her own nice bed, but as soon as she is better she'll be glad to see old Nanny again. And now poor Miss Susan and Master Robin, come along and let Nanny wash your faces and hands and get you some tea. Would you like tea with us, sir, in the nursery? I expect they are busy downstairs.'

Richard gratefully accepted and they went up to the nursery. At the sight of Jessica's empty bed in the night-nursery Nanny's tears began to flow again but hospitality won the day, and in putting the kettle on and getting tea and washing her ex-charges' faces and hands, which she insisted on doing herself, she forgot the worst of her fears. Richard was rather afraid that she would want to wash him too, but though she cast longing eyes at his hands, she allowed him to go to the bathroom alone. After a good tea Robin got out his clockwork train and they were all very happily on the floor when Mr Fanshawe came in.

'Jessica is doing nicely, Nanny,' he said, 'and you can go and see her for a moment. Richard, I'd like to shake hands if it wouldn't embarrass you. I'm afraid you'll have to make up your mind to a good deal of gratitude. I only wish I had had your chance, or that having it I could have been as cool as you were.'

'Thank you very much,' said Richard, taking Mr

Fanshawe's proffered hand, 'it was really Modestine—Neddy, I mean.'

'Mr and Mrs Dean want to see you,' continued Mr Fanshawe, 'and so does Helen. You'd better go and get it over.'

Rather unwillingly Richard left the safe haven of the nursery and went down with Mr Fanshawe. On the way he found courage to ask how Mrs Dean was, half fearing that she might be ill with the shock, but Mr Fanshawe said she was extraordinarily well, and Richard thought, but couldn't believe it, that there was a faint sound of amusement in his companion's voice. They found Mr and Mrs Dean in her sitting-room. Mr Dean grasped Richard's hand painfully, said he would like to talk to him later, and went quickly away. Mrs Dean, no longer in tweeds, but even more lovely in a tea-gown than she had been in her coat and skirt, was lying on the sofa. She took both Richard's hands in hers and with tears in her eyes thanked him for saving Jessica's life.

'That's all right, Mrs Dean, there wasn't really much danger. Mr Palmer's cowman said he was quite a good-tempered bull and wouldn't hurt anyone,' said Richard, but Mrs Dean scorned the suggestion. All bulls, she said, were mad, and how could Richard know that this one wasn't.

'I simply can't tell you what we feel,' she went on. 'Frank and I owe you everything. We are having my doctor down tonight to see her. The man here is quite sure that it's only mild concussion, but we want to be absolutely certain. Laurence has gone up in the car to fetch him. We were very lucky to be able to catch him on a Sunday. Oh, Richard, what should we have done if you hadn't been there?'

'Oh, Susan would have done it. She kept her head more than anyone. She sent Robin for Mr Dean. I think I'd better go home if you don't mind. If my people hear about it they'll be worrying.'

'Of course, dear Richard, of course. Come and see us tomorrow, and God bless you.'

As Richard left the room Helen, whom he hadn't noticed in a corner, slipped out after him and took his arm.

'Oh Richard, you are marvellous,' she said. 'I was such a fool and I am so ashamed. I was afraid Mother would faint or something, and I didn't know whether to go backwards or forwards or scream or run away, and you simply went and saved Jessica's life. I'm— Oh, I don't know what to say to you.'

'Well, don't forget you are going to show me how to take down the car,' said Richard, and went to collect Modestine.

'What good stuff there is in that young Tebben,' said Mr Fanshawe to Mrs Dean when Richard had left the room.

'High praise from you, my sardonic Charles.'

'Sometimes I think it's time I left off being sardonic, but there isn't much to encourage me,' said Charles, a little wearily. 'Try living with undergraduates and dons, and you'll know what I mean. You are one of today's surprises, Rachel. I was quite prepared for you to die on the spot after the way you tried to frighten me about yourself. You are a bit of a fraud, my dear.'

'I must have been getting better without knowing it,' said Rachel, meekly.

'By the way, how long is it since Masters overhauled you?'

'I don't know. About six months, I suppose.'

'Now, listen to me. I know exactly what you have been doing. You have put off seeing him because you were frightened. When he has seen Jessica, let him have a good look at you. He will probably say that you are ever so much better and are to stop being silly. Then you can tell Frank how foolish you have been, and everything will be all right. We middle-aged people tend to think too much about ourselves perhaps, and our hearts.'

'I wish you would get married, Charles.'

'I have been waiting for that. I think you say it three times a week at least whenever I am staying with you.'

'Well, I wish you would. But you never look at any young women except Helen.'

'And Helen looks at Richard,' said Charles Fanshawe. 'Well, if I can't be of use, I'm going for a walk.'

And off he went to the nursery and took Susan and Robin over the hill and down through a very muddy valley and through a wood and past the ruined mill and home again, and was more than usually amusing.

8

Essay in Criticism

Betty and Mrs Tebben had passed an extremely pleasant afternoon. Margaret, with aching eyes and heart, was trying to help her father to arrange some notes for a lecture he had promised to give to the Snorri Society, so Mrs Tebben and her young guest had the drawing-room to themselves. At first Mrs Tebben, who was not used to much consideration from the young, was rather diffident, but as Betty plied her with questions about Miss Pitcher-Jukes and the delights of Oxford, she became eloquent in praise of St Mildred's, her old college. Her description of her own student days, which she still mistakenly considered the happiest period of her life, became more and more enthralling, and all her shyness fled away, as did her loyalty to Miss Pitcher-Jukes.

'To tell you the truth,' said Mrs Tebben reflectively, 'I always thought her one of the rudest and most conceited women I have ever known. But there must have been something about her. She was one of those people that other girls always seemed to get what we used to call a pash for.'

'A bit of a Lesbian, I suppose,' said Betty.

'Oh no, my dear,' said Mrs Tebben, who was secretly frightened of the word and thought it had perhaps something to do with drugs, 'but she certainly had a very great influence over her fellow-students. A girl called Ivy Punch tried to drown herself in the bath because Effie Pitcher-Jukes wouldn't sit next to her at the lectures on the banking system, but the bath was out of order and she could only get boiling water, so she couldn't manage it. Afterwards she took a good degree and became secretary to a very well-known man in the literary world, but—'

Mrs Tebben stopped, remembering that the rest of the unlucky Ivy Punch's story was not suitable for young girls.

'Oh, I know all about her,' said Betty. 'Her girl was at the same school I go to. She was called Brynhild Punch, but of course, everyone knew who her father was. I say, Mrs Tebben, do tell me how you wrote your first book.'

On these pleasant lines the afternoon passed away till tea-time. As Mrs Phipps had gone home, Mrs Tebben and Betty got the tea, and such friends did they become that Mrs Tebben could almost believe that she was again making tea at St Mildred's. Mr Tebben and Margaret joined them, both in low spirits. Mr Tebben's lecture was not shaping well, and he saw that he would have to spend at least a day in town at the British Museum. Margaret, although she had tried very hard to feel an interest in Icelandic procedure in the case of Outlawry, could not control her thoughts. Laurence's wretched, hang-dog expression in the Palmers' pew was in her mind all the time, and she had confused the two Snorris quite shamefully.

Betty inquired what they had been doing, and was kind enough to explain some of her own feelings on the subject.

'I always feel,' she said, 'that the attitude of the Sagas towards religion is the only real attitude. To know that the gods' hands are always against you and to laugh in defiance; and then at the end to go laughingly to death in the defence of the gods in whom you hardly believe, seems to me very splendid, and perhaps the only true happiness. Do you know Mr Moxon, the curate?'

'Unfortunately, I may say, yes,' said Mr Tebben.

'Mother asked him to lunch today. He's a fool.'

'I sometimes wish,' said Mr Tebben, 'that Moxon, with his irritating zeal, had been a missionary to Norway in pagan times. He would undoubtedly have been spread-eagled.'

'Too good for him,' said Betty. 'Hullo, Richard.'

'My dear boy, you are back early,' said his mother. 'Why, how the time has flown! It is nearly six. I thought it was much earlier. Did you have a nice time? And will you have a cup of tea?'

'No, thanks, Mother. I had some tea at the Dower House.'

'I suppose I ought to be getting along,' said Betty. 'I said I'd pick up the others at Aunt Louise's.'

'Oh, they aren't there,' said Richard.

'But they were going there to tea. Are they back?'

'They came back early. Jessica had a fall.'

Under a severe and thoroughly annoying cross-examination

from his mother, who had a passion for what she called Getting at the Root of Things, Richard grudgingly recounted in part the story of the afternoon's adventure. From his account his parents gathered that Jessica had fallen off Modestine because she saw a bull, and that Richard was somehow to blame. To their interested and well-meant inquiries for further details, he opposed the rather offensive reserve to which they were well accustomed. Margaret was too unhappy to care, but Betty was not only curious, but entirely free from the inhibitions which beset her host and hostess.

'You might tell us what *did* happen, Richard,' she said indignantly, 'instead of snubbing everyone. It isn't every day that one meets a bull on the road. Did you wave a red flag or anything? Don't make shutting-up faces at me, because I want to know. People's reactions to a crisis are always of value.'

'Well, it wasn't a crisis, and I haven't any reactions.'

'My dear boy!' said his mother.

'Is Jessica all right?' asked Margaret.

'Of course.'

'Have you seen her?'

'No, but the doctor said so.'

Upon these words Betty pounced, and gradually elicited that the local doctor had been called in, that Jessica had mild concussion, and that a London doctor was expected that evening.

'Oh, poor little Jessica!' cried Betty, suddenly becoming human. 'Richard, you were a beast not to tell us before. I'll go back at once. How could you let her fall off Neddy?'

'I didn't.'

'Well, where were you then?'

'Excuse me,' said Richard, to the company in general, 'as I don't seem to be popular here, I think I'll go and do some work. And I wish to goodness people wouldn't fuss so much,' he added in an aside that was audible to everyone.

As he got up the front door, which was never locked in summer, was heard to open and shut, and into the room came Mr and Mrs Palmer, with Gunnar walking among their legs.

'My dear Winifred!' cried Mrs Palmer. 'What a day! Thank God, Jessica is all right, but what *do* you think of Richard?'

'Think of him, Louise?'

'Well, aren't you bursting with pride?' asked Mrs Palmer, as quick to generous admiration as to wrath. 'If I'd a son and if he had been like Richard, oh, I'd throw my hat over the house.'

'But what has happened?' asked Mr Tebben, who was accustomed to being perplexed by his family, and while usually resigned, felt that there was now an opportunity, with visitors present, before whom he could not be snubbed, to discover what they were all talking about

'Why the bull, my dear man, the bull!'

'Showed presence of mind, great presence of mind,' said Mr Palmer, and stepping forward he wrung Richard's hand. 'We're all very grateful to you, my boy, more grateful than I can say. It would have broken my sister's heart if anything had happened to Jessica.'

'But, Aunt Louise,' said Betty, 'what *did* happen? Richard said Jessica fell off the donkey because she saw a bull.'

Mr and Mrs Palmer, speaking together, but with Mrs Palmer well ahead in her exposition, told the story as it had reached them through their cowman in whose admiring narration it had lost nothing. From the Palmers' strophe and antistrophe Betty and the Tebbens gathered that a mad bull, if not a herd of mad bulls, deliberately let loose by Lady Bond for the destruction of the Dean family, had come charging down the lane. The head bull, an animal of gigantic size weighing several tons, had hurled himself with lowered head and threatening horns upon Modestine. Jessica had been thrown several hundred yards and rescued by Richard, who had then interposed his body between Jessica and the bull till Lady Bond's myrmidons, despairing of accomplishing their fell design, had, with John's help, for they were too overcome with terror and remorse to be able to move, dealt with the bellowing monster, who was now chained hand and foot in the half-acre paddock.

'And it didn't surprise me in the least,' said Mrs Palmer emphatically. 'Lucasta Bond is capable of that, and far worse.'

'Do I understand, then,' asked Mr Tebben, 'that you saved Jessica from the bull, Richard?'

'Oh, that's rot, Father,' said Richard, going bright red and kicking his own feet. 'It was really all Modestine. And anyway the bull wouldn't have hurt Jessica. It was Susan that kept her head and sent Robin to fetch Mr Dean. Well, I really think I ought to do some work, if you'll excuse me. Goodbye, Mrs Palmer. Goodbye, sir.'

Stepping over Gunnar he made for the door and disappeared.

As the Palmers repeated the story, the actual facts began to emerge, the bulls in buckram dwindled to one, and that one not mad, but none the less was it clear that Richard had shown great coolness and courage in a situation that was really dangerous and but for him might easily have had a tragic ending. Mrs Tebben nearly cried with joy and pride, and could hardly be restrained from running first to Richard's room to see if he was gored, and then to the field to see if Modestine was any the worse. Mr Tebben said that Richard was certainly no Skraeling, a statement which afforded him immense satisfaction and had the additional advantage of being unintelligible to most of his hearers. Mr Palmer did make an inquiry as to what his host was talking about, but his niece silenced him by saying 'Kipling', at which Mr Tebben winced.

'Well, we must be getting along,' said Mrs Palmer. 'It's dress rehearsal on Wednesday, you know. I'm afraid I was very thoughtless about Mrs Phipps, Winifred. You must forgive me. Why didn't you remind me?'

'It was quite all right,' said Mrs Tebben magnanimously. 'Margaret managed beautifully and Laurence was such a help in the kitchen. He is quite like one of the family.'

The day on which Richard had saved her youngest niece from a bull was not, Mrs Palmer felt, the day on which to tell his sister to leave her eldest nephew alone. All the same she was annoyed when she said goodbye to find that Margaret had quietly slipped out of the room. Margaret had gone up to find Richard and hear from him what really happened, and after a little pressing he thawed, and gave her a pretty accurate account of the affair, explaining again that the bull was not at all mad. In an outburst of confidence he told Margaret that the person who had behaved best was Mrs Dean.

'She isn't frightfully strong, you know,' he said, clearing his throat, 'and I thought she'd crock up or something. In fact, I wouldn't have been a bit surprised if her heart had played up, but she was perfectly splendid. She looked awfully white, but somehow she looked even more ripping than she does ordinarily. She was marvellous to me about it afterwards. She said,' added Richard reverently, ' "God bless you".'

'I should think she did,' said Margaret. 'Oh Richard darling, I am so proud of you that I could burst.'

'One would do absolutely anything for her. You may as well know, Margaret,' said Richard in a hoarse croak, the effect of emotion, 'that I love her.'

'Oh, Richard,' said his sister, not critically, but with just the right blending of admiration and awe.

'She makes one feel a clumsy, clod-hopping booby,' said Richard, who appeared to consider this a high recommendation of his beloved, 'and I know I'm not fit to be near her, but somehow she lifts one up. Inspiration I suppose you might call it. I've written heaps of poetry about her, but I had to tear most of it up, because one can't do her justice, and there are no rhymes to Rachel. But I did a little thing yesterday that I think is pretty good. Would you like to hear it?'

Margaret, immensely flattered, begged to hear the poem, and curled herself up on Richard's bed.

'It isn't really finished yet, but I think the idea is good. She had a kind of heart attack that evening when Susan and Robin got on the roof, and she looked so pale and lovely, and the shadows on her eyelids,' said Richard, musing, half to himself, 'were just the colour of those violets one gets down by the railway. It was that that made me think of the poem. It begins like this:

'Strew no roses round her bed,
Roses are too white, too red.'

Here his voice cracked, and he had to go to the bathroom and get a drink of water.

'Shall I go on?' he asked when he came back.

'Please do. It's wonderful.'

'Strew no roses round her bed,
Roses are too white, too red;
But the cloudy violets bring,
First-fruits of a tardy spring.

'Do you like it?'

'I think it's lovely,' said Margaret.

'All her roses now are fled,
Rue must deck her lonely bed,
And on those—

'No, that's wrong, I couldn't quite read it, it ought to be

'And upon those sealèd eyes.
Violets fall, from Paradise.'

At the end of this poem Richard was so overcome by the events of the day, his love for Mrs Dean, and the letting loose of his long-pent passion that he choked. Tears stood in his eyes with combined asphyxia and emotion, and he had to go and get another drink. When he came back he asked his sister if she had really liked it. Margaret thought it very beautiful and sad, almost as good as Keats and Shakespeare, and said so.

'Did you notice that line "Roses are too white, too red"? One might easily have written "Roses are too white and red", but repeating the "too" makes a good effect, don't you think?'

'Yes, it does.'

'"Cloudy" violets is a good epithet too, isn't it? I'm not quite sure about "first-fruits". I did think of "children" or "nurslings", but on the whole I think "first-fruits" is best.'

Margaret said she did too.

'How do you like "sealèd eyes"? Of course the whole thing still wants a lot of polishing, but I do feel it has the feeling.'

Margaret also felt that it made one feel the feeling. While her brother discussed at length the Craft of Poetry, with special reference to his own works, Margaret gave herself up to day-dreams. It was very wonderful that Richard was in love with Mrs Dean, and very kind of him to tell her about it; but much as she would have liked to be comforted, she had not the courage to tell Richard her own secret, and in any case she didn't think he would have listened just at present. Of course she didn't really love Laurence, in fact she hated him, and would like to see him and tell him so. As for Richard and Mrs Dean it was one of those very wonderful things like Tristram and Iseult, or Lancelot and Guenevere, that only happened to people like her brother; beautiful because impossible. If Mr Dean did suddenly die, and Richard did happen at the same time suddenly to be earning a very large salary, they might get married, but it all seemed improbable. And even if they did, she could hardly imagine Richard as a stepfather to nine people, some of whom were older than he was, and three of whom he had never even seen. Besides, if Richard married Mrs Dean she would be Mrs Dean's sister-in-law, an unreasonable state of things. Also she would automatically become Laurence's step-aunt, a relationship that did not seem calculated to lead to matrimony, if indeed it were not within the forbidden degrees. No, on the whole, it would be better that Mr Dean should remain alive, though without prejudice to Richard's earning a large salary. From these thoughts she was roused by her brother's voice, raised in some impatience.

'I say, Margaret, you might listen. Do you think I should call the poem "To Rachel", or simply "Rachel", or "Requiem"?'

Margaret said she thought 'Requiem' would be very nice, but wasn't it rather like Stevenson.

'Gosh, yes,' said Richard, 'and we've had enough of that with Modestine. I'll tell you what, I'll call it simply "Strew no roses".'

Margaret said that was a lovely name, but if Richard didn't mind her saying so, she thought perhaps that line was rather doubtful English, like 'Deliver no circulars', because you couldn't order people to do a thing that meant not doing a thing. Richard said of course if she was going to *carp*, but very handsomely forgave her and decided to call the poem 'Requiescat', or failing that, 'Shadowed Eyes'. They then went down to Sunday supper and for the rest of the evening Richard treated his parents as human beings indeed, but of an inferior order, and everyone was glad when bed-time came, except Margaret, who lay awake crying all night, distinctly hearing the clock strike twelve.

'I suppose you thought it funny to tread on my tail last night,' said Gunnar to Modestine, down in the field.

'Your tail?' said Modestine. 'My good cat, there's hardly enough to tread on.'

'What's all this about a bull?' asked Gunnar.

'Oh, nothing.'

'Well, the Palmers were talking about it at tea. What did you do?'

'Hardly worth talking about. I was taking Jessica for a ride, very kindly, and letting Nanny walk beside her, when a mad bull came rushing at us. He tried to gore me, but I simply looked at him. Not a finger did I move, but just looked. No bull can stand up to a brave man's eye. He cringed, the bully, and I finished him off with my heels and teeth. Properly punished him, I did. He won't show his face again in these parts for a long time.'

Gunnar was perplexed. He knew that it was unlike Modestine to tell the truth, but he had no means of disproving it. And had not Richard himself said in the drawing-room that Modestine had saved Jessica's life? He decided to try another form of attack.

'I thought you were going to kick the cart to pieces and throw old Ma Tebben over the hedge and kick old Tebben to death and join the army,' he said.

'My dear fellow,' said Modestine in a refined voice, 'on Sunday? What are you thinking of?'

Next morning Richard found two letters at his place at breakfast. One was from his Oxford tailor, reminding him in a gentlemanly way that a settlement of his outstanding account of seventeen pounds, nine shillings and sixpence would be welcome. The other bore the postmark of Winter Overcotes, the nearest sorting office. Richard opened it, glanced at the contents, and sat gaping. His parents were too well trained to dare to ask what had happened, and would probably never have known, had not Richard's excitement been such that he had to share it.

'I say, Margaret,' said he, speaking rather to his sister than his father and mother, as more likely to understand what he said, 'what do you think? Mr and Mrs Palmer have sent me a cheque for fifty pounds.'

The success of this announcement was instantaneous and gratifying. Everyone had a suggestion to make for spending the gift, and it shows how really nice Richard's family were that not one of them said he ought to bank it, or give a penny to the poor. Mr Tebben advised a walking tour abroad and the purchase of quantities of books. Mrs Tebben thought an Icelandic or Hellenic cruise and a portable wireless for his bedroom. Margaret said she would get a lot of new clothes if it were hers. But what use would new clothes be, she added to herself, if Laurence were not there to see them. Richard refused to make any plans, but promised to consider carefully the use he would make of it. His first job he said, was to go and thank Mr and Mrs Palmer. Accordingly he set off for the Manor House across the fields. Entering by the back way he met Sparrow in the passage and asked if Mrs Palmer were in.

'Mr Palmer and Mrs Palmer are still in the dining-room, sir,' said Sparrow. 'Excuse me, Mr Richard, but I would like to be allowed to offer my respectful congratulations. When John told us in the Hall, for on this occasion we could not but allow him in, and came ourselves from the Room to hear it, of the spectacular way in which you had tackled the bull, I said to him, "Mark my words, John, a young gentleman that can hold a ball like Mr Richard did at the match against Skeynes will do anything and," I said, "he will go far." I should very much appreciate the honour of shaking hands, Mr Richard.'

'Oh, thanks awfully, Sparrow,' said Richard, shaking the butler warmly by the hand, 'but it wasn't so bad as all that. John told me himself the bull was quite harmless. But thanks awfully.'

He hurried past the kitchen regions, nervously conscious of admiring giggles from behind corners, and emerged through the swinging baize-covered door into the hall. In the dining-room he found the Palmers still at breakfast, and poured out his thanks for their generous gift.

'I really don't think I ought to have it, sir,' he said. 'It was just as much the Bonds' cowman and John. I mean, if they hadn't taken the bull away, I couldn't have done anything.'

'Stuff and nonsense,' said Mr Palmer. 'Sit down and have

some breakfast. Had some? Well, have some more. You'll be glad to hear that Lady Bond has sent a very handsome apology, very handsome. Says she never meant to keep the bull, but her cowman was laid up with lumbago on Saturday. That's why he brought it over on Sunday. Well, what are you going to do with this little windfall?'

'First, sir, I've got to pay my Oxford tailor,' said Richard rather shamefacedly.

'Bad plan, bad plan. Never pay the fellows. Makes them get above themselves. Something on account regularly, yes, but never settle the bill.'

Richard felt young and rather damped.

'Don't take any notice of Fred,' said Mrs Palmer. 'Pay your tailor and don't get into debt again. Any plans for the balance – if there is any?' she added sharply.

Richard said there would be a considerable balance, but before deciding what to do with it he had to consult some people. Mr Palmer began advising him on investments, but Richard, alleging an engagement, escaped, with further grateful acknowledgments.

'Going to the Dower House, I suppose,' said Mrs Palmer, watching Richard as he ran across the lawn. 'I wonder who it is, Fred. It can't be Betty or Susan, it must be Helen. What do you think, Fred? Lucasta Bond is actually taking six seats for the play. It shows she knows she was wrong about that fence.'

As he came out of the Palmers' drive Richard cannoned into the curate, who said he must absolutely congratulate Richard on his top-hole performance. Richard, he said, absolutely must come and talk to his scouts about it.

Chivalry, Mr Moxon considered, and self-sacrifice, were ideals which too few of our younger men had before them, but it was his aim, through fellowship, to cultivate in his Boys the knight-like spirit. Richard, he considered, was as much a true knight as any paladin of the olden time. Richard must also, he said, if he would allow an older man to speak from his heart, and as a friend, remember whence strength to combat bulls, both of the flesh and of the spirit, came. Richard thanked him awfully and ran on again till he got to the Dower House, where the big car was at the door. Mr Dean and a middle-aged man were talking on the steps. When Mr Dean saw Richard, he called him.

'This is Richard Tebben,' said Mr Dean, 'to whom our debt is so great. Richard, this is Dr Masters. I am thankful to say that he is pleased with Jessica. We shall have her about again in a day or two.'

Dr Masters, shaking Richard's hand, said he had heard all about his presence of mind and would like to congratulate him. He then got into the car and was taken away. Before Richard, terrified at the thought of any more congratulations, could escape, Mr Dean had asked him to come to his study. Here, to his great relief, Mr Dean, instead of talking about the bull, asked him a good deal about himself, what he had done, what he meant to do, what his interests were, what, very delicately put, were his circumstances. Richard, who had only looked on Mr Dean as the husband of Mrs Dean and father of Laurence, Helen, Betty, Susan, Robin and Jessica, not to speak of Gerald and the twins, found that he was having an extremely interesting conversation with a man of wide experience, and even heard himself saying what sounded to him rather sensible things. After half an hour's talk Mr Dean got up.

'I would like another talk with you,' he said. 'Can you come and see me on Thursday morning about eleven?'

Richard said he would. As he was leaving the room he fidgeted with the handle of the door and asked if Mrs Dean was all right.

'I only asked because once, that time Susan and Robin got on the roof,' said he nervously, 'Mrs Dean was rather faint, and I had an idea . . . '

'That she had a heart? So she has, but no more than hundreds and thousands of other people. Dr Masters says she is really very well and stood the shock splendidly. Of course at nearly fifty one can't expect the health of twenty. You will find the others in the garden, I think.'

Richard went round to the stable-yard with the words 'nearly fifty' sounding unpleasantly in his ears. He had never thought of his divinity having any particular age, but now he came to think of it, if Laurence, as he happened to know, was twenty-seven or nearly twenty-eight, Mrs Dean could hardly be much less than fifty, unless she had married unusually young. Fifty was rather a drab word. Of course age meant nothing with such a woman as Mrs Dean, but one oughtn't to have to think of it.

Helen was in the garage alone, cleaning her sports car, which she would not allow Mr Dean's chauffeurs to touch. Richard offered to help and was allowed to polish the glass; the paint Helen preferred to do herself. Here alone with Helen, Richard was able to unfold to her a plan for which her help was indispensable. Helen listened kindly, promised to give all possible assistance, and by way of a start suggested that Richard should come out in the sports car with her at once, taking lunch to be eaten on the road. This suited Richard's impatience admirably. Helen sent a message to the kitchen by the second chauffeur to say that she wanted the small lunch-basket packed for two as soon as possible, and put away her cleaning kit. Mr Fanshawe then came into the yard with Susan and Robin hanging on his arms.

'We never got our walk last night,' said Mr Fanshawe to Helen. 'What about now?'

'Oh Charles, I do wish I could, but I'm just going out with Richard.'

'Well, after lunch?'

'I don't know when we'll be back. We're having an adventure together.'

'What about tomorrow then?'

'I'm terribly sorry, Charles, but we may be out tomorrow too. I simply long for a walk, but I promised Richard, you see.'

'I see.'

'I say,' said Robin to Susan. 'You know that boy called Morland I told you about at school that says he can mesmerise bulls by looking at them. Well, that's what Richard did. He looked at the bull and it got mesmerised. I bet Morland will be sick when he hears he's not the only one. Morland's mother writes books, Uncle Charles, but he says they aren't much good, they're like novels. I'll ask John to let me mesmerise the bull.'

'No, you won't,' said Mr Fanshawe. 'You are neither of you to go near that bull unless I am with you, or your father, or Mr Palmer. Or, of course, Richard,' he added generously.

'I say, can we come with you?' Robin asked his sister.

'No,' said Helen. 'I'm awfully sorry, but Richard and I have some rather private business,' a remark which did not make Mr Fanshawe any happier.

The lunch-basket now arrived, Helen and Richard got into the car and drove away. Mr Fanshawe, after promising Susan and Robin a bathing-party in the afternoon, went round to the front of the house where Rachel was lying on a chair under the mulberry tree with her husband beside her. Charles sat down cross-legged on the grass.

'How easily you do that,' said Mr Dean enviously.

'It's all brain,' said Charles, and without uncrossing his long legs got up and sat down again.

'I said you were young,' said Rachel. 'I couldn't do that if I burst myself.'

'If being physically active were to be young . . .' said Mr Fanshawe. 'Well, Rachel, what is the verdict? You look extremely well.'

'This foolish girl,' said Mr Dean, laying his hand on his wife's, 'has been passed as in excellent condition by Masters. She just has to take a little care, that's all. She tells me that she has been worrying about herself, and you gave her good advice.'

'She is a self-dramatiser,' said Charles. 'I told her to pour out her troubles to you, Frank. You appeared to me a more suitable recipient for them than an old bachelor.'

'I wish,' said Rachel plaintively, 'that you wouldn't call yourself old so often. It isn't flattering to me, considering our ages are so near. And after all, to be nearly fifty isn't really old at all.'

'It depends on the point of view,' said her husband. 'Richard, for instance, doesn't think it is so young.'

'What devilment are you up to?' asked Charles.

'None. Richard was making inquiries as to Rachel's health after the fright of yesterday. I told him, not exactly in so many words, that at fifty one wasn't so young as one had been, but she was doing nicely.'

'You are a cold-blooded devil,' said Charles amiably.

'Possibly. But Rachel is a warm-hearted angel who lets people impose themselves on her. It's time Richard stopped kicking his heels and had some work instead of hanging around the Dower House. I propose to liquidate a little of the debt we owe him, a debt which nothing could repay, by offering him a start in business and removing him from the snares of this weak-minded siren who can't protect herself against her admirers.'

'You see, Frank knows all,' murmured Rachel, giving her husband such a look of affection that Charles got up.

'I am henceforward a misanthrope,' he announced. 'To see you and Frank making eyes at each other fills me with a mixture of nausea, scorn, and envy that I can't describe. And I meant to do something for Richard myself, and here you come, Frank, cutting the ground away from under my feet.'

'Then sit down again,' said Rachel.

Charles sat down and lit his pipe; Mr Dean retired into some papers. Rachel, looking up from her novel now and again, thought that if she hadn't had the good luck to have Frank for a husband, she could think of no one nicer than Charles. But as Frank, most fortunately for her, was there, she wished very much that Charles could be kept in the family. He would be exactly the person for her difficult Helen, the child she least understood. A little old, perhaps, but no one younger that she could think of would be able to handle the child. That Charles, the woman hater, cared very much for Helen, she was pretty sure, but whether he knew that he cared was another question. She thought not. And now Helen had made friends with Richard Tebben, a nice boy and one to whom her eternal gratitude was given, but not brilliant or good-looking enough to rouse in Charles the jealousy that might reveal his own mind to him. She thought of Frank's serpent-like remark to Richard about her age, laughed, sighed, and went on reading her book.

Rachel Dean was not at the best of times a very good judge of character, and her reading of Charles was more inaccurate than usual. Not only was he very much aware how much Helen meant to him, but he was at the moment bringing all his experience, logic, philosophy and common-sense to bear upon the question of jealousy. It had been easy enough to give Helen good advice when she confessed to jealousy of Margaret. What had been remarkable was that she had listened to him patiently. Knowing her quick, difficult temper he had quite expected her to fly out at him, or deliberately to go against his advice. Her confidence in his help, her promise to try what he suggested, her brief moment of self-pitying abandon against his shoulder, these had touched him profoundly. As profoundly had he admired the way she had taken herself in hand and mastered some of her weakness. Then Richard had turned up, youth had called to youth, and there was the only woman he could ever care for preparing to throw herself away on a penniless cub several years younger than herself.

He checked himself. Cub was a word he had no right to use. Richard by his courage yesterday had proved himself a man and had acted where he, Charles Fanshawe, had done nothing. What Helen thought, as between him and Richard, he had no doubt. Richard had saved Jessica from probable death or injury. Charles Fanshawe, who had never failed in a crisis, had failed in this. That there had been no time, that the whole thing had been over in a moment, was no excuse. He ought to have been in Richard's place, and Richard in his, among the women. Not only had he failed in this, but after telling Helen and Mrs Tebben that he could help Richard, and taking their gratitude complacently, he found that Frank Dean, without any words, had already done what he had only talked about. All he could do now was to renounce, and try not to feel wounded, or even worse, noble about it all. Richard's admiration of the mother had been patent enough, and suitable to his age, but when he realised as he must, that the daughter cared for him, how could he but care for her? To be loved by Helen would be the most enchanting mixture of safety and adventure that anyone could conceive. Once given, her heart would be as sure as a rock, but what quicksands, what morasses there would be around it. To love her would be to hold in one's hand a black opal, dull sometimes on the surface, fire flashing in its depths. Well, that must be put out of his mind. Richard would get his job and marry Helen, and Mr Dean would be the benefactor that he himself had meant to be.

'I sometimes wish I'd had a scientific education,' he said aloud.

'Why, Charles?' asked Mrs Dean, looking up from her book like a very soft, attractive owl, with her large spectacles.

'It seems to lead to deeds, not words,' was all Charles's answer as he got up and went away.

The bathing-party consisted of Mr Fanshawe, Betty, Susan and Robin. Mr Fanshawe loathed bicycling and utterly refused to consider the loan of a bicycle from the second chauffeur, so it was decided that they should walk to the little chain of pools known as the Dipping Ponds, and perhaps take the motor-bus back. Their way lay by Lamb's Piece, and as they passed they saw Mrs Tebben and Margaret working in the front garden.

'Good day, good day,' cried Mrs Tebben, waving a gauntleted hand. 'You aren't going to Winter Overcotes, are you? Oh, I just thought you might, because the bus starts about now, and if you were I was going to say would you be so very kind as to get me some of Picker's sausages. I always get Picker's, because really he is more reliable than anyone, especially in the hot weather. I never think Pollett's at the shop are really fresh. But if you are going bathing, of course that makes all the difference. Margaret, why don't you go too, and bring them all back to tea?'

Mr Fanshawe, seeing that Margaret was made very uncomfortable by her mother's well-meant foisting of her on the party, hastened to say, with perfect truth, that they would like it very much if she would come and bathe with them. Margaret got her bathing things and they all set off again. The Dipping Ponds are about two miles from Worsted, and were probably stew ponds for the little abbey of Beliers, long since fallen to untraceable ruin. The ponds are fed by a streamlet, tributary to the Woolram, and the largest, surrounded by beeches, makes a very pleasant summer bathing-place. True, the water is nowhere more than four feet deep, the bottom muddy and the surface matted with water-lily leaves, but the Deans were still young enough to like water for its own sake, and enjoyed the romantic setting. The way was secluded, entirely through field and woodland, and Mr Fanshawe had ample leisure to reflect as they strolled along how an undisciplined heart can spoil summer, sunshine, trees and streams by its own discontent. He wondered what Helen and Richard were doing, and reminded himself that it was no business of his.

'I hope your mother will let me come again,' said Betty to Margaret when they had crossed the stile and got into the woods. 'I enjoyed my time with her awfully yesterday, and she's going to give me some very good introductions when I go to Oxford.'

Margaret, who was rather shy of Betty because of her scholarship, said she was sure her mother would love it.

'It's very good for Mummy,' she said, 'to have someone to talk to who is keen on her sort of things. I'm no good, because I never went to college.'

'I don't think it would have done you any good,' said Betty dispassionately. 'Some people develop as far as they are ever likely to go on their own lines and others need the extra stimulus. You would always be just the same and college would have been wasted. In my case I am very much repressed at home, and college will probably develop my personality. I admit that it is in a way a waste of time, and I could learn in one year what they spread over three, but that can't be helped.'

While Betty discussed her own personality Margaret was able to wonder exactly what Betty meant by being repressed. She had never seen a family suffering less from repressions than the Deans, and wondered how Betty would like to have to live at Lamb's Piece, and what it would be like to exchange mothers, but remembering that to have Mrs Dean for a mother would make her Laurence's sister, she dismissed the thought at once. Her attention was recalled by the sound of Laurence's name.

'Of course,' Betty was saying, 'Laurence is a good example of repressions. He wanted to be a musician, but my father wanted him to go into the business. As you have probably noticed, he is always playing his little guitar. It is a kind of release.'

Margaret's heart melted at the thought of Laurence, his soul in music, his body in the office, solacing himself with an occasional chord on the guitar. No wonder he was rather thoughtless with such turmoil in his being. And she had thought him so happy.

'If he'd gone in for music,' Betty continued, 'he would probably have met some Real woman. Laurence ought to have been married by now, or at least engaged, but the kind of society girls he goes about with are not what he needs, and he has never thought seriously of one of them. He is an example of an extremely unhappy man, ruined by repressions, but unluckily he does not realise it.'

Margaret said wasn't it a good thing perhaps that Laurence didn't know how unhappy he was, as it might make him unhappy, but Betty inclined to the sterner view that if he knew how unhappy he was it would do him good, and he would be better able to release himself.

'Any form of drama sublimates unhappiness,' she said. 'If only Laurence realised his own unhappiness he could pour it all into Hippolytus.'

'Could I sublimate unhappiness into Phaedra?' asked Margaret timidly.

'Of course, if you had anything to be unhappy about,' said Betty. 'Now, if Aunt Louise had let *me* do Phaedra—'

She stopped, remembering that Margaret was doing the part, unaccountably feeling sorry for her and not wanting to hurt her feelings.

'I do wish you were doing Phaedra,' said Margaret truthfully. 'I'm only doing it because Mummy and Mrs Palmer wanted me to. I'd really much rather not. Couldn't I retire and you do it?'

'That is very nice of you,' said Betty, in one of her human outbursts, 'and I'd accept at once, but it would mean such a rumpus with Aunt Palmer that one could hardly sublimate it into the part. But if you did get ill or anything,' she added hopefully, 'I know the part backwards, and I've been to all the rehearsals, and Dr Thomas has given me the most wonderful coaching.'

They pursued their way in silence, Margaret thinking how noble it was of Laurence never to have thought seriously of any of the girls he knew, Betty indulging in a mad hope that Margaret might have a slight and painless illness before the performance. When they got to the large Dipping Pond, Susan and Robin flung off their scanty upper garments and appeared in bathing things. Margaret and Betty found a hawthorn brake to undress in. Mr Fanshawe suddenly felt very old and said he wouldn't bathe, turning a deaf ear to the reproaches of the young Deans. Susan and Robin, who had brought a collapsible rubber ball, blew it up and organised a game of water polo. The air was thick with shrieks in no time, the water thick with churned-up mud, and Margaret the heart-broken and Betty the repressed screamed and splashed as violently as any. Mr Fanshawe, accustomed to the voices of the athletic young, stretched out his long legs and went to sleep on the bank. Presently, through his sleep, he was conscious of someone near him. He opened his eyes and became aware of the curate in a speckled hat, looking down at him.

'Am I intruding?' asked Mr Moxon.

'Not at all. The water polo-party are in the pond. I am here. Will you smoke?'

Mr Moxon said that if Mr Fanshawe didn't mind he would prefer his pipe. Though he had no prejudice himself against cigarettes, he considered a pipe more manly and an example less likely to be followed by his Boys. He added that he dared say Mr Fanshawe was wondering what brought him to this spot.

'Not to share Actaeon's fate, I hope,' said Mr Fanshawe, courteously indicating the bathers.

Mr Moxon laughed understandingly, and said he had

been choosing a course for the Scouts' paper chase on Saturday, and hearing voices had approached. He regretted that he had not his bathing things with him when he saw the young people enjoying themselves.

'Take mine,' said Mr Fanshawe.

Mr Moxon, with great presence of mind, thanked him, but said the chance of a talk with Mr Fanshawe was too valuable to waste. He would like Mr Fanshawe's considered advice. He had heard that there was to be a very good curacy vacant at Clacton-on-Sea. He felt that Worsted, much as he loved that old-world place and the dear people and that real saint, Dr Thomas, hardly gave him enough scope. Had Mr Fanshawe any idea whether Clacton-on-Sea was the sort of place where there would be opportunities for fellowship. He would have hesitated to trouble Mr Fanshawe on so slight a matter, had he not known that his experience in helping men younger than himself was very great, which emboldened him, he said, to approach Mr Fanshawe.

When Charles was able to get a word in he said that judging by his only experience of Clacton, a day's visit some years ago to see into a piece of college business, a visit which had unfortunately coincided with three very long excursion trains packed from end to end, it was his considered opinion that Clacton offered boundless opportunities for fellowship, opportunities which today would be, if possible, even more boundless than ever. He also thought, but did not say, with some satisfaction, that Clacton was a very long way from Worsted. Mr Moxon thanked him very much and professed to be considerably easier in his mind.

The water polo had now come to an end, owing to a leak in the ball, and the players came out. As soon as Susan and Robin caught sight of the curate they snatched up their clothes and rushed away, while Margaret and Betty, feeling too grown-up to follow their excellent example, came to greet the unwelcome addition to the party.

'It will be extremely embarrassing for Mr Moxon if you dress here,' said Mr Fanshawe, taking a malign pleasure himself in embarrassing the curate, 'so he and I will walk slowly on towards the bus and wait for you there.'

When he and the curate got to the crossroads they found Susan and Robin already sitting in the bus, a ramshackle little affair that ran backwards and forwards, for no particular reason, between Worsted and the Ram and Twins, a small public-house on the edge of the forest. The bus was not yet due to start on its homeward journey to Worsted, so the driver, who is also conductor and owner, was talking to a friend outside the Ram. Mr Moxon, scenting fellowship, detached himself from Mr Fanshawe and approached the men. The driver nudged his friend and both attempted to escape, but Mr Moxon was too quick for them and had a hearty conversation about cricket. In this conversation Jim Pollett, the driver, took part with sulky resignation, but the friend very basely became a prey to dumb forgetfulness, and was no help at all. Presently Jim Pollett strolled over to the bus. As he took his seat he made a hideous face at Robin, expressive of contempt for the lower clergy, at which both Robin and Susan grimaced horribly in the direction of the unconscious curate.

'I should laugh if the Reverend got left behind,' said Jim,

preparing to start the bus. 'Four fifty-seven now. Let's call it five o'clock.'

'Good egg,' said Robin appreciatively. 'I'd love to see old Moxon haring along with his coat-tails flying.'

'Sorry, Jim, you'll have to wait,' said Susan. 'My sister and Miss Tebben are coming. Hang on a minute, they won't be long.'

Jim nodded. At this moment Mr Moxon got into the bus and sat as near Mr Fanshawe as possible, evidently with the intention of resuming their helpful talk about Clacton, but Jim Pollett, starting his engine vengefully, caused the bus so to shake and rattle and to make such explosive noises that the passengers were bounced about in their seats and conversation became impossible. Margaret and Betty came out of the wood and got into the bus, and Jim started.

'I say,' shouted Robin to Susan, 'I've got a jolly good idea. I'd put the old League of Nations in this bus and not let them get out till they'd settled everything. I bet that would stop them talking.'

This novel view of a well-meaning body so interested Mr Fanshawe that he was about to ask, though doubtful of his own powers of out-roaring the engine, for a further exposition of Robin's ideas, when Mr Moxon, his face grim with indignation, intervened.

'Hardly can I credit,' he began, when Jim, suddenly going into low gear as they climbed the very steep winding road marked 'Narrow and Dangerous', made the bus leap forward with such a shattering roar that though Mr Moxon did indeed go on angrily opening and shutting his mouth, no one could hear what he said.

By the time that speech was again possible Susan and Robin were playing tennis across the bus with Robin's damp bathing-suit as a ball, and in a few moments the bus stopped at the gate of Lamb's Piece. Passengers usually paid their fares on alighting, and if Jim had not enough change, or they had forgotten their purses, they paid him next time they used the bus. The bathing-party got out and Mr Fanshawe felt in his pocket for some money.

'You are all coming in to tea, aren't you?' asked Margaret. To everyone's horror, Mr Moxon took the invitation as including himself, and bearing no malice, also got out of the bus.

'One more fare, please,' said Mr Fanshawe to Jim.

Mr Moxon said he must protest. Mr Fanshawe paid the fare, and Jim went off with a final wink at Robin.

'Welcome, welcome,' said Mrs Tebben as the party came in. 'Margaret dear, will you see if Mrs Phipps has left the kettle on. I am afraid it is rather a Monday-ish tea, but I told Mrs Phipps to make some of those little cakes we like so much and use up a few currants that were left over. I don't think you've been here before, Mr Moxon.'

Mr Moxon asked if this was where Mrs Tebben worked. Mrs Tebben said Yes, if you could call pot-boiling work. Mr Moxon said he had never read any of Mrs Tebben's books, but would now at once get one from the library.

'They aren't novels,' said Betty. 'They're textbooks on economic sociology. They only cost one and six, so you could easily buy one.'

Mr Moxon made a joke about church mice. Betty and Robin obtrusively exchanged looks of contempt, and made much of Gunnar. Mr Tebben was then summoned to tea. He was not enjoying his holiday very much, but when he saw Mr Fanshawe he cheered up, and as soon as they had drunk a cup of tea he carried him off to his study, there to get at the bottom of the ex-Bursar's history. Mr Moxon chatted gaily to Mrs Tebben and Margaret about the play, while Betty, Susan and Robin sat in hostile silence. Mr Moxon, while admitting whole-heartedly that Mrs Palmer was an inspired producer, said there were one or two little things on which he could perhaps have given expert advice, had he been asked. When he and his East End Boys did the *Hippolytus*, a shortened version of which he himself had arranged, in Epping Forest, they greatly increased the value of the henchman's part by making him come running from a great distance to tell Theseus the tidings of his son's death. Mrs Tebben could hardly imagine, he said, the tension among the audience, splendid boys whose families were in the most appalling state of destitution, when the henchman was seen approaching from the direction of the Chigwell Road, heavy with Doom. Mrs Tebben said that a barn was of course not so big as Epping Forest. Mr Moxon said no, of course not, by any means, but if the henchman came running, say from the old potting shed across the back drive into the barn, it would greatly heighten the effect.

'I quite know what you mean,' said Mrs Tebben. 'Doom. We did try that one year with *As You Like It*, though that was not so much for doom as for pastoral effect, but we found that as soon as anyone had to run they forgot their words and had no breath. It is difficult enough for them to remember what they are saying in any case. I fear it would be impracticable.'

Mr Moxon said that, without wishing to criticise, the feeling of Doom was hardly pronounced enough in Mrs Palmer's production. When he produced *Hippolytus* the feeling of Doom had been so strong that one of his Boys, a very clever and sensitive little Jew with a crooked spine, had to be withdrawn from the cast, because of his inclination to epileptic fits.

'I could see the boy from where I lay,' said Mr Moxon, 'literally trembling from head to foot with the feeling of Doom.'

'I expect he was going to throw a fit,' said Robin, suddenly taking an interest. 'I wish I could have seen him. When people have epileptic fits you have to put corks in their mouths or else they bite their tongues off. There's a boy at school called Morland and his mother's cook had an uncle that bit the tip of his tongue right off and they kept it in a bottle. I wish I could see it.'

'Were you acting Hippolytus yourself then, if you were lying down?' asked Margaret hastily.

Mr Moxon smiled modestly, with all his teeth.

'The real Hippolytus was my second-in-command, a splendid young fellow, the son of an undertaker. He trained the Boys to carry him on a stretcher which his father very kindly lent, and one of them was apprenticed to the business in consequence. But if he had any urgent work, I took his place, I hope not unworthily. Ah! I could still say every line of the part even now. Wonderful old Euripides!'

As Margaret could see that Robin was bursting to ask

231

about the undertaker's work, and probably to contribute items of general interest about embalming, she plunged into the conversation again, by saying what a pity it was that Mrs Palmer didn't know he knew the part, as then he might have done it alternately with Laurence. Mr Moxon looked gratified and said they had but to call on him if need were. Returning to the question of Doom, how remarkable, he said, was the character of Phaedra as presented by Euripides. Here we had a woman of untamed nature whose passions, he said, lowering his voice because of Robin, could not be called guilty because she was Doomed to be unhappy.

'There,' said Betty, 'you are perfectly right.'

'Please, Mrs Tebben, can I put the wireless on for the cricket news?' asked Robin. 'I'll only do it gently.'

While Robin and Susan listened to county cricket, Mr Moxon and Betty, for a brief moment in agreement, discussed Phaedra, with several references to the original Greek. Insensibly their voices rose in argument as Robin abstractedly turned the wireless on louder, and Margaret was heartily glad when Mr Fanshawe came in and summoned his young charges home. When she had seen them all off she came back to the drawing-room to turn the wireless off. A record of dance music was being played and Margaret suddenly felt very sad and neglected. She turned the music lower and its sad throbbing made a background for melancholy thoughts. If Laurence did not come and find her, how could she ever tell him what she thought of him, or find out what he really thought of her. Her conscience smote her for having been both priggish and unkind. As she slowly turned the knob and the dance music gently melted away, she felt it was an allegory of her life; joy and pleasure departing, nothing to come. Her father was still in great difficulties over his lecture, so she went and did some typewriting for him, but whenever she came to the word 'Outlaw', or 'Outlawry', it made her think of Laurence, who was an outlaw from her heart; a conceit which blurred the page before her eyes.

9

Rehearsal with Catastrophe

Tuesday passed uneventfully. Jessica got up and the hospital nurse left, much to Nanny's satisfaction. As Jessica was not to ride for a few days Richard was free to go on with his secret plan, and he and Helen were out from after breakfast to nearly dinner-time. Mr Fanshawe heard them arranging for another expedition on Wednesday and did his best not to think of it.

'I think I'll have to leave you on Thursday,' he said to Rachel.

'Oh, but why? I thought you were staying another week at least.'

'So did I. But I have done my good deed and made you have a little sense, and now is a good moment to make an effective exit.'

'Helen will be disappointed. She wants to have that long tramp with you.'

'She could take Richard instead,' said Mr Fanshawe quite

naturally, and thanking heaven that Rachel was not very observant.

'So she could. But it wouldn't be the same thing,' with which poor comfort Charles had to be content.

Wednesday came. Mrs Palmer telephoned at intervals during the day to remind the Deans that the dress rehearsal was at a quarter to eight and that she particularly wanted all the performers there by seven. All day she and Mrs Tebben had been working at the dresses and receiving reports at intervals from Mrs Phipps about Doris's condition. To her mother's great pride she had become hysterical again, and had giggled so uncontrollably in the Dower House kitchen that the cook had spoken sharply to her and made her cry.

'I can't blame Mrs Dean's cook,' said Mrs Palmer to the outraged Mrs Phipps. 'You know what Doris is, Mrs Phipps, when she's like that. But if she comes in with a red nose and swollen eyes it won't be much help. Winifred, where is Theseus's fillet?'

'I put it in his left boot, so that it wouldn't be lost. Oh, there is Sparrow with a telegram. I hope it isn't for me,' said Mrs Tebben, to whom telegrams still meant death or disablement for all her dearest.

'It's from Lucasta Bond,' said Mrs Palmer. 'She wants to come to the rehearsal and bring her son. The wire was sent from London, so I suppose she is coming down and sent it before she started. Sparrow, send a telegram to Staple Park and say I'll be delighted to see Lady Bond and Mr Bond. Why they don't have a telephone I don't know. She might at least have made it Reply Paid. Which boot did you say, Winifred?'

235

'The right; or else the left. I know I put it in one of them. You ought to stop, Louise. You look tired.'

'What time is it? Five o'clock? Good gracious, I'd no idea. Winifred, I'll send you home in the car, and mind you get a good rest. If you don't mind picking up Dr Thomas on the way I'll send the car again to fetch you at half-past seven. I did want you at seven, but it can't be helped. You and Margaret can dress quickly.'

The car took Mrs Tebben home and was just turning in the little space before the house when another car was heard hooting outside. A small four-seater came down the drive and in the car sat Richard and Helen. The small car appeared to take fright on seeing Mrs Palmer's large car, but quickly recovering itself it drew up with its front wheels in the flower-bed, leaving room for Mrs Palmer's car to finish turning and go out.

'How nice of you to bring Richard back,' said Mrs Tebben. 'Richard, you must hurry. The performers and chorus are called for seven o'clock. I'm not going till half-past because Louise is sending the car for me and Margaret, but she wants you there at seven.'

'No need for Mrs Palmer to send her car,' said Richard off-handedly. 'I'll run you up.'

Mrs Tebben looked at her son uncomprehendingly.

'Father,' called Richard, putting his head in at the front door, 'Father, do come and see. It's important.'

Mr Tebben came out.

'What is it, Richard?' he asked, rather peevishly. 'I am trying to get that lecture finished.'

'Well, Gilbert dear,' said Mrs Tebben, 'we'll have to have

236

supper early if you don't mind, because Richard and Margaret and I have to get to the barn early. Margaret and I are going in Louise's car, which she is sending for us at half-past seven, but Richard will have to walk or bicycle as he has to be there at seven. So early supper. Or as it's hot we can have it cold when we come in if you like. Or perhaps just a kind of high tea, boiled eggs and coffee, at a quarter-past six and then some paste sandwiches when we come in. I could tell Mrs Phipps to wrap them up in a damp napkin to keep them moist.'

'But Mother, do listen one moment—'

'I am, dear boy, I am, but I'm sure Helen wants to go. You can tell me whatever it is afterwards. Is that a new car you are driving, Helen?'

'Oh, Mother, do stop fussing,' said Richard. Then making a valiant effort to master his irritation he said, addressing his parents, 'It's really for you. Helen helped me to choose it second-hand and it's awfully cheap and in quite good condition, she says. And she is in with the police and we got my driving licence fixed up and I've been driving all today, and it didn't go so badly, did it, Helen?'

'Quite well,' said the expert. 'You needn't be afraid to go with him, Mrs Tebben.'

'But is it really yours?' asked his father.

'Well, I bought it with some of the Palmers' cheque. I thought it would be nice for me to take you and Mother in sometimes. Nicer than Modestine anyway, when it's raining.'

'But my dear boy,' said his mother, more touched than she would admit but more than ever her anxious, well-meaning self, 'the upkeep!'

'It's all right, Mother. It does about forty to the gallon. It's a wonder. I'll run you and Margaret up for the rehearsal and come back for Father. Mrs Palmer doesn't really need me for the chorus, as they don't come on at the beginning.'

'Did you really think of us?' asked Mr Tebben. 'You shouldn't have done it, Richard. We do very well with Modestine.'

Richard, knowing that his father would be constitutionally unable to express gratitude till he had first examined all the possible reasons against having a car, kept his temper admirably.

'I thought it would be nice for you and Mother,' he said again. 'Of course I shall use it if I want to go off anywhere for weekends, but I could run you to the station, or to Winter Overcotes to save changing, or run Mother over to the Manor House. Of course, if I go to London I shall take it, but Margaret can learn to drive and take you about while I'm here.'

'Or I might learn myself,' said Mr Tebben, eagerly.

'Well, you might,' said Richard doubtfully. 'I'm going to run Helen home and then I'll be back here for you.'

With some skill he turned the car and drove off.

'He is a good boy,' said Mr Tebben. 'I wish to goodness he had some work, or that I knew what would become of him.'

'It was extraordinarily generous of the dear boy,' said his mother and both Mr and Mrs Tebben felt deeply moved. That their acceptance of the gift had been in any way ungracious never struck them, just as it would never strike Richard that a car which he proposed to take to London

238

and use for weekends was not wholly for his parents' benefit.

Mr Dean and most of his family were under the mulberry
tree when Richard drove up with Helen. Robin, who first
spotted the new car, came tearing across to see what it was.

'I say, that's a decent little car,' he said. 'Where did you
get her, Helen?'

'She's mine,' said Richard.

'Can you drive her?'

'Yes, Helen taught me.'

'I bet you'll have an accident,' said Robin. 'You have to
have seven accidents before you can drive properly. Can I
drive it?'

'No,' said Helen.

'I say,' said Susan, coming up, 'that's a good little car.
Whose is it?'

'Mine,' said Richard.

'Lucky dog. Can I drive it?'

'Certainly not,' said Helen.

Betty, who felt it beneath her to show any interest in cars,
now strolled up with her father and looked at the car in
silence.

'It's my new car,' said Richard proudly.

'What do you call it?' asked Mr Dean.

Richard hesitated. He wanted to call it Rachel, but so
unusual a name would provoke comment. Everyone then
made more or less ingenious suggestions for a name. Blondel
because of Richard, Minotaur because of the bull, Neddy
the Second from Robin, who had violent giggles at his own

239

wit, were among those put forward. Mr Dean inquired how he got it, and on hearing that it was part of a gift from his sister- and brother-in-law, suggested Palmerston.

'I'll tell you what,' said Susan, 'we'll christen it tomorrow. We'll put all the names into a hat and Jessica shall pull one out and that'll be the one. Make her go, Richard.'

Richard obligingly drove her round the gravel sweep and nearly ran into Mr Fanshawe, who had as usual been walking.

'Sorry, sir,' said Richard, as he put on the brakes so violently that he nearly hit his teeth on the wheel.

'Is that a new animal?' asked Charles Fanshawe.

'Yes, sir. Mr Palmer awfully kindly gave me a present, and I spent a bit of it on this. Would you like to drive it?'

'Even if I did, I couldn't,' said Charles. 'It's very kind of you, but I know nothing about cars.'

'You prefer Shanks's mare, like Mr Moxon, don't you, Charles?' said Helen. 'Richard and I have had a marvellous time today and been all over the world, haven't we?'

'It was ripping,' said Richard, looking at her with an expression of gratitude that Mr Fanshawe found difficult to bear. 'I've never had such a time. Helen was marvellous.'

'Well, so were you,' said Helen. 'I've seldom had a quicker pupil – amateur, I mean. I must rush off and get ready for Aunt Palmer's rehearsal now, but we'll meet again at the barn and tomorrow we'll do another tour.'

'I'm sorry we didn't get our walk,' said Charles to Helen.

'Oh, but we must. What about tomorrow?'

'I thought you were arranging a plan with Richard. Besides, I'm off tomorrow.'

'Oh, Charles! How flat. Don't go. Where are you going?'

'Anywhere,' said Charles, and walked away.

Helen felt chilled. When Richard had asked her to help him to find a good second-hand car and get his driving licence, she had agreed more in the hope of smoothing Laurence's path with the Tebben family than because she wanted to, though it interested her to teach Richard who, from the very beginning of the holidays, had shown a real aptitude for driving. But Richard with his new-found confidence since the affair of the bull was a far more agreeable companion than she had expected. They had had a good deal of fun, first in choosing the car under her professional eye, then in testing it all over the county, but if she had known that Charles was going so soon, Richard could have found his car for himself. She regretted the two or three days she had given to Richard with an intensity that surprised her. Anxiously she considered how she might make amends to Charles, and suddenly thought that if he really had to go the next day, she might suggest a moonlight tramp, a treat to which she knew he was partial. After the rehearsal they could drive to the downs and walk as far as they liked under a moon only just past the full. Charles had vanished, but she determined to ask him at the rehearsal.

There was one very important person who had not yet seen the car.

'Do you think, sir, that Mrs Dean would like to see my car?' Richard said to Mr Dean. 'I'd love her to see it if she isn't tired or anything, and if she likes it perhaps she'd let me take her and Jessica for a run sometime.'

Mr Dean was touched by Richard's thought of Jessica and

knew that Rachel would like to give Richard pleasure. He said he would see where she was and tell her Richard was there. The others had all gone in and Richard was left alone. He sauntered along the front of the house on the grass edge, feeling that life was better than it had been for a long time. That he had been able to do something to help Mrs Dean was almost too good to be true. Then Mr Dean had hinted vaguely at interesting things, and the Palmers had given him that munificent gift. Perhaps from now onwards life would be quite different. He congratulated himself upon having kept his temper with his parents and hoped that he would be given fortitude to continue, or that a miracle would happen and they not be so trying; perhaps both. Reflecting on these things he stood idly by one of the long drawing-room windows and plucked a piece of heliotrope which he smelt with pleasure. From inside the room, he heard the voices of people, invisible behind the thick silk curtains drawn against the afternoon sun.

'Oh, there you are,' said the voice of Mr Dean. 'I thought you were in your sitting-room.'

'No, darling, I was here. Come and talk to me,' said the voice of Mrs Dean.

This was the moment for Richard to move away or make his presence known, but he was arrested by hearing his own name.

'Richard wants to know if you could come and see his new car. Fred gave him a cheque after the affair with the bull, and he has got a little runabout. Helen, I gather, helped him to choose it.'

Now Richard should have spoken, now he should have

gone on noiseless feet across the grass. Now he should have been far away.

'Darling,' said Mrs Dean, in a tone of affection that Richard did not know, that thrilled him to the quick, 'I would so much rather not. I shall never stop being grateful to him about Jessica, but he is so devoted that it is quite trying. It has been bad enough with cricket talk, and if it is to be car talk too, I shall burst. I don't want to seem ungrateful, but if you could tell him that I am dressing for dinner, or anything you like—'

What Mr Dean said in reply Richard did not know for he had fled from the window. This betrayal was far worse than bulls, or examination results. The goddess whom he thought favourably inclined had suddenly sent thunder on his unhappy head. Nothing could disguise the fact that Mrs Dean found him a bore. And this was not the worst. If it had not been for his own despicable and ungentlemanly conduct, he need never have known it. Under the mulberry tree he paused and leant his head against its gnarled trunk. He was now entirely disillusioned and his whole life shattered. His heart's devotion had been at Mrs Dean's feet, and she had found it trying. He would have liked to pick up the despised offering and jauntily carry it elsewhere, but it was too heavy, it weighed him down with unutterable sadness. Besides, he couldn't think of anyone else who would want it. Perhaps he was a failure after all, a miserable young man who slacked at Oxford and didn't try to be nice to his parents, who made a nuisance of himself to the most enchanting person he had ever seen. He had even fancied that if he could get as far as mentioning his feelings to Mrs

Dean, she might lend a not unfavourable ear. But in her few words to her husband he had realised, though the note was new to him, that she loved Mr Dean very much indeed, which made his presumption in caring for her, his ingratitude to Mr Dean, all the greater. Accustomed to his parents' bickering, whose underlying affection, born of difficulties faced together and also of long habit, he did not understand, he had naturally never considered that grown-up married people could go on being in love. Any suggestion of this in his people would have shocked him, but in the Deans, surrounded by wealth and comfort, it seemed a beautiful thing. If he could ever hope to hear anyone speak to him as Mrs Dean had spoken to her husband, thinking they were alone, he could go on living, but trying to consider himself dispassionately, he saw no reason why anyone should look more than once at a lanky young man who hadn't even got a job. Once more he saw Mrs Dean lying in the chair, cloudy violets on her closed lids, and in his misery he made a noise like a groan.

'Hi!' said a voice from above him. 'What's up, Richard? I'm coming down. Look out for mulberries. We got some ripe ones on us this afternoon. It isn't safe to sit under the tree any longer.'

There was a slight crashing and rustling among the branches and Susan, in her bathing dress, jumped down and stood beside him with a basket of mulberries.

'They're ripest on the top,' she explained, 'but one gets everything stained, so I put on my bathing things.'

Richard looked at her. She had evidently been taking toll of the mulberries. Her face was smeared with purple, her arms splashed, her hands incarnadined. He looked at his clothes and saw a large stain on his grey trousers.

'Blast,' he said, pointing to it.

'Oh, that'll clean,' said Susan. 'Anything up? You look all peculiar. It's been a dull day with you and Helen away. Laurence wouldn't stop working and come out. He looks a bit peculiar too. I say, I must hurry. It's old Aunt Palmer's dress rehearsal and she wants me and Robin for audience. Cheer up.'

She hit Richard very hard on the arm in a friendly way, leaving another mulberry stain, and went into the house. Vaguely comforted by her violence, he got into his car, whose radiance was now completely obscured, and drove back. His mother, as usual, was too much absorbed in her own affairs to take much notice of him, and even Margaret, on whom he was relying for sympathy, was absent-minded, and showed a preoccupation which was unlike her. Richard was thankful for his mother's obtuseness, and perhaps it was as well that Margaret shouldn't notice, for what could one say to her? Only two days ago he had confided to her his exquisite secret. How could he now tell her what had happened? How could he explain without letting her jump to the conclusion that Mrs Dean was a monster in disguise? For a moment, in self-defence, he wondered if Mrs Dean were a little selfish, but put the thought resolutely away. After all it was entirely his own fault for eavesdropping. He hadn't been a gentleman, and this was his immediate punishment. It might be best to know the truth, but truth was bitter, so bitter that he made another groaning noise. Luckily his mother and Margaret, whom he was driving to the rehearsal, thought it was his anxiety over his new car, and took no notice. He dropped them at the barn and went back to fetch his father.

The barn was being arranged for the performances which were to take place once on Friday and twice on Saturday. Chairs were already placed, and some of the scouts were fastening numbers on them. Mr Moxon, in an unclerical flannel shirt, was superintending them, and lightening their labours by giving them something to laugh at when his back was turned. From behind the scenes came a confused noise of people losing their sandals and borrowing one another's safety-pins. Mrs Palmer had snatched a cup of tea when Mrs Tebben left her, and since then had been hard at work, overlooking the wardrobe and dressing the chorus as they arrived.

The heat was overpowering in the dressing-rooms. The basin was leaking again, and Doris Phipps had arrived with a blotched, scarlet face and neck, the result of a beautifying lotion recommended by Mrs Dean's second housemaid. Mrs Palmer's temper, deeply tried by her relations, had been fraying all day, and was now rapidly ravelling into nothing.

'Very well, Doris,' she said, when the tearful kitchen-maid was brought by her mother to be inspected, 'I hope this will teach you to leave beauty creams alone.'

'That's what I tell her,' said Mrs Phipps. 'I don't know what her dad'll say when he sees her. If I'd messed my face about like that when I was a girl, my dad'd have had the strap to me.'

'Well, now it's done,' said Mrs Palmer. 'I shall have to put white lotion and powder on, that's all, and if you touch that rubbish again before the performance, Doris, I'll read your part myself.'

'There you are,' said Mrs Phipps to her daughter with gloomy satisfaction. 'You just hark to Mrs Palmer, Dawris.'

'And if you cry any more I'll give you sal volatile,' continued Mrs Palmer. 'Put your dress on and then come to me.'

Doris, subdued by the threat of sal volatile, which she conceived to be some form of corporal punishment, withdrew to get dressed.

'Well, Louise, here we come with our sheaves!' said Mrs Tebben, entering with a flourish.

'Have you seen Doris Phipps's sheaves?' asked Mrs Palmer. 'That little fool has been trying to beautify herself, and has red spots all over her face in consequence. I shall cover her with powder, even if she gets skin disease and dies of it. But how did you get here, Winifred? I was going to send the car for you.'

'My dear!' said Mrs Tebben dramatically, 'that foolish boy of mine, with part of the gift that you and Fred so nobly sent him, and for which I do hope he adequately thanked you, has bought a small second-hand car. I can't tell you what Gilbert and I felt when he said he got it thinking of us, and though I shall still use Modestine a great deal, it will be the greatest help to have the car for wet days. He drives beautifully already, and he ran Margaret and me here in no time, and has gone back to fetch his father.'

'That's all very nice, Winifred, but you might have remembered that the car was coming. If you had let me know it could have gone straight to Dr Thomas instead of wasting time going to you when you aren't there. I might catch it now before it starts.' She walked onto the stage and parted the curtains. 'Ernie! Ernie Phipps!' she called. Ernie in his scout uniform came smartly up to the platform.

'Ernie, run and find my chauffeur and tell him not to go to Mrs Tebben's, only to the Rectory and hurry up.'

'Is there anything my Boys can do for you?' asked Mr Moxon, coming up. 'We are all ready for our good deed you know. Ernie, where are you off to?'

'He is going on a message for me,' said Mrs Palmer.

'Quite right. We aim at service,' said Mr Moxon as if he were advertising a large department store, 'but discipline, Mrs Palmer, discipline. All my Boys take their orders through me. What are you to do, Phipps?'

'Tell Mrs Palmer's chauffeur not to go to the Rectory.'

'No, Ernie,' said Mrs Palmer. 'Listen. Tell the chauffeur to GO to the Rectory and NOT to go to Mrs Tebben. Now don't dawdle. Thank you for your good deed, Mr Moxon. Those boys understand nothing till you tell them twice.'

She went back to the dressing-room where Mrs Tebben and Margaret were nearly dressed.

'I've sent Ernie to tell my man to go straight to the Rectory,' she said. 'Heaven knows how the message will reach him, but I've done my best. I do wish you had let me know, Winifred. I'm run off my feet as it is, without having that fool Moxon interfering.'

'Well, Louise, I forgot. I simply forgot,' said Mrs Tebben. 'What with one thing and another I forgot. I'm sorry. I thought it would be cooler this evening, so I put on a thin long-sleeved vest, but I can easily turn the sleeves up.

Margaret dear, just pin my vest up, will you? That's better. I dare say it wouldn't matter at rehearsal, but it's the *spirit*. And now I think it's going to be hotter.'

Mrs Tebben was by now mobled in grey veils and draperies, and looked exactly like a person who was going to act in a Greek play. Margaret was oppressed and self-conscious in her white robes. She realised acutely that she was no actress, and that the most she could hope for was to speak her lines clearly and correctly and not disgrace herself. It was going to be horrid to say Phaedra's part, because it was all about being in love with Hippolytus, and goodness knew she wasn't in love with Laurence. Being only a play made it different, of course, but being amateurs made it worse. If one were a real actress it wouldn't matter what one said, but the whole village would hear Miss Tebben making very passionate and unladylike remarks about young Mr Dean. And then Hippolytus would make very rude cold-blooded remarks about Phaedra, and though she knew it was all a play and very improbable at that, she would not enjoy hearing young Mr Dean announcing to the world his indifference to Miss Tebben. One could always take refuge in the dressing-room, or go right out of the barn into the rickyard, but people might wonder where one was, or Mrs Palmer might be annoyed, or one might be late for one's entrance. Besides, even if one hated Laurence, one must in fairness admit that he spoke very well, and there was something so endearing about the way his hair grew at the back of his neck.

She went out onto the platform and looked through the curtain. The favoured people who had been invited to the dress rehearsal were assembling. Miss Thomas and Miss Dolly were settling their father in comfort before dressing for their parts. Miss Thomas had brought her father's special detestation, the little black knob to put into his ear, connected by a thin wire to a small black box, held in the hand, placed on the table, or slipped into a capacious pocket, that was supposed to help him to hear.

'You'll hear better if you use it, Father,' said Miss Thomas, thrusting the little box at him.

'Take it away,' said Dr Thomas, suddenly asserting himself. 'I may be a little deaf occasionally, and would be less deaf if people didn't mumble, but a machine like that is an insult to humanity. Besides our dear Betty speaks beautifully. I can always hear every word she says.'

'But Betty isn't acting, Father,' said Miss Dolly.

'I can't hear you,' said her father.

'Father's wonderful,' said Miss Dolly proudly to Mrs Dean, who had come to sit with the Rector. 'Once he gets an idea into his head nothing will get it out. He thinks Betty is going to act Phaedra. We must be off now and dress, Mrs Dean. Don't let Father be too much for you, the dear old soul.'

Of the rest of the Dower House party Margaret could see no sign. She was just going back to the dressing-room when Robin careered onto the stage.

'I say, have you seen Ed?' he inquired. 'Richard's car has stuck in the back drive and no one can get it to move.'

'Why don't you get Helen?'

'Oh, she's dressing, and Aunt Palmer hooshed me out.'

'Try the men's dressing-room.'

Robin careered away again. In the men's room he found Bert and Ed preparing to get into their Greek tunics. Luckily they hadn't got further than shirt sleeves and were able to accompany Robin to where, within sight of the barn, Richard's car had stopped in the narrow road, holding up Lady Bond's and several other cars. Mr Tebben was giving ignorant advice, while Richard, vainly fumbling with knobs and handles, was getting every moment more nervous and annoyed.

'I say, Helen's dressing,' shouted Robin, 'but I found Ed. He'll do it.'

'That's okay, Mr Richard,' said Bert, 'Ed'll do it. He's a wonder with cars, aren't you, Ed?'

A corroborative murmur came from the audience who had been enjoying Richard's discomfiture, though in no unkindly spirit, some saying that Ed would do it, others that Ed was a wonder with cars.

'Come on, Ed,' said Bert, 'make her move, and then we'll go and say your line.'

Thus kindly encouraged Ed opened the bonnet, made a swift examination with fingers in which all his woolgathering wits seemed to be concentrated, got into the driving seat, and with no effort made the car move on to the barn, backed it, and parked it among the cars of the other performers.

'Thanks awfully, Ed,' said Richard gratefully. 'You're a marvel. What was wrong?'

Ed, pleased to be famous, explained at length to Richard and the bystanders exactly what had happened. The Hon. C. W. Bond, who had been parking his mother's car, strolled over to join in the discussion. In him Ed found an intellectual equal, and technicalities flew to and fro. But just as the Hon. C. W. Bond was elaborating a plan by which Ed should come down the line to Skeynes after work and see the new tractor, Mrs Palmer's voice was heard.

'What are you all doing?' said she, scattering the group. 'Bert and Ed, get dressed at once. It's a quarter to eight already and we ought to be beginning. Richard, I want you to sit at the very back of the hall and tell me how the chorus sounds. Oh, Mr Bond, how do you do? Your mother is waiting for you in the barn.'

'I'm very well, thank you,' said Mr Bond. 'I do want to see your *Hippolytus*. I did it myself last year at Oxford.'

'And Laurence hasn't turned up yet,' said Mrs Palmer to Richard, ignoring her old enemy's son, who went off to join his mother. 'And Doris has only just stopped crying, and I'm not even dressed myself. Tell everyone we shan't be long now. I will never do another play again, if people can't take it seriously.'

She hastened back to the stage, where her husband met her.

'That basin's still leaking, Louise,' he said, 'still leaking. I went round to look and it's as bad as ever. Where's Bert? I want to tell him to let his father know that he must send up at once and have it put right.'

With very little ceremony Mrs Palmer gave her husband to understand that Bert was even now changing into his costume, or she hoped he was, that she herself was on the verge of a breakdown and that the basin would have to wait.

'Well, I'll go and talk to Lady Bond,' said Mr Palmer. 'Ask

her what Bond thinks of his Root Vegetables Bill now. I expect he wishes he had left it alone since the by-election. I could have told him exactly what would happen. By the way, Louise—'

But his wife had gone, so he went down into the hall and sat between his sister and Lady Bond.

Margaret, finding the dressing-room very full and stuffy, came out onto the stage again. The sunlight was beginning to come in shafts through the open side of the stage, and a golden ray touched her as she stood disconsolately against the white pedestal on which Doris was to stand. Laurence, who had dressed at home and driven himself over, came across the rickyard in his hunter's tunic and cloak, carrying a spear and the green wreath which he was to place on the altar of Artemis. He saw Margaret, no passionate Phaedra, but a girl, perplexed and tired at heart, drooping against the pillar. Margaret looked up at the sound of footsteps and saw Laurence, a glory of sun about him, dazzling her eyes. Their hearts leapt. Self-consciousness claimed them both.

'Oh, I think Mrs Palmer is asking for you,' she said, holding a hand above her eyes to shade them from the level beams of light. How was it possible that Phaedra should not have been consumed by her desire for Hippolytus?

'I expect she is,' said Laurence, 'but Aunt Palmer can wait a moment. Here am I, dressed all exquisitely in white with my nosegay in my hand, and not even a chorus to greet me. What's the world coming to?'

(You are not Phaedra, you are chill Artemis whom I worship. If I weren't rigid with fear of annoying you again, I'd go down on my knees and lay my garland at your feet.)

'You look very nice,' said Margaret feebly.

'Not bad,' said Laurence, 'a bit hairy about the legs, but I dare say the Greeks were a hairy lot. I like all your white draperies and whatnots.'

'I wish I weren't doing it,' said Margaret.

(To say I love Hippolytus is like showing my heart to the world.)

'Oh, you'll be all right. I don't much fancy lying on that hard stage for half an hour while Pollett forgets his part.'

(To die for you, especially if one could do it as Hippolytus always does, with not a hair out of place, might be a blissful pain worth enduring.)

There was a pause in which Mrs Palmer could be heard mustering the chorus of huntsmen. Desperately Laurence approached his love, his face suddenly assuming the haggard look that so tore her heart.

'I say, Margaret, you didn't take it all too seriously, did you?' he inquired anxiously.

Margaret felt her heart leap and fall with sickening violence. As she had at times surmised, Laurence had only proposed to her because of those cocktails. He was sorry for what he had said and wanted to get out of it. He should get out of it; and she would somehow get through the evening and then run away, go to the flat in London, find a job, go back to Grenoble where her French family would be glad of her help.

'Seriously?' she said. 'Of course not. No one takes proposals seriously at midnight. I'm afraid it is you that are serious. Have you actually been worrying? I'd forgotten the whole affair.' And she managed a creditable imitation of a laugh.

'My God, I didn't mean that, Margaret, you know I didn't. The proposal holds good till doomsday, and you know it.'

'But I don't,' said Margaret, weak from the incredible lightening of her heart's sorrow, hardly knowing what she said.

'Margaret, enchanted bird, it's everything and for ever. Oh, must I say it again? Damn these clothes. How the ancient Greeks ever did anything in yards of sheeting I don't know. If I could get my arms out of this foul cloak . . .'

He dropped the spear and wreath, threw his cloak angrily back from his shoulders and advanced on Margaret. In a moment she would have been in his arms, had not Mrs Palmer appeared at the back of the stage.

'Oh, there you are, Laurence,' she said, in a voice of final exacerbation. 'Do you mind picking up your things and going behind? I have to get Aphrodite in her place. We are nearly half an hour late already. Margaret, you'd better wait a minute.'

Laurence, with a conspirator's look at Margaret, disappeared. Doris Phipps, looking very effective with her face heavily whitened, took her place on the pedestal, too frightened even to giggle.

'Keep absolutely still when the curtain goes up and don't start your lines till you see me nod my head at you from the side,' said Mrs Palmer. 'Now, Margaret, you go behind, and I must ask you,' she said following Margaret off the stage, 'not to interfere with Laurence any more this evening. He was late to start with, and you kept him there while I was sending everywhere to look for him. There has been too much of this sort of thing, and if your mother realised how you are behaving she would be as annoyed as I am. I must say I was surprised at the way you and Laurence were behaving at her dinner party, and thoroughly ashamed.'

Even as Mrs Palmer spoke, she knew she was being unjust. The heat, the long hours, the countless irritations of the amateur producer, the reaction from Sunday's alarm, Doris's hysterics, Mr Moxon's interference, her husband's concern about the basin, the insubordination of Bert and Ed, all had come to a head at an unlucky hour, and Margaret was at hand. It would have given Mrs Palmer great satisfaction to go working herself up as an outlet for her general annoyance, but she was uneasily afraid that she had already gone too far. Margaret looked at her with expressionless eyes and went into the dressing-room. Mrs Palmer could not waste any more time. She gave the signal, the curtains were drawn aside and Doris, her own permanent golden curls shining above her white face and draperies, evoked a buzz of appreciation from the audience. After some seconds Doris cast an agonised eye in Mrs Palmer's direction, Mrs Palmer nodded, and Doris began, quaveringly at first, but with more assurance as she realised that all the people in the barn were looking at her with admiration, to go through her part.

Mrs Palmer was beginning to breathe again, Doris was half-way through her speech, when Margaret appeared from the dressing-room in her ordinary clothes, carrying a white bundle.

'I can't act, Mrs Palmer,' she said, laying the bundle on the floor. 'Betty will be very glad to do Phaedra.'

256

She vanished. Mrs Palmer stood frozen, and so uncomfortable that even her spirit had to own it quailed. Margaret's entirely unexpected rebellion roused a thousand questionings and doubts in her. There was no time for repentance or restitution. That would come later, but now the rehearsal must go on. She saw Doris falter for a moment in her speech and look with more than a goddess's interest at the audience. Doris had seen Miss Tebben, who was all dressed up to say her lines a minute ago, come into the barn in her day dress and make signs to Miss Betty, who had got up and gone out. Reflecting that the sooner she was off the stage, the sooner she would know what was happening, Doris got through the rest of her part with ever hastening tempo and made her exit. As she went out, she passed Mr Laurence, followed by Bert and Ed and the rest of the hunters, Mr Laurence looking nearly as nice as Ben Hur. Bert, by a well-placed witticism, made her giggle so much that Mrs Phipps, who had been hovering about watchfully, took her off to the dressing-room, made her drink the sal volatile supplied by Mrs Palmer, and then sent her off home to get her dad's supper, saying there was no sense in wasting her holiday if Mrs Dean didn't want her back till half-past ten.

Hippolytus and the huntsmen were already grouped round the altar of Artemis when Mrs Palmer became aware of Betty.

'Margaret says she can't act,' said her niece. 'I don't know what's up. She says I'm to do Phaedra. Are these the things?'

She picked up the bundle and went behind, where she found Helen, slinging Artemis's quiver over her shoulder.

'Give me a hand, Helen,' she said. 'I've to do Phaedra. Margaret says she can't act, and I can't make out what's up. It's something to do with Aunt Palmer, but what I don't know.'

Helen began to wonder, as she helped Betty to robe herself, but could do no more than guess. She could not question Mrs Palmer, who was even now marshalling her women to lead them on. Mrs Tebben came in anxiously.

'Is Margaret here?' she asked, 'it's time for her to be ready. We have to go on together.'

'Oh, Margaret asked me to do it,' said Betty. 'She said she couldn't act tonight, but you weren't to worry. She didn't look ill or anything. Will you show me, Mrs Tebben, how we go when we come on? After that I know what to do.'

Mrs Tebben was uneasy, but there was no time for questions. The chorus had made their pause, indicative of doom. Mrs Palmer's voice was heard, heralding the approach of the Queen and the Nurse, and Betty, leaning on Mrs Tebben's arm, took the stage.

'How noble dear Betty looks,' said Dr Thomas, proudly, to Mrs Dean. 'Why did Dolly say she wasn't acting?'

'Betty?' asked Mrs Dean.

It was indeed her second daughter, looking incredibly handsome. On the stage and at a distance, her dark hair and heavy eyebrows, her rather large mouth, her statuesque build, told admirably. She was managing her draperies as to the manner born, and her clear delivery had an assurance to which Margaret was a stranger, and quite as much passion as was suitable for eighteen. Dr Thomas surreptitiously put on his acoustic machine and listened with unfeigned pleasure. Mr Moxon tried to express his enthusiasm to his Rector, and was frowned down and silenced. Mr and Mrs Dean and Mr Fanshawe, though a little perplexed, were astounded at the metamorphosis of Betty and full of admiration. Lady Bond asked Mr Palmer who she was. Her son whispered to Richard that he had never thought a Phaedra could look more tragically handsome than the man who had taken her part in their college performance, but this girl was even better. Richard, interested and surprised, entirely forgot about the chorus, and paid no attention to Mrs Palmer's frenzied signals. Betty, only interested in her part, entirely unaffected by the whispering among the audience, continued very effectively to sublimate herself, enjoying it hugely and carrying Mrs Tebben along with her.

'I am eager to see how Betty will take Hippolytus's entrance,' said Dr Thomas. 'That is a considerable test, but I believe she will rise to it.'

As he spoke, Laurence appeared from the back of the stage. He came forward, turned to face Phaedra and saw Betty. Looking wildly round for Margaret he caught his foot against the altar of Artemis, lost his balance, and fell down the platform steps. He was up in a moment, but had to sit down again with a very white face.

'I'm sorry, Aunt Louise,' he said, while Betty stood suspended in her last words, 'but I'm no good. It's my ankle. Oh, hell!'

For a few moments there was confusion. Mr Dean came quickly from his place, saw that the ankle was badly hurt and Laurence in considerable pain. Richard offered to go for the doctor in his car, an offer which Mr Dean accepted.

'Tell him to go straight to the Dower House, Richard,' he said, 'and I'll bring Laurence. Tell Mrs Dean not to worry. Come along, Laurence, we'll get you to the car. Bond, will you give him an arm?'

Mr Moxon put in a word for his scouts who, he said, would jump at the chance of service, and could make a stretcher from two of their poles and a couple of jackets in no time, and was shouldered away by Mr Bond. Between them he and Mr Dean got Laurence to the car. Helen, who had not at first known what was happening, came running out in agony for her brother.

'Shall I come too?' she asked. 'I'm used to ankles and things at Brooklands.'

'You carry on,' said Laurence. 'Tell Aunt Palmer I'm sorry to let her down. I'm done for the next few days. I say, Helen,' he pulled his sister nearer to him, 'look out for Margaret. I don't know what's happened. We seem to have lost her between us, Aunt Palmer and I. A plague o' both our houses.'

He then fainted and was driven away with his father.

'I am sorry,' said Mr Bond with real concern. 'Can I do anything, Miss Dean? If you need a Hippolytus, might I help? I'm a bit rusty, but I did the part last year and your sister would be splendid to act with.'

Helen thanked him and they returned to the barn. Mrs Dean, partially reassured by the message that Richard had brought from her husband, was so sorry for Mrs Palmer that she had decided to stay on. Robin and Susan volunteered to go home on their bicycles and bring back word as soon as the doctor had been, a piece of consideration inspired in

Robin's case by a devout hope of seeing the ankle. Charles Fanshawe admired Rachel's courage, refused to think that she was perhaps not acutely sensitive, and contemplated with displeasure Helen's controlled anguish.

Mrs Palmer and Mrs Tebben came down to hold a consultation.

'We must decide at once,' said Mrs Palmer to her husband, 'whether we are to go on or to drop it. Betty is doing admirably, and now we have the question of Hippolytus. I suppose there is no chance of Laurence being able to act by Friday?'

'None,' said Helen.

'I'm sorry about Laurence,' said Mr Palmer. 'Bad luck, very bad luck. Didn't look where he was going. Always ought to look where you're going. Poor boy.'

'Louise,' said Mrs Tebben. 'Mr Moxon told me at tea the other day that he knew the part. He acted it at Epping with the East End Boys.'

'What was that?' asked Mr Palmer. 'Pierrots or something?'

'No, Mr Palmer, his troop of scouts. Perhaps he would be kind enough to fill the gap.'

Mr Moxon said that none regretted more than he the accident which had just occurred. If young Mr Dean had but followed the scout motto, Be Prepared, this might not have happened. Any poor effort that he could make was at their service. He might be able to give Miss Betty, who had taken on the part in a way which showed that she indeed was prepared, some helpful hints about her rendering of Phaedra.

Betty, who had come down to join the discussion, said

she would prefer to follow her own reading, and if Mr Moxon had been prepared he would have gone for the doctor himself. Her mother said, 'Hush, Betty,' but Betty, after kissing her mother affectionately, remained defiant.

'Do be reasonable, Betty,' said Mrs Palmer, almost in tears.

'Aunt Louise,' said Helen, 'Mr Bond knows the part. He did it last year at Oxford.'

Mrs Palmer stood irresolute. She disliked Mr Moxon, though not so heartily as her nieces and nephews, but she felt that after his offer she could hardly turn him down for Mr Bond, though she would like to have Mr Bond as a sign of restored amity with his mother. Dr Thomas asked what they were all talking about.

'Mr Moxon wants to act Hippolytus,' said Betty taking no trouble to disguise the hostility in her voice. 'But Mr Bond did the part last year at Oxford, and I should prefer to act with him.'

'Moxon act Hippolytus? Certainly not, I forbid it,' said Dr Thomas, who like many deaf people, was unaware how far his voice carried. 'He helps me into the pulpit, *helps* me! The idea cannot for a moment be considered.'

'Where authority speaks, I must obey,' said Mr Moxon, slightly chagrined, though not so much as Betty would have wished.

'Well, will you help us, young man?' said Mr Palmer. 'Never remember your name. Never remember names.'

'We always call him C. W.,' said his mother. 'Of course he will, won't you, dear?'

Mr Bond, his eyes glued on Betty, said he would be

delighted and made an apology to Mr Moxon, who accepted it in such a spirit of fellowship that Mr Bond nearly took it back.

'Well,' said Mrs Palmer, 'as it's nearly ten o'clock we'd better run through the rest of the play and we must have another rehearsal tomorrow, if everyone will be kind enough to come. C. W., you'll have to act in your own clothes tonight, and tomorrow we'll have Laurence's for you. Rachel, you go home, you must be tired. Come on, principals and chorus.'

10

Another Way of Love

'What happened to Margaret?' asked Mr Palmer when they got back to the Manor House. 'Nice girl that. Little Betty did well, though, very well.'

'I'm afraid it was my fault, Fred,' said Mrs Palmer, looking old and tired. 'I can't forgive myself. I was nearly at the end of myself with worry and the heat, and I found her and Laurence amusing themselves when they ought to have been getting ready. I spoke very harshly and unfairly to Margaret and she said she couldn't act. I don't blame her, I blame myself.'

'What did you say?' asked Mr Palmer, lighting a cigar.

'Fred, you know I always hoped Laurence would marry someone we both approved of. After all, this place will be his, and we must want to see him with the right sort of wife.'

'Margaret would be a very good wife, a very good wife. It's time Laurence settled down. He must have children, you know, Louise,' said Mr Palmer taking his wife's hand. 'Bad plan having no children, bad plan. Not our fault, but there it is.'

'I know, Fred, I know, but I would have liked Laurence to marry well.'

'What exactly is "well", my dear? He doesn't need money. Margaret is a very nice girl, and Tebben and his wife are clever people. And Richard is a good boy, a very good boy.'

'I dare say you are right, Fred. Well, if Laurence has made up his mind he must go his own way. I like Margaret and I admit I was wrong to scold her. Now I suppose she will be offended, and she will tell Laurence, and that will be the end of his affection for me. I'm an old fool, Fred, and there's nothing like that.'

'She won't tell him,' said Mr Palmer. 'Not the sort to make mischief. You write her a letter and say you're sorry. She'll come round all right. It's the heat. Don't be unhappy, Louise, I don't like it.'

'Very well, Fred,' said Mrs Palmer, with a sigh. 'I'll write it now and send it round first thing tomorrow. I shan't sleep tonight. Oh, how sorry I am!'

'Never mind, you're a very handsome woman, my dear, and a fine one,' said her husband. 'Send the letter round tonight. If she's awake it will do her good. If she isn't, she'll get it all the same tomorrow. It's only half-past eleven. John and the boy are up with a cow; the boy can take it over.'

When the rehearsal was over Helen changed into her own clothes and with a sigh of relief was getting into her car to go home, when Laurence's words came back to her, 'Look out for Margaret.' That was her first duty.

Susan had come back with the welcome news that it was

not a complicated ankle, but Laurence would have to keep his leg up for several days. Robin had been allowed to see the doctor at work and had stayed at home to tell Nanny all about it. So Helen did not feel unduly anxious about Laurence. Where to find Margaret was the next question, and sensibly considering that her own home was the most likely place, she drove to Lamb's Piece. In the drawing-room she found Mr and Mrs Tebben and Richard, eating the paste sandwiches and drinking the cocoa which Mrs Tebben had for once succeeded in forcing upon them.

'I came to ask after Margaret,' Helen said. 'I hope she's all right.'

'She told Mrs Phipps she felt so sick, poor child, that she couldn't go on,' said her mother. 'She had to go straight to bed, and when we got back I took up some cocoa, but she wouldn't open her door. Her light is still on. Would you like to go up and see her?'

Helen knocked at Margaret's door and went in. Margaret was lying huddled up in bed with the reading light on, pencil and paper at her side, looking so miserable that Helen felt very sorry for her.

'I came to see how you were,' she said. 'May I sit down? Laurence wanted to know. He was anxious about you.'

'I don't suppose he noticed if I were there or not,' said Margaret sullenly.

'He did. He noticed to such an extent that when he saw Betty doing Phaedra he fell off the platform and hurt his ankle.'

Margaret sat bolt upright in bed, staring speechlessly.

'I don't know yet whether it is broken or only sprained.

266

Mr Bond is doing his part. He asked me to see what had happened to you and then he fainted and Father took him home,' said Helen, her voice shaking perilously. 'He said he thought he and Aunt Louise had lost you between them. I don't know what he meant.'

'Oh, Mrs Palmer!' cried Margaret angrily.

'I don't want to be curious,' said Helen, 'but Laurence is very anxious, and if I could take him a message that you are all right I think he would sleep better. It hurts a good deal and I expect he will have a temperature.'

Margaret's defences were down at once. She poured out to Helen the whole story, part of which Helen already knew and part suspected. How Laurence had asked her to marry him, how she had thought he wasn't serious, and that there had never been an opportunity to meet and explain things.

'And then tonight,' she went on, 'he came up the steps in his white cloak and I loved him so much I could hardly bear it, and then I thought he was laughing at me and then I thought he really meant what he said, and then just as I thought everything was going to come right, Mrs Palmer came in, and when she had sent him away she said the most dreadful things to me about Laurence. And I couldn't find Laurence to help me and I didn't know what to do, so I took off my Phaedra things and gave them to Mrs Palmer and told her I couldn't possibly act, and I came home secretly and went to bed. And I was trying to write to Laurence and tell him I couldn't ever see him again. Oh, Helen, it has been so awful.'

Helen felt a wave of indignant anger against her Aunt Louise, first on Laurence's behalf and then even more on behalf of the victim before her. Without wishing any evil to her aunt, she determined to back Margaret up against her, both for Laurence's sake and for her own.

'Of course I can't ever tell Laurence, because I dare say Mrs Palmer didn't really mean it and I don't want to be unfair to her,' continued Margaret, in tears, 'but it is so awful to be told that you haven't been behaving well. I shan't tell Mummy or anyone, except you of course.'

This exception touched Helen very much.

'Aunt Palmer is very uppish sometimes,' said Helen. 'I expect she is having tortures of remorse now, thinking you will tell Laurence and he will hate her.'

Margaret felt that it would be as easy to tell Laurence that she had been scourged and branded as to tell him of his aunt's cruel aspersions.

'I think,' Helen continued, 'Aunt Louise forgets that Laurence is not her own son, not that any son would stand for the way she would like to bully Laurence. Margaret, Laurence will be terribly unhappy till he has seen you. Won't you come over tomorrow? If you don't he is quite capable of coming to see you and knocking himself out completely. Besides, you could see him alone at the Dower House.'

Margaret, still startled and unnerved, needed a good deal of persuading, but at last, partly lured by Helen's suggestion of seeing Laurence alone, she consented to come over about eleven o'clock.

'Only I don't know what to do about Mrs Palmer,' she said anxiously. 'How can I see her again?'

A tap, somehow of very annoying quality, at the door,

heralded Mrs Tebben, walking on tip-toe in case Margaret –
and hence presumably Helen also – was asleep.

'A note from the Manor House,' she exclaimed dramatically, waving it in the air. 'One of the cowman's boys
brought it. Shall I read it?'

'Is it for me?' asked Margaret.

'Yes, dear. About the next rehearsal I suppose. Wouldn't
you like some cocoa now?'

'No thank you, Mummy.'

'Well, good night. Don't keep this girl up too long,
Helen. If she is really going to be sick, the sooner the better.'

As the door closed, Margaret was opening the envelope
with shaking fingers. Then she laid the letter on the bed.

'Do you think she is suddenly scolding me again?' she
asked.

'I don't think so. She isn't full of malice, only of impulse.
Would you like me to read it?'

'Oh, please. It somehow makes things worse if one sees
them written.'

Helen looked at the letter.

'It is very short,' she said, 'and whether you like or not I
am going to read it to you. "Please forgive," she says, "an old
woman who is sorry and ashamed. When you can call me
Aunt Louise, I shall know that you bear me no grudge."'

'What does she mean?' asked Margaret in a whisper.

'I'm only a reader, not an interpreter. Will you go to sleep
now? And can I tell Laurence to expect you tomorrow
morning?'

'Please,' said Margaret.

Helen bent over and received a hug which improved her

opinion of Margaret still further. On her way out she looked into the drawing-room and told Mrs Tebben that Margaret was much better, dissuading her from visiting her daughter again with cocoa, cake, biscuits, or chocolate, or even a banana. She asked Richard, who was seeing her off, how the new car was going. Richard told her how it had stuck in the back drive and been rescued by Ed, but that he had no further difficulty, and his parents were delighted with it.

'I've got to go over and see your father tomorrow morning,' he said. 'He wants to see me, I don't know what for.'

'Probably to offer you a job,' said Helen.

'I wish I thought so, but I don't think he will. Your people find me a bit of a bore, I think.'

Helen, as indignant as a slight feeling of guilt could make her, disclaimed the suggestion.

'They would do anything for you,' she said. 'First you saved Jessica, and then you got the doctor for Laurence. You are rather a hero in our family, Richard. Cheer up.'

She drove home, put her car away and went up to see Laurence. He also was awake with his light on.

'Did you find her?' he asked.

'Yes, at home, in bed. No, not ill; just to escape from her mother I think. She is coming to see you tomorrow morning, so good night and go to sleep. Is it hurting?'

'Oh, it's all right, just pretty foul. Helen, are you sure she wasn't ill, or angry, or anything?'

'Not ill, not angry. Laurence, for goodness' sake be kind to her. She is rather young.'

'Kind? What else would I be?'

'Oh, thoughtless, exacting, selfish, difficult; yourself.'

'Helen!'

'You can't bully me, Laurence. You could bully her. I give you a solemn warning that I am on Margaret's side, now and for ever, because I love you so much. Go to sleep now. Do you want a drink, or aspirin, or anything?'

'I only want tomorrow. Did she look very lovely in bed?'

'Go to sleep.'

'You are a bully yourself, Helen, but a pearl of sisters. All right, I'll lie down and go to sleep. Good night.'

'Good night, darling; and goodbye.'

She left the room. On the stairs she stopped by a window and looked out on the moonlight. This she reflected was the end of her life with Laurence. She had done his last bidding, she had found his lost love and comforted her. Now her work was done and she could go. Tomorrow Laurence would belong to Margaret. She was thankful that she had never let Laurence see how bitterly she had once thought of his future wife. That she had been able to control herself was Charles's doing. It was he who had listened to her self-pity, who had set her feet upon the right path, who had let her cry upon his comfortable shoulder. Her secret would be safe with him, just as Aunt Louise's would be safe with Margaret. How many secrets in people's hearts! Richard too had his secret trouble that she had tried to solace, though why he should suddenly think her people found him a bore, she could not guess. And Charles. Why had Charles to go so suddenly? She remembered her vain promise to walk with him. Tonight she had meant to offer him a moonlight walk to make amends, and in running Laurence's errands she had forgotten her intention. Softly she went to the door of his room. It was open and the room empty. He might have gone out alone, or he might be in the library, though she had seen no light as she came in. Softly she went down the stairs, along the passage. The library was in darkness, except for moonlight pouring through the high windows. The door into the garden was open and she stepped out into the strange brilliance of the moon. The grass was soft to tread, the night-scented flowers heavy on the air. She walked across the lawn to where the lily-pond lay, molten silver with a marble edge. On the curved stone seat at its further end sat Charles Fanshawe. Softly she trod the stone walk towards him, the faint sound of her footsteps drowned by the splash of the little fountain that flung diamonds towards the moon. She sat down beside him and had nothing to say. Only night sounds of distant birds and animals stirred the silence of which the fountain's constant diamond splash was a part.

'What have you been doing to make you so late?' said Mr Fanshawe.

'Laurence was very unhappy about Margaret and asked me to go and see her. She was very miserable, some kind of misunderstanding, but when I told her I had come from Laurence she cheered up. She is going to see him tomorrow, and I think all will be well.'

'Will it be well for you?'

'For me? I don't know. I said good night to Laurence, and goodbye. He didn't know what I meant. You will.'

'You are a good girl, Helen; a very good girl.'

'Outside, perhaps, Charles, not inside. I am raging like a lion inside.'

'Well?'

'You see, Laurence wanted me to speak to Margaret for him before. I couldn't very well do that, but I thought if I were very kind to Richard, it might make the Tebbens think what a nice family we were. So when he asked me to help him to choose a car, I took a lot of trouble.'

'Is that what you have been doing for the last three days?'

'Of course. And helping to get his licence, and giving him tips. But what makes me rage, Charles, is that I wasted all that time on Richard. Margaret and Laurence seem to have had some kind of row, and now they are going to have a glorious reconciliation, and all the trouble I have taken over Richard hasn't really helped a bit. And all the time I was thinking how I wished I was walking with you. And now you are going, and Laurence will have Margaret, and I shall have nothing left. Nothing.'

Charles Fanshawe remained silent, divided between annoyance at his own misjudgment of Helen and Richard, and relief at the simple explanation.

'But if you must go,' said Helen, 'I came to ask if you would like a moonlight walk. I couldn't bear to feel I had disappointed you.'

'You haven't. If ever I thought you did, it was my own stupidity. I don't think I need go after all, so let's have our walk tomorrow.'

'I'd love to. And I'm very glad it's not tonight, because what with the rehearsal, and Laurence and Margaret, I am so very tired. Let's go in.'

They walked back, a little apart, to the house. At the library door they paused and stood looking at the strange world under the moon.

'Helen,' said Mr Fanshawe, and stopped.

'What do you want to say?' asked Helen, urgently, wondering why speech was suddenly so breathless, so difficult a thing.

'To say it in one word, or rather in three,' said Mr Fanshawe, deliberately putting on his spectacles, 'I love you.'

'Love?' said Helen questioningly. 'Oh, I have heard so much about love tonight. It is all foam and sunlight.'

'So was Aphrodite,' said Mr Fanshawe. 'But she is irrelevant. Will you marry me?'

He took off his spectacles and put them away, as he was used to do after interviewing undergraduates.

Helen said nothing, but as she turned to go into the house she caught at his hand and kissed it. Then she was gone into the shadow. Mr Fanshawe stood alone, between the cold moon and the earth.

'Humility doesn't seem very possible after this,' he remarked to the world.

A Case of Conscience

In the dewy morning Gunnar came walking past Modestine's shed.

'Any news?' asked Modestine.

'I've been out all night with Kitty Dean from the Dower House. We got a nice young rabbit.'

'Disgusting!' said Modestine.

'That's according to taste. Kitty Dean tells me that Mr Dean is going to give young Richard a job. No one offers me jobs. Favouritism, that's what I call it. Nepotism, too.'

'That's only your ignorant way of speaking,' said Modestine. 'I'm thinking of retiring myself.'

'Retiring?'

'That's what I said. Now young Richard has got a car I can take things easier. I may do a little light village work, or take Jessica for a ride occasionally, but no more station work for me.'

He hummed a few bars of 'Non più andrai'.

'Don't make that noise,' said Gunnar. 'I've got a frightful hangover.'

'It comes of eating uncooked meat. Stick to a vegetarian diet, and you'll be like me.'

'That clinches the matter,' said Gunnar, and went up to the house.

After breakfast Mr Fanshawe found Helen in the garden.

'Alluding to our conversation of last night,' he said, 'do you know that I am about twice your age?'

'That's just about the right age,' said Helen. 'Do you think we ought to mention it to my people now?'

'I did mention it to your father. He seemed not displeased, and said your mother would be delighted.'

'I shouldn't think she would notice very much. Dear Charles, I do think you are extraordinarily pleasant to be with.'

Under a sycamore, the mulberry being now so dangerous, they found Betty reading.

'I think, Betty,' said Mr Fanshawe, 'you may as well know that I am your future brother-in-law.'

Betty looked up from her book and uttered a few well-chosen and well-modulated words of congratulation, winding up with the hope that they would be married at a registrar's office, as she could not reconcile it with her conscience to go through the mummery of being a bridesmaid.

'I don't know,' said Mr Fanshawe. 'There is something about the words "the service was fully choral" which I find inexplicably attractive.'

Robin then came careering on his bicycle over the grass,

as he had been so often forbidden to do, calling Charles and Helen to come and bathe.

'I can't,' said Helen. 'I'm waiting for Margaret. Let's bathe after tea.'

'Oh, all right,' said Robin. 'I thought you were going, Uncle Charles.'

'So I was, but I'm not. I'm going to marry Helen instead.'

'Oh,' said Robin. 'I say, Uncle Charles, what do you think I did? I rode my bike round the churchyard wall, on the flat top. Old Phipps told me not to, but he was sextoning and didn't see. He's awfully bucked because Mr Patten's old mother died last night and she's to be buried in the new bit of cemetery. I wonder if he'd let me help to dig the grave.'

And off he careered.

'Darling Charles, as we are going to spend practically the rest of our lives together,' said Helen, 'forgive me if I desert you for a moment. I see Margaret, and I must take her up to Laurence. After that I shall come down in walking shoes and go to the end of the world with you.'

She ran across the grass to meet Margaret and took her upstairs.

Laurence, much to his affectionate annoyance, had been delivered to the tyranny of Nanny, who was vastly enjoying her power over her eldest baby. By bullying and cajoling he had made Nanny help him to dress and shave, and was sitting in the window with his leg on a cushioned stool, looking romantic.

'Here is Margaret,' said Helen. 'I'm going for a walk with Charles, so I'll leave her here for the present.'

Margaret stood by the door, full of delightful, but frightening feelings.

'One step at a time does it,' said Laurence encouragingly. 'I hate to seem discourteous to a lady guest, but would you mind bringing that little chair with you, and then you can sit and talk to me. I mustn't exert myself.'

'Laurence, did you really faint?' asked Margaret, installing herself at a decent distance from her host.

'I did. There I lay, till next day,' said Laurence, with great enjoyment, 'an ashen hue on my cheeks, my bright hair dabbled in blood. That's the worst of dark hair, the blood doesn't show.'

'Did you really bleed?' asked Margaret, her mental eye seared with a vision of Laurence in a swoon of death.

'No, not a drop. What happened was I thought it was you and it was Betty, so I tripped up on the altar and fell down the steps and twisted my foot till it was back to front.'

'Laurence!'

'Not really back to front,' said Laurence hastily, seeing her look alarmed, 'only a nasty wrench. Would you like to see it?'

'No, no,' said Margaret and shut her eyes tightly.

'That's a pity. I wouldn't show it to everyone. Margaret, what happened to you last night? Why did you go away and make me fall off the platform?'

'You know I didn't make you fall off the platform. I went away because I was miserable and I went on being miserable till Helen came.'

'And then was it better?'

'Oh, yes. She said you wanted to see me.'

'So I did. So I do and evermore shall. If I could get up and kneel down I would, and ask you to forgive me for everything you imagine I've done. And then we could— What is it, Nanny?'

'I've brought you a nice plate of mulberries, Master Laurence,' said Nanny. 'Miss Susan gathered them last night and they're all nice and ripe. You ought to have plenty of fruit when you're not taking exercise.'

'That is quite enough of a repellent subject, Nanny,' said Laurence. 'And while I am about it, I may as well say please don't bring me any more treats, medicinal or otherwise, for the present, because I want a little peace. I'm going to propose to Miss Tebben.'

Nanny smiled tolerantly, and telling Margaret to take no notice of Master Laurence's ways, left them alone.

'I had it all beautifully arranged in my mind,' said Laurence, 'but Nanny drove it away, so I'll have to start again. Miss Tebben, I love you to distraction. Could you possibly give me any hope?'

Margaret was unable to speak.

'Of course,' continued Laurence, 'I simply love to see you sitting there, going pink in that delightful way but it doesn't get us anywhere. Could you come a little nearer? Or shall I risk mortification followed by gangrene and amputation and come to you?'

He made as if he would rise, but Margaret with a swift movement was kneeling at his side, laying both her hands on his arm, begging him to keep still.

'I'll lie here for ever if you ask me to,' said Laurence, putting his arm round her and gently pulling her to him.

'You will find a kind of hollow in my shoulder, eminently suitable for people to put their heads in. I've never cared much about having it used, but if you would just give it a trial and tell me what you think of it— Well, Susan, and what do you want?'

'I suppose you're engaged,' said Susan looking at Laurence and Margaret without much interest. 'I'll be a bridesmaid if you like. I say, Laurence, do you know where Robin's pocket comb is? He thinks he dropped it in your room last night when the doctor was here, and he wants to comb the stable cat. She's been out all night and got full of burrs. Are you better?'

'Much better. And tell Robin I don't know where his comb is, and he'd better ask Nanny, but not to tell her what he wants it for. And I am engaged, and in a moment Margaret will be engaged too. And I don't want to see you or Robin till lunch-time.'

'All right,' said Susan and left the door open.

'They do put one off one's stroke, don't they?' said Laurence. 'Is that bit of my shoulder right for you, darling?'

Margaret's reply was a muffled 'Laurence!' which appeared to give complete satisfaction to the invalid.

At that moment Doris Phipps, who had no business to be upstairs, came past the door with the beauty cream, which she was taking back to the second housemaid's bedroom. She looked in, gave a shriek and disappeared.

'You are now compromised, Miss Tebben,' said Laurence proudly, 'and will have to marry me at once. My precious bird, have you any objection?'

Margaret was understood to say that she hadn't.

'Well, Doris will doubtless spread the news about,' said

Laurence, 'so we needn't worry. Now I think you might kiss me – but not unless you really want to.'

'I do,' said Margaret.

Richard, once more a prey to despondency, arrived at the Dower House and asked for Mr Dean. His underhand conduct in listening at the drawing-room window had been so preying on his mind that he could hardly force himself to keep his appointment. Until the early hours of the morning he had lain awake, debating with himself whether he ought to tell Mr Dean. If, as Helen said, Mr Dean was going to offer him a job, would it be fair to take it after so basely betraying his hospitality. The question was still undecided in his mind. An impartial observer would have said that he had been quite enough punished for a momentary lapse from the strict path of honour by his own tormented conscience, but Richard was gloomily inclined to torture himself still further.

In the library Mr Fanshawe was writing a letter. The parlour-maid said Mr Dean was expecting Mr Richard, and would be down in a moment.

'Well, Richard?' said Mr Fanshawe. 'I have a kind of idea why you are here, and if it's what I think, I will say that you have all my good wishes.'

'Thanks awfully,' said Richard, knowing what a black monster of dishonour he really was, and how unworthy of anyone's good wishes.

'I say, sir,' he continued, measuring a paper weight against an A.B.C. with meticulous care, 'could I ask your advice about something?'

'Well?'

'Supposing someone heard something about themselves that wasn't very nice, and they hadn't exactly been listening, but just happened to hear, and then went on listening without meaning to, do you think they ought to do anything about it? I mean, do you think they ought to tell the person that said the thing that they heard it, so as to be more truthful? I mean, suppose the person that said the thing, or at least the person that the thing was said to, was going to do something rather kind for them, do you think they ought to take it or not?'

'My advice to your friend,' said Mr Fanshawe gravely, 'for I have noticed that it is always a friend called "they" who is involved in these cases, would be to say nothing about it, try to forget what he had heard, and take the offered benefit. Nothing is served by emotional muck-rakings. He, if they is a he, would only give pain to his potential benefactor and do no good to himself. I hear Helen calling me for our walk. Good luck.'

Richard breathed more freely as light came to him. He began to realise that his impulse to a noble confession was a piece of showing off which would have made both Mr and Mrs Dean very uncomfortable. When Mr and Mrs Dean came in, he was able to face them with a mind almost at ease. Mrs Dean had only come for a book. She smiled divinely at Richard and went out again. He discovered, as he held the door open for her, that though she was still the loveliest woman he had ever seen, his heart was now his own, and after the upheaval of the last few weeks he was pleasantly relieved.

He and Mr Dean then had a short talk, the upshot of which was that Mr Dean's firm would be willing to take Richard into the business side on a small salary, with the prospect of doing well as he rose in the office. It would mean a year's training in London, possibly followed by some years abroad, and an assured future, as far as could be seen. Mr Dean wanted him to start the following week, if his parents were willing. Richard knew that, beyond his mother's natural anxiety about the washing, there would be no difficulty and thanked Mr Dean most gratefully.

'Then that's settled,' said Mr Dean. 'I am more indebted to you, Richard, than you can ever be to me, and I look forward very much to seeing you do well. You will report to my secretary at the office next Wednesday at eleven. Now you might go and find some of the children. They will be delighted to hear that you are coming into the family business.'

In the stable-yard Robin was combing the unwilling Kitty Dean, and Susan was sitting on the horse-block, watching him.

'I say,' said Richard, sitting down beside her, 'what do you think? Your father is going to have me in the business.'

'Oh, golly, that's good,' said Susan. 'I'm frightfully, terribly, *ghastlily* pleased.'

'I have to begin work next week,' said Richard importantly, 'and very likely I'll be going abroad.'

'Well, I'll be here when you come back. Richard, I simply knew something would happen for you when you saved Jessica's life. You were perfectly marvellous, and I've thought about it ever since.'

'Oh, rot,' said Richard. 'You were the one that really kept their head. You were splendid. I'll always come and see you when I get back from abroad. I say. I was thinking of calling my new car Susan.'

'Oh, Richard!' said Susan and hit him violently on the leg, and they sat in the sunshine in great contentment.